CINNABAR

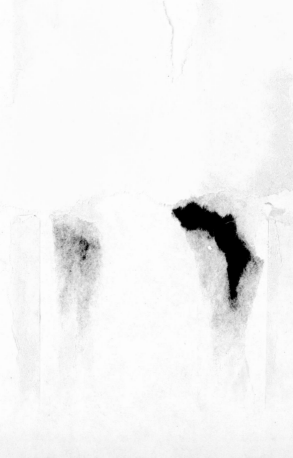

CINNABAR

LEE RODDY

WORD PUBLISHING

DALLAS LONDON VANCOUVER MELBOURNE

PUBLISHED BY WORD PUBLISHING

DALLAS, TEXAS

Published in association with the literary agency of Alive
Communications, Inc. 1465 Kelly Johnson Blvd, Suite 320
Colorado Springs, Colorado 80920

Book design by Mark McGarry
Set in Garamond

LIBRARY OF CONGRESS CATALOGING-IN-PUBLICATION DATA
Roddy, Lee, 1921–
Cinnabar / Lee Roddy.
p. cm. — (Giants on the hill:bk 2)
ISBN 0–8499–3832–5
1. California—Gold discoveries—Fiction.
I. Title. II. Series: Roddy, Lee, 1921– Giants on the Hill:
bk. 2 PS3568.0344C56 1995 813.54—dc20
95-30289 CIP

567899 RRD 654321
PRINTED IN THE UNITED STATES OF AMERICA

To the memory
of my father,

T.L. "Jack" Roddy
October 21, 1885 – June 24, 1995

AT THE TOP of the last mountain peak, the man who called himself Yancy Tate stiffly dismounted from his skinny mule. Dropping the lead rope to a second animal packed with his meager belongings, the dirty, unshaven man rushed to join the dozen other young riders standing at the granite rim.

Around them immense granite knobs showed above the timberline. Here, the sky was clear, but the air was already sharp with October breezes. Below, a few scattered and scraggly conifers grew between the massive boulders. This was the last peak in California's high Sierra Nevada Mountains. From here, the trail led down through stately Jeffrey pines to the great Sacramento Valley, which spread out in the distance.

The other equally unkempt young riders whooped joyfully at the sight. As always, Tate, really Alvin Brakken, remained aloof. He no longer felt the aches of having traveled two thousand miles by mule, the fastest way possible from the Missouri River to California.

Brakken's gray, expressionless eyes swept the distant scene below. Somewhere down there were two people he had come west to find.

He would rob one and kill the other. The sooner, the better.

At the thought, his excitement increased. He licked his lips and his breath came faster. He glanced down at his badly worn boots, the fourth and last pair he had brought with him from Independence, five months before. The cuffs on his pants were badly frayed, and his knees showed through the patches he had made himself. His shirt was dirty and perspiration-soaked, as was his slouch hat that had once been gray.

But all that will change, he told himself with satisfaction. *All I have to do is find those two.*

To confirm his thought, he reached into his pocket and removed a double eagle. Cupping the twenty-dollar gold coin in his callused, grimy hand so that no one else could see, he cursed under his breath. It was the last of all those coins she had given him before she headed west two weeks ahead of him.

Brakken felt a secret excitement in fondling the coin, knowing now that she must have had many more like it hidden in a false bottom of her canvas-topped wagon. There had probably been plenty of similar pieces sewed into heavy blankets or secreted in the flour barrel along with her good china. He hadn't discovered the cache in time to prevent her from rolling west with it, but now he intended to have it. She surely hadn't had time to spend all that gold, but even if she had, there were other reasons for finding her.

She was a looker, both in face and form, with long blond hair, tempting green eyes, and a taunting smile that seemed to hint at more than friendliness. He was a good-looking twenty-five-year-old who knew his way around women. He didn't think she would resist, but if she did, he had a way of changing her mind.

What little of Brakken's face that showed above the untidy brown beard was almost blackened from the merciless sun. His sunburned nose had never really stopped peeling. But those were small discomforts to be endured for the double satisfaction he soon anticipated.

He thoughtfully took a final sweeping look at the valley spread out before him, then he shoved the coin back into his pocket. Two weeks after the woman had left for Sutter's Fort, Brakken had met a discouraged miner returning home after giving up on the California gold rush that had started this year of 1849. From the miner, Brakken had learned that the man he had sought for seven years had been seen in San Francisco. That gave Tate two reasons to head west. It had taken him a fortnight to get ready, and now the end was in sight.

His old hatred made him reach up and absently feel his whisker-covered throat. Sometimes he thought he could almost feel a rope around his neck; the same rope that had taken his brother's life. He and his twin, Alben, had started as one egg. There had always been a oneness about them. Kinfolk and neighbors in Texas who knew them claimed that the Brakken twins were exactly alike in good looks, mean ways, and passionate feelings.

On the morning his brother was secretly hanged, Alvin awoke, fighting for breath and with a sense of unease about his twin.

There had been no trial, only one angry man and his rope around the other brother's neck. The hangman had fled, but now vengeance was at hand.

Yes, it's close now! Brakken had worked it all out in his mind. He would find his brother's killer, but he wouldn't rush the final encounter. Instead, he would possess or ruin everything the man had. Only when that was done would Tate take all that the man had left: his life.

Brakken's weariness dropped from him. He squared his aching shoulders, hurried past the other men, and checked his pack animal's load. It included a noose he had brought along. It was ready. Satisfied, Brakken seized the pack animal's lead rope, then swung into the saddle of his riding mule.

"You boys will have to get along without me," he said in a distinctive, raspy voice. "I'm riding on alone."

Brakken urged his animals down the mountain.

CHAPTER I

S HILOH LET her gaze drift to the Marin headlands on the opposite shore. She drew her cloak about her shoulders against the October breeze blowing through the Golden Gate.

Clay leaned toward her in the buggy. "Please," he said with a hint of a drawl, "don't turn away from me. We came out here to discuss our situation and make some decisions, so let's do that."

Shiloh Laird sighed, trying to find the words that would make Clay understand her feelings. She realized it was difficult for a naturally quiet, taciturn man like Clay to say much. Words didn't come easily to him, yet he'd been making a strong case for moving their office from San Francisco to Sacramento.

"It's one option," he said gently. "All the major stage lines are either in Sacramento or Stockton. We're losing business being here."

"I know that." In the few short months since they'd started the Laird and Patton Stage Lines with an ancient springless wagon and a team of mules, expenses had exceeded income. "But," she continued, "major businesses are locating here by the bay."

"Not all of them. Sacramento's getting plenty. That's why both Jim Birch and Bob Crandall have their stage lines head-quartered there."

Shiloh made an impatient gesture. She was tired of hearing about the two most aggressive and thriving stage-line owners. Independently, their two companies were outdistancing the many other small lines trying to get a piece of the booming passenger, mail, and banking business.

Stagecoach demand would increase dramatically if the delegates who met at Monterey earlier this month had their way. They voted in favor of petitioning the U.S. Congress to admit California to the Union as a non–slave-holding state.

Shiloh conceded, "That's true, but if we move we'll have to take in a silent partner to provide the money to expand: to buy new equipment and teams and hire drivers. I think we should go slowly, paying as we go."

"I would prefer that, too, but in order to, we've got to take in a whole lot more than we've been doing up to now. The one thing that could pull us out of this would be to get the mail contract that the U.S. government will award to a stage line."

For a moment, Shiloh was hopeful, for everything really depended upon being awarded that contract. She asked, "I know, but how in the world can we get that?"

"We've still got time. They're going to make the decision on December tenth here at the courthouse. That gives us a chance to show them we're solvent and can buy the equipment necessary to do the job. If we can't do that . . ."

Shiloh broke in. "We're not going to lose the company!" Her words were as firm as her inner conviction. "That's all I have left of Aldar, his dream for this stage line." She paused, glancing down at her body. Silently, she added, *And his child.*

At twenty weeks, her unborn child was a constant reminder that Aldar had been murdered just days after she had conceived. To marry Aldar, she had left her childhood home in Pennsylvania, her parents, and everything familiar for an exciting new life. She had never doubted that marriage would bring her happiness and security. However, Aldar Laird's death had shattered that belief and thrown her life into turmoil. Now, her only recourse was to develop the stagecoach business to provide financial security for the child and herself.

"We've got to be realistic, Clay. We're both misplaced in this situation. You're obviously not happy in the office or out trying to drum up customers. You belong in the open air, driving a team or supervising other drivers. That's what you do best, and that's what you love."

The breeze ruffled Clay's dark wavy hair. "True. When Aldar and I used to talk about staging, it was agreed I'd handle the field work, and he would take care of the business end."

Clay fell silent, studied Shiloh intently, and shook his head. Was this the same vulnerable young woman who had arrived in San Francisco just months ago? Now she sounded so determined, so sure of her convictions. He knew that under that facade was the same frightened girl who was so abruptly left alone when Aldar was murdered. Clay was determined to help Shiloh make his best friend's dreams come true. More than anything, he wanted to see Shiloh happy again.

"I don't belong in the office either." Shiloh broke into his thoughts. "No woman is in the stagecoach business, especially in this town of mostly men. They don't like dealing with me, especially now. I overheard some of them talking about what they call my 'delicate condition.' I'm a burden . . ."

"Don't ever say that," Clay interrupted, his deep brown eyes showing his concern. "You didn't ask to be a partner. You inherited it. Aldar brought brains, charm, and business sense to the company. Now he's gone. But we're alive and we're here . . ."

He interrupted himself. He wanted to take Shiloh in his arms and reassure her, but he knew she wasn't ready for that. He added, "I'm sorry, Shiloh. I didn't mean to bring up a lot of memories."

"It's all right," she assured him, turning away so that he would not see the sudden moistness that leaped unbidden to her eyes.

But it's not all right, she admitted to herself. *I don't know if I can ever learn to trust life again, to have what Aldar and I had for those few months.*

Clay prompted, "We've got to make some decisions."

"I know." She took a deep breath and turned back to him. "But . . ."

He waited for her to finish. When she didn't, he prompted, "But what?"

"It's just so hard to know what the right thing to do is."

Her eyes skimmed the western horizon from south to north, seeking the words to explain her concerns. Suddenly, she sat straight up on the seat beside him and pointed toward the entrance of the bay. "There's a ship! But look at her!"

Clay leaned forward to peer past the mare standing patiently atop the bluff. "That's one of those fast new clippers, but it's barely afloat."

The vessel limped into the bay at dead-slow speed.

One of her three tall masts was missing, and the shredded sails on the midship and foremasts flapped loosely. The hull rode low in the water, indicating her imminent danger of sinking. The deck slanted sharply, forcing the crew and a few passengers to cling to ropes to keep from sliding overboard.

Clay reached for the reins. "She's in really bad shape." He slapped the lines across the mare's back. "We'd better tell them at the presidio. They'll sound the alarm for the rescue if it's needed."

The mare's hooves thudded in the sandy soil as the light, four-wheeled carriage left the bluff and picked up speed. Shiloh twisted in the seat to peer through the tiny window in the back of the buggy.

"Oh, those poor people!" Shiloh cried. "Will they make it?"

"I don't know. They still have to get around the point to the docks. From the way her master's heading her toward shore, I'd guess he's getting ready to abandon ship if he has to."

Shiloh had only seen one of the speedy clippers earlier this summer, shortly after she and her late husband landed at Yerba Buena Cove. That ship had presented a glorious sight with all three masts grandly supporting the acres of white canvas that made clippers the fastest ships afloat.

Everyone had talked about the majestic ship that had sailed down the Atlantic, around the Horn, and up the Pacific in under one hundred days. The first such clipper had been launched just four years earlier, in 1845. Built for speed, clippers were breathtakingly beautiful, with long overhanging bows and great clouds of wind-filled canvas sails. Easily the fastest vessels afloat, they showed pride in every slender line.

But not the one creeping into sight. Ocean storms had obviously taken a heavy toll, snapping one mast and carrying away great sheets of canvas sails. Apparently the early season storm of the past few days had sealed this ship's fate.

Shiloh tried to make out what she saw. "There's something lashed on her deck, back where the mast is missing. Looks like a stagecoach." Shiloh abandoned the tiny window to lean her head out and look back.

A puff of smoke erupted from the fort's cannon where it overlooked the harbor's entrance. This was followed by a dull boom that made Shiloh jump. She looked up questioningly at the man beside her.

"Somebody at the presidio has also spotted her and is signaling that a ship's in distress." He pulled back on the reins, stopping the horse, then assured Shiloh, "They'll have small craft alongside her in a few minutes to save the passengers and crew if necessary."

"Isn't there anything we can do?"

"Not right now. This is where men trained in such matters take over. But when they get to shore, the crew and passengers might need our help."

"Then let's go!"

He pulled on the right rein to turn the horse east, so the clipper would again be in sight. "We'll circle inland past those hills and meet her at the wharf."

"I wonder if there are any women or children aboard?"

"I don't see any, but from this distance, I can't be sure." Clay's voice suddenly rose. "Say, that *is* a stage on her deck! But it's not just any stage! That's a Concord! There's no mistaking that kind of beauty!"

Shiloh knew about the most famous stages in America. Aldar had dreamed of having fleets of them crisscrossing California and maybe, eventually, the two thousand miles of wilderness to Missouri.

Clay said softly, "Aldar wanted us to be the first out here to own a Concord, but it looks as though either Birch or Crandall beat us to it."

Both Shiloh and Clay fell silent. Only the soft thudding of the horse's hooves in the sandy hills marred the quiet, but an awful thought invaded Shiloh's mind. If the ship sank, the stagecoach would go down with her. It seemed symbolic of the problems facing Shiloh and Clay.

Forcing the possibility aside, she reflected on her dilemma. Was Clay right, or was she? What was the correct business decision? Aldar would have had no hesitation in choosing. His acute sense of commerce decisions matched his vast vision. Shiloh searched her memory, trying to remember if he had said anything that would help now. In the few short months during which they had met, married, and moved to California, Aldar's enthusiasm had infected Shiloh. Yet, the far-flung stage-line concept was not Shiloh's original vision. Instead, she had dreamed of a home with a loving husband and children.

Those simple things represented happiness to Shiloh, and she had thought they would be fulfilled with Aldar. His violent death had left her afraid to again trust intrinsic things. But she could do her best to turn Aldar's dreams into reality. He had anticipated that his stage lines would make him a millionaire in three short years. Then he would build them a beautiful mansion on Fern Hill, the largest of San Francisco's hills now home only to wild goats. Aldar had said that someday the men who would become giants in California would live there. That's where he and Shiloh would have their real home. All that was possible, he had stoutly claimed, through developing a network of stagecoach lines.

Clay's voice jarred her from deep introspection. "Here comes another carriage. Looks like Jefferson Locke."

Shiloh suppressed an annoyed sigh. There weren't many people she didn't like, but Locke was one of them. She forced herself to be pleasant as a sorrel gelding was reined in and the driver spoke to them.

"Mrs. Laird," he said, showing crooked teeth. "Clay." Locke reached across from his buggy, and the men shook hands.

Shiloh didn't speak but merely nodded to the short, balding Locke.

"Out for a little ride, were you?" he asked with a hint of a smirk.

The implied meaning annoyed Shiloh. She resented Locke's insinuating that Clay was more than a business partner.

If Clay also caught Locke's meaning, he let it pass.

"We have our eyes on that clipper ship down there. It's in trouble."

Locke squinted, following Clay's pointing hand. "I hadn't noticed," Locke replied. "Been out looking for choice lots to sell. But let's take a look." He reached down to the seat, picked up a brass telescope and extended its sections.

Shiloh noticed that the forty-two-year-old land speculator had on the same rumpled black suit he had worn every time she had seen him.

"Hmm. You're right; she looks ready to sink." Locke moved the telescope forward to scan the long, graceful hull. "She's called the *Summer Cloud*. Take a look, Clay."

Clay took the glass and offered it to Shiloh. She shook her head. Clay placed the instrument to his eye and studied the ship in thoughtful silence before handing the glass back to Locke. "Much obliged, Jefferson," he said.

"Be too bad if she sinks with that stagecoach on board, Clay. It'd be a mighty fine way to replace that old broken-down wagon you've been driving."

"Sure would," Clay admitted.

Locke shifted his eyes to Shiloh. "I imagine you're feeling mighty happy about the way things went at the Monterey Convention this month."

"Yes, I am."

"Too bad women can't vote, isn't it, Mrs. Laird?" There was a touch of sarcasm in Locke's voice.

"They didn't need my vote," she replied evenly, trying to keep her annoyance from showing.

The former lawyer from Tennessee had strong pro-slavery feelings. These were repugnant to Shiloh, who had grown up in a Pennsylvania home of staunch abolitionists. Locke turned his eyes to Clay. "As a Texan, how did you feel about the convention voting against slavery?"

"My political beliefs don't matter," Clay answered a little crisply. "I'm putting all my thoughts into how to run a stage line."

Shiloh raised an eyebrow at those remarks. Clay and Aldar had often discussed politics, and Clay was quite knowledgeable although he could be reserved and keep his opinions to himself.

Locke exclaimed, "Ah, but your beliefs do matter, Clay. Any thinking man can see that this slavery issue is going to bring on a war between the states. Everybody's got to take sides."

Shiloh reminded him, "But at Monterey, your side lost, Mr. Locke."

"Not necessarily. Just because those delegates voted for statehood doesn't mean Congress will see it that way, not with the way things are now: fifteen free states and fifteen slave-holding states, and no other territory except California seeking admission. So you can be sure there's going to be a long fight in Washington before California's status is settled."

Shiloh wasn't interested in pursuing the subject. Her concern was with the crippled ship and the people on board. "Clay," she said quietly, "I think we should go."

He nodded and loosened the reins, but before the mare could move, Locke spoke again.

"In fact, Congress could reject the convention's petition for statehood or even vote to admit California as a slave-holding state."

Shiloh asked, "What if Congress admits California as a free state?"

Locke's eyes narrowed. "Then I'd join the movement to have California secede from the Union and become a separate nation."

That statement startled Shiloh. "Are you serious?"

"Very," he assured her. "I'd join Denby Gladwin in that."

She protested, "But his idea for a Pacific Empire didn't even get consideration at Monterey."

"Those fools!" Locke's tone turned bitter. "Well, they may live to regret that. The separate nation movement is alive and well. This time, we'll not make the same mistakes as before."

Clay asked, "What mistakes were those, Locke?"

"Three basic ones, including the one we secessionists made. First, there was no newspaper to carry the message to the right people. Next, there was no means of reaching interested men because there is no real organized staging system in operation."

Shiloh and Clay exchanged glances, but neither spoke.

"Finally, there needs to be a force of arms to back up the demand for a separate nation."

"You mean an army?" Shiloh blurted in disbelief.

"At least six thousand well-armed men," Locke assured her.

"But that's impossible!" Shiloh protested.

"I beg to differ with you, Mrs. Laird. You will live to see the day when what I say comes true." He picked up the light buggy whip and flicked it over the gelding's back. "Well, I must be getting on." He tipped his hat with his free hand and drove off.

Shiloh asked Clay, "Do you believe that?"

He shrugged. "Locke does, and that concerns me."

"But why would he tell us something like that? I would think such plans would be highly confidential."

"They should be, but Locke talks too much. Or maybe he was trying to impress you."

"Scare me is more like it," she admitted. "Ever since I landed here, I've seen men grasping for money and power. But he's the only one who has always worried me."

"He failed in his efforts to have the delegates vote in favor of California being admitted as a slave-holding state. He could fail again in this separate nation idea."

Shiloh pondered that in silence as the mare rounded the last hill and Yerba Buena Cove came into sight. About five hundred ships rotted in the harbor, abandoned by thousands of passengers and crews headed for the gold country.

At the extreme northeast corner of San Francisco's peninsula, swarms of men, alerted by the cannon and the semaphore on Signal Hill, had joined the Chilean residents at the foot of the hill. In silence, they all faced north, shading their eyes against the bay's glare.

Shiloh's gaze swept past the newly erected wharfs at Clark's Point to the glistening white rock called Alcatraz, then left, toward the sea. "There's no sign of that ship."

"She's gone down."

Shiloh spun to face him. "So quickly?"

He nodded. "See those small boats pulling for shore? They're full of people the rowers have just rescued."

Shiloh stared at the bay's choppy water. There was no ship of any kind in sight. "I pray they all made it!"

"Me too."

Shiloh closed her eyes to shut out the pathetic sight of shipwreck victims, but another vision remained: the beautiful Concord stage had gone down with the ship.

She tried to banish the image, but it remained burned into her mind like a personal omen of what lay ahead.

ᨀ CHAPTER II ᨀ

ALL OF THE passengers and crew from the sunken clipper came safely ashore without serious injury. The survivors huddled out of the wind wrapped in hastily gathered blankets while hundreds of curious people crowded around.

"They've lost everything!" Shiloh exclaimed. "Let's go see if we can help some of them. I've got room at the house, and there's plenty of food."

"You stay here, and I'll see what we can do."

"Find out if there are any women or children," she called after him. He nodded without looking back.

She watched his six-foot-four-inch frame tower above everyone else as he moved through the spectators. *We didn't make any decisions,* she reminded herself. *They've still got to be made, and soon.*

The ocean breeze increased, forcing Shiloh to pull her shawl tighter about her shoulders. She shivered in spite of the cloudless sky and bright sun. She closed her eyes, but the thought of unresolved problems stayed in her mind. So did the image of the magnificent Concord coach lashed to the deck of the sunken ship.

ᨀ

A few miles away, south of Market Street, a strikingly beautiful mulatto woman paused outside a dusty shack with a sign proclaiming, "Lots for Sale." She hesitated only momentarily before opening the door and peering inside.

Jefferson Locke, back from his drive, looked up from the far side of a cluttered table to take in her perfect figure, pale, creamy tan skin, and intense eyes as black as her hair. He started to smile, then frowned, studying her closely.

"No coloreds allowed in here," he said curtly without rising from his chair.

Except for a momentary flash of anger in her eyes, the woman showed no emotion.

"I'm called Mara," she said, examining the short, balding man in the rumpled suit. "I'm a friend of Shiloh Laird's."

Locke showed crooked teeth in an uncertain smile. *This is an uppity nigra, calling herself a friend of a white woman.* Instead of inviting the visitor to take the empty chair opposite him, Locke commented, "Oh, yes. I saw her a while ago. She sent you with a message?"

"No. I came on my own."

The smile vanished. "What do you want?"

Mara ignored the question's bluntness. "I understand you have some property for sale over by what's called Portsmouth Square, or the Plaza."

"Yes, I do. Does Mrs. Laird want to buy it?"

"No, but I do."

Locke stared, then laughed. "Your kind of people can't buy land around here."

The light again flashed in her eyes, but she kept her voice calm. "I am exactly half white and half black, Mr. Locke, just as William Alexander Liedesdorf was, and he owned considerable property in San Francisco and elsewhere."

"But that was in the Mexican period, which ended when we beat them in the war. Besides, Liedesdorf's been dead about five years. Anyway, you could be a runaway slave for all I know. Slaves are property, and property can't own property."

Mara kept her temper. "You know Shiloh Laird, so you know that I have my freedom papers. I suspect that the real reason you're being so difficult is because I'm a woman. I've heard that you don't have much respect for women, white or colored."

He nodded appreciatively, his eyes sliding from her flawless face to caress the body not entirely hidden under the long dark dress. "You're a woman, all right."

"A woman with cash to buy property." Determinedly, Mara

pushed ahead with her goal. She touched the handbag clutched against her full breasts. "Gold, in fact."

His eyes returned to her face. "Where did a gal like you get gold?"

"I earned it. I set up a small bakery in front of a tent saloon and baked pies and biscuits. I only accepted gold dust, nuggets, or coins minted in the United States."

His eyes half closed to mask his greed. "I heard about that. So that was you. Weren't you going to run a boardinghouse with the profits from your little venture?"

"I intend to do more than run it, Mr. Locke. I will own the boardinghouse as well."

Slowly, he shook his head. "Not in this town, you won't. Women can't own businesses in their own names, and colored women can't own anything at all."

She reached into her pocketbook and pulled out a handful of coins. "Double eagles," she said softly, letting the twenty-dollar gold pieces clink temptingly. "Minted this year of 1849 by the U.S. government."

He stared at the heavy coins. "Mara," he said, using her name for the first time, "do you know how many of those it would take to buy a lot by Portsmouth Square?"

Mara replied coolly, "You recently told Shiloh that a hundred and fifty-foot square lot there went from $16.50 two years ago to $6,000 last year and is now worth about $50,000."

"That was some time back. Now, it's more."

"How much more?" She shook the coins gently in her palm.

A hint of sarcasm showed in his reply. "Are you going to stand there and try to make me believe you have that kind of money?"

"Try me."

The simple declaration carried such conviction that Locke believed her. For the first time, he stood and leaned across the table. "If you're lying to me . . ."

"I brought enough for a deposit," she interrupted brusquely. "Draw up the papers, and I'll return within the hour with the balance. The whole thing."

His eyebrows worked up and down, and he licked his lips while his eyes dropped again to the gold coins. Then, reluctantly, he shook his head. "Even if you're telling the truth . . ."

"You know I am!" she broke in sharply.

"It's not logical, but . . ." He turned and walked a couple of quick steps from the table. "I just can't. I can't sell to a nigra!"

She did not reply, but when he turned to face her again, her beautiful face was drawn and tight.

"Remember this day," she said coldly, her black eyes alive with passion, "because the time is coming when I will be able to buy and sell you, and everything you own!"

"Are you threatening me?"

She interrupted sharply. "Just remember what I said!"

The door slammed behind her, and he heard her footsteps rapidly fade into the distance on the newly installed boardwalk.

Before coming to California, Locke had owned slaves and ordered all black people around with a casual, insolent air, having no fear of retaliation. But there was something about Mara that was different. There was a cold, firm determination in her that bothered him. Slowly, he sank back into his chair and stared into space.

◌

Alvin Brakken's hunger pangs forced him to leave the trail and turn toward a small gold-rush, foothill community of tents and shacks. He avoided the main part of town and turned his mules down a narrow path toward a river. He circled the burgundy manzanita and pushed through the dark green chaparral toward the sound of shallow water rushing over stones. He hoped to find a lone man to rob, but reined in when he came upon two young miners panning for gold in the stream.

Neither was armed although a pistol lay on a flat boulder within reach of the taller, more slender miner. Brakken forced a friendly sound to his raspy voice and asked, "Any luck?"

"Lots of it," the shorter, stockier miner answered, looking up with the pan in his hands. He wore a faded blue shirt. "All bad. Barely getting enough color to make day wages."

That wasn't what Brakken wanted to hear. He glanced around casually and noticed a buckskin pouch on top of a boulder a few feet away from the river. Confident that the poke contained gold, Brakken casually slid out of the saddle. Maybe he wouldn't have to risk getting shot if he was careful. He squatted on his heels in the shadow cast by the mule, facing the miners but keeping the buckskin poke in sight.

The blue-shirted miner commented, "From the looks of you and your animals, you've come a far piece."

"Far enough," Brakken admitted, letting his eyes take in the canyon, the whitish boulders in the river, and the green forested hills beyond. "You two the only ones around?"

Both gold panners laughed before the tall one replied, "There must be five hundred men within a couple miles of here. Can't see them because they're down in the rivers and gulches, like us. Can't hear them over the water rushing by, either."

That meant the sound of a gunshot might alarm the others, so Brakken knew he couldn't risk firing or being shot at. But he had to have money. His stomach was rubbing against his backbone with hunger. Well, if these two weren't good prospects for robbing, maybe they could help him in his search.

"Either of you from down Texas way?"

The tall miner straightened up and arched his back to ease aching muscles. "I've seen men from nearly every place in the Union, not to mention foreigners, like Dutchmen, Englishmen, Eyetalians, Australians, and Irishers. But I can't say that I've met any from Texas." He turned to his companion. "You recollect anybody?"

When the second man shook his head without looking up from his gold pan, the slender one asked, "You looking for somebody special?"

"A friend of mine told me to look him up if I got out this way," Brakken lied. His eyes again drifted to the poke, then lifted to check the surrounding area.

"What's your friend look like, Mister?"

Satisfied that no one else was around, Brakken turned back to the miner. "He's a long drink of water, but broad shouldered and muscular."

"Taller'n me?"

Brakken studied the miner. "You must be close to six feet, same's me."

"Six even."

"My friend is six-four or -five." Brakken slowly stood, preparing to make his move. "You seen any women coming through from the east?"

Both miners laughed as though the question was a big joke. The taller man explained, "We ain't seen a woman in so long I hardly remember what they look like." He paused, then asked, "You looking for any particular woman?"

Brakken nodded. "You could say that."

"Might be some in Sacramento City or Stockton." He pointed over the next ridge. "More'n likely, San Francisco. Probably ain't a single one you'd want to take home to meet your ma, though. 'Course, I heard tell that some decent women folk are coming overland, but the trail don't come near here, so I ain't seen none."

Brakken nodded. "I got to be moving on. Much obliged, anyway." He readjusted his sweaty hat on his mop of uncut hair and deliberately turned his two mules to momentarily block the miners' view. He walked around to the far side of the riding mule, ready to snatch up the poke.

But before he could reach for it, a third man rushed out of the chest-high chaparral.

"Hey!" he called, waving his hat and running as fast as his worn-out boots would allow. "I seen a woman's clothes hanging on a line outside a wagon over by Coyote Diggins!"

"A woman? You sure?" the tall miner demanded from where he stood waist deep in the river.

"Got a glimpse of her with my own eyes!" The third man's excited face showed that he was sincere. "She can't be no more'n twenty years old."

The two miners rapidly waded out of the shallow water. They dropped their gold pans on the rocks and rushed past Brakken and his mules to meet the new arrival.

"What'd she look like?" the tall miner demanded, his back to Brakken.

He casually eased his hand down and let his fingers touch the poke. He had never felt gold dust, but he was sure that's what it was. He deftly palmed it, satisfied with the hefty feel.

"Purty as a spotted pup," the news bearer cried. "Slender, she was, with long blond hair down to her waist. And blue eyes, with skin white as milk in a pan."

Brakken was suddenly very interested. "Where did you see this woman?" He had slipped the poke into his pocket and swung into the saddle, ready to ride out.

"Over yonder." The messenger pointed. "Two ridges over, off the wagon trail. Can't miss her. Well, I got to pass the word along." He turned downstream, broke into a run and shouted at the top of his voice. "A woman! I seen a real young American woman!"

Brakken clapped dusty boot heels to his mount and nodded to the two miners. They obviously had not seen him pilfer the gold, for the tall one called, "Reckon we'll see you there real soon."

Brakken's skin tightened with the anticipation that the miners might notice the missing poke and fire a shot at him. He didn't relax until the chaparral closed about him and the sound of the miners' voices was lost in the mountain stillness.

Blond. Blue-eyed. Young. Probably lots of women like that, so it's not likely to be her, he told himself. *Besides, she should be a lot farther down the trail by now. But something could have happened to delay her.*

He rode as fast as his jaded mule could move, wanting to see the woman and make up his mind long before the miners showed up. In spite of their excitement, they might miss their sack of gold. *Well, they got off lucky. I didn't have to shoot them.*

By the time he topped the first ridge, he heard voices. In a few minutes' ride, he came upon unshaven, untidy miners pouring away from the rivers and gulches and headed the same way he was.

"Hey, Mister," a heavyset man called as Brakken rode past, "I'll give you this nugget to borrow one of your mules for an hour." He held up an irregular piece of gold. "It probably weighs, two, maybe three ounces."

Brakken was sorely tempted, but he knew that he had to get away with the stolen poke of dust. "Sorry," he replied. "Thanks, anyway."

I can't believe men are so desperate to see a woman, he told himself, thumping his heels against the mule's sides. *What kind of a place is California, anyway?*

He rode on, passing the many men who emerged from the surrounding hills. He was offered two other pouches and another smaller nugget for his mules before he passed the foremost men and glimpsed the dusty canvas cover of a wagon ahead.

He eased back on the reins upon sighting the garments strung between the wagon and a lodgepole pine. There was no doubt that they belonged to a young woman.

Anxious to discover who she was, Brakken rode boldly to the front of the wagon, calling out. "Anybody in there?"

He pulled the mule sharply to a halt when a musket barrel eased out from the darkened interior.

"Stop right there, mister!" The man's voice was weak, but he aimed the weapon steadily at Brakken's chest.

"I'm coming peaceful," Brakken called with a smile. He kept the mule in check with one hand and lifted the other to show it was empty.

"Ride on up, real slow-like."

Brakken decided that there was a slight tremor to the man's voice. Old or sick, he decided, but protecting that pretty gal. Brakken loosened the reins and the mule walked forward.

When he drew even with the wagon tongue which rested on the ground, the voice spoke again. "That's far enough. Now, state your business."

"There's a few hundred miners coming this way," Brakken explained, twisting to point the way he had come. "They haven't seen a woman in a mighty long time, so I thought you should know."

He thought he heard a startled exclamation from inside the wagon's dark interior, but he couldn't be sure. He waited, anxious to learn if this was the woman he sought.

Brakken squirmed in the saddle, aggravated by the delay. "Uh . . . those men will be here soon. If you want, I'll side with you in case any of them get out of hand."

The musket was drawn inside and a gray-bearded man moved his head into the sunlight. "We had this happen once before," he said in a tremoring voice. "Last week, fact is. Harmless, they were. Polite as in a church. They just want to get a look at my daughter."

Brakken waited, unsure of what to say, but becoming increasingly uneasy at the sound of the approaching miners.

The old man continued, "Last time, the boys took up a collection. A dollar apiece they was willing to pay, just to see my girl stick her head out like this."

There was a movement inside the wagon and a woman's head appeared beside the old man. She was blond, all right, blue-eyed, too, and reasonably good enough looking. But she wasn't the woman Brakken sought.

"Then you'll be safe," he said, touching the brim of his grimy hat and digging his heels into the mule's side.

The young woman gave him a warm smile and spoke for the first time. "Thank you for stopping. It was very kind of you."

"My pleasure." Riding even with the wagon seat, he had the feeling that she wouldn't mind if he stopped. Brakken smiled to himself. Women were always attracted to his rugged good looks.

The old man called, "You look like you ain't et in quite a spell. Me'n my girl are soon fixin' to. You're welcome to join us."

The invitation was powerfully tempting to the hungry rider, but he shook his head. "Thank you both, but I've got to be getting along." He kicked the mule into a lope and looked back at the pack mule where the hanging rope was secure and ready.

⤜

Clay reappeared from the crowd of spectators milling around the shipwreck survivors. "There are no women or children," he told Shiloh.

She closed her eyes and whispered, "Thank God."

"All the survivors have been cared for except one man. He seems to be sick, and none of the local men . . ."

She interrupted, "I'll take care of him."

Clay hesitated, frowning. "He may need more care than you can give him, especially now."

"If the man is ill and needs care, the Christian thing to do is care for him. Besides, Mara will help me. Please, Clay, get him."

He nodded and again disappeared into the crowd.

⤜ CHAPTER III ⤜

CLAY RETURNED a few minutes later accompanied by a clean-shaven, auburn-haired man of medium height. He appeared to be in his late twenties. Thin and pale and shivering with the cold, he held on to an old horse blanket someone had thrown over his shoulders. Clay carried the man's large carpetbag.

"Shiloh," Clay said, "this is Jared Huntley. Mr. Huntley, Mrs. Laird."

"Mr. Huntley," she said, "I'm sorry this happened."

"Thank you," he replied weakly, momentarily letting go of the blanket. It fell open, revealing a dress coat and vest. Lacking the typical deep V front, his buttonless vest was squared off a couple of inches below his chin.

He replied, "I'm grateful that all of us safely reached shore. It is very kind of you to offer your hospitality."

Shiloh broke in, anxious to save the shipwreck survivor any more talk than necessary. "I have a separate building with living accommodations at my place. You're welcome to them."

"Thank you. To ease your mind, I am not afflicted with anything contagious. The ship had a shortage of everything, including fruits and vegetables, and what food there was had a most disagreeable odor and taste."

Shiloh smiled. "You will not have to endure any such problems in my home." Without waiting for his reply, she turned to Clay. "There's only room for two in the buggy. You take him, and I'll hire a carriage."

"I'll get a carriage," Clay offered, "but first, Mr. Huntley, you'd better sit down."

"God bless you for your kindness," Jared said, "but I am feeling stronger, so I believe I'll stand."

"Suit yourself," Clay answered. "I'll be right back." He strode off and quickly blended into the crowd of spectators.

Shiloh smiled warmly at the man. "Did I notice a hint of accent in your voice?"

"I'm proud to hail from Virginia." Jared seemed talkative and sounded well educated. "I apologize for the inconvenience.

I'll only need a few days to recuperate. My wife and I became quite ill while rounding the Horn."

"Wife?" Shiloh repeated. "Where is she?"

"She died last week. We buried her at sea."

"Oh! I am so sorry!" Shiloh's own recent loss made her ache with sympathy for this man.

Jared said, "I am grateful to you and your husband . . ."

Shiloh interrupted, "Clay is not my husband."

Jared looked uncertainly at her face. "I . . . I thought . . ."

"My husband was killed in June. He and Clay were very good friends and business partners."

"Oh."

Shiloh turned to look for Clay, but he wasn't in sight. Shiloh returned her attention to Jared. "What happened to your ship?"

"Ah, the *Summer Cloud*. At first, she was a thing of beauty and fast as a bird on the wing. Then we lost the stern mast in a violent storm rounding Cape Horn and started slowly taking on water. It wasn't so bad until last week when more bad weather increased the leaking alarmingly. Fortunately, we had a ship's master with an iron will. He was determined to reach San Francisco in spite of our perilous situation. We all joined him in praying for that."

Jared smiled ruefully and glanced toward the bay. "Perhaps we should have been more specific and prayed that we would safely dock at the wharf."

Clay arrived with the horse and buggy, followed by a springless wagon pulled by a sway-backed brown mule.

"Nothing available but hotel omnibuses," he explained. "I hired that wagon, but it'll shake a person's teeth loose. Shiloh, if you'll take Mr. Huntley in the buggy, I'll follow in the wagon."

When the buggy began to move, Jared's talkativeness ended. He leaned back, closed his eyes, and seemed to nap. Shiloh's heart went out to him. In silence, she directed the horses inland, admiring how many brick and other permanent buildings had been erected downtown since she had arrived in late May. She started to comment on that, but her passenger seemed to be asleep.

He didn't stir until Shiloh turned the mare down a side street. Jared opened his eyes and sat up, gazing toward the only house at the end of the road.

The one-story adobe structure had a look of comfort and solidness. Red tile roof and stout wooden beams protruded from the ends of the eaves. Clay pots hung suspended from leather thongs in the partly enclosed veranda. Summer flowers had withered in the pots. A small garden graced both sides of the path leading to the front door.

When Shiloh quietly reined in the horse, Jared exclaimed, "What a lovely home!"

"Thank you. It was built by one of the last Spanish *rancheros,* Don Diego Alvarez. He now lives down the coast. He sold it to my husband. I share it with Mara."

"Mara?"

"Yes. She and I have been like sisters since we were little girls. You'll meet her in a moment. She slept in the building out back until my husband died. Then she moved to the main house with me."

Clay arrived in the wagon, paid the driver, and reached the buggy in time to help Shiloh alight. Jared unsteadily climbed down by himself, accepted Clay's offer to carry the carpetbag, and followed him and Shiloh toward the house.

Jared said, "I can see part of a building in back. I presume that's where I will have my quarters?"

Shiloh nodded. "It's the cookhouse, but it also has sleeping quarters and a small parlor. I'm sorry it's not better."

"I'm sure it will be fine," Jared interrupted. "Would you think it terribly rude of me if I asked to be excused so I may go there now?"

"Please make yourself comfortable, Mr. Huntley."

"I'll help you get settled," Clay volunteered as the guest continued along down the path.

"That's not necessary."

"It's locked," Clay interrupted, falling into step beside him. "I'll show you where the key is. Besides, I've got your bag."

Mara opened the door where Aldar had carried Shiloh across the threshold as a bride.

"Who's that?" Mara asked in her straightforward way.

"Jared Huntley of Virginia. His ship sank," Shiloh replied, entering the home where the fireplace glowed with pleasant warmth. She removed her cloak and hung it up by the door. She walked on through the room and down the hallway to the bedroom opposite Mara's, explaining how she and Clay had met her guest.

Shiloh wanted to rest, but she forced the need aside. She checked her appearance in an oval mirror on the tall armoire and ran her hands down her body, grateful for Mara's expert sewing skills. The skirts of Shiloh's dresses fell softly and loosely. Two petticoats also helped conceal the fact that she was five months pregnant.

Shiloh told Mara, "Mr. Huntley seems like a very nice gentleman. He'll be back in a moment and you'll get to meet him."

"I only got a glimpse of him. He is rather nice looking," Mara commented. "I just hope he's not like that other Southerner, Jefferson Locke."

Still seething over her encounter with him, Mara explained what had happened. "If he's right, I can't even own my own boardinghouse. But I'll find a way to beat him," she concluded.

Shiloh put her arms around Mara. "Knowing you, I'm sure you will. But you've heard how some of the men at the Monterey Convention made an effort to exclude free Negroes from even living in California."

Mara's voice took on an iron sound. "But others voted

down a provision that working beside a Negro, free or slave, would be degrading."

Shiloh's strong antislavery feelings had made her aware of the convention's makeup. Twenty-two of the delegates had been born in northern states. Fourteen were natives of southern states, and only one of those had come to California from a free state. Other delegates included six native Californians and four foreign born.

"I'll help you get your boardinghouse," Shiloh assured Mara as footsteps sounded on the small back porch. "And we'll find a way for you to own the real estate. We'll talk after we get our guest settled."

Shiloh walked toward the back door to admit the two men. She introduced Mara and Jared with the same trepidation she had felt when Mara and Clay had met. Shiloh was never quite sure how a southerner would react to Mara, even out here in California.

Shiloh observed two things about Jared although both lasted only a second. His eyes opened slightly in surprise because Shiloh had not told him that her childhood friend was a Negro. She also recognized that Mara's beauty had startled him. However, he quickly masked both by saying softly, "Mara."

She merely nodded, then said, "I was just starting supper preparations. If you'll excuse me."

"Ah!" Jared exclaimed, "You're the maker of those delicious fragrances that wafted in from the other end of that building." He motioned toward the cookhouse.

"I am," Mara replied shortly and went out.

Leading the way back to the parlor, Shiloh explained to Jared, "There's such a danger of fire that the cooking is done in that separate building. But Mara won't disturb you; there's another room between the kitchen and your living quarters."

"So I noticed through the windows out there," Jared replied.

Shiloh indicated that the men should sit in the horsehair

upholstered chairs. She took a straight-backed chair as she found it more comfortable.

Shiloh asked, "Will those accommodations do for the time being, Mr. Huntley?" When he assured her they were fine, she queried, "What was your occupation back home?"

"I was admitted to the bar last year. Before that, I worked with a stagecoach line in New York."

Shiloh exclaimed in surprise. "You did?"

"Yes. That provided the necessary resources to earn my law degree."

"My husband had a dream about starting a stagecoach company that would serve California and eventually connect it with the East."

"Mr. Patton told me a little about that. He must have been a real visionary, Mrs. Laird."

"I realize that now. However, at the time, it just seemed to me that it was Aldar's dream, which he and I would share together." The words started another flood of memories. She fell silent.

"If it's too painful to talk about . . ." Jared began, but she shook her head and spoke quickly.

"It's all right. Aldar and Clay had planned to be partners in this venture. Now, Clay and I are trying to carry out Aldar's plans, but neither of us has his great understanding of the details on how that could be done."

"Perhaps I can be of help to you," Jared volunteered, then turned to Clay, who was his usual taciturn self in the presence of most people. "Mr. Patton, I came to California because I have great expectations of what a man can do in such a rich new land of opportunity."

He turned his eyes on Shiloh. "I'm very interested in what's been happening politically these last few months. I'd like to ask Clay a few questions. Do you mind?"

"Not at all. In my parents' Pennsylvania home, I listened in on countless conversations of a political nature. Mostly about the slavery issue."

Jared commented, "You came from a northern home, so I assume your father was against slavery?"

"Yes. Well, he and his wife adopted me. They were strong abolitionists. I never knew my birth parents. It's only fair to warn you that I share the views I grew up with. You Virginians hold contrary ideas about slavery."

"I see nothing wrong with it," Jared admitted, shifting his gaze to Clay. "I dare say that, as a Texan, you probably agree with me?"

Clay didn't answer, but stared thoughtfully at his boot for a long moment.

Shiloh suddenly realized that she and Clay had never discussed this sensitive issue. She really didn't know where he stood on the topic.

"I'm not much on voicing my personal opinions on most things, Jared," Clay finally answered. "But if you'll ask questions, I'll answer as best I can about the political situation here in California."

"I'd appreciate that."

Shiloh stood up, saying, "Please excuse me. I'll go help Mara."

She walked out the back door and across the ten feet to the cookhouse. Through the window on the far left end, Shiloh could see Mara moving about as she prepared the meal.

As Shiloh entered, Mara turned her attention from the contents of a big iron kettle on the black cookstove. "That man has hungry eyes," she commented.

"Jared?"

Mara nodded.

Shiloh pulled an apron from a wooden peg by the door. "His wife just died a week or so ago."

Mara made a derisive sound. "The way he looked at me, I wouldn't think he was married." She picked up the coffeepot from the back of the stove and poured two cups while Shiloh seated herself at the small table by the front door.

"Do you think my reputation will be ruined if Mr. Huntley stays here, even in a separate building?"

"You know what folks will say." Mara sat her cup on the table. "But don't worry. I'll be here."

"For all your hard reputation, Mara, you're always looking out for others."

Mara smiled and tried to look sternly at Shiloh.

"I'm looking out for myself, and don't you ever forget it!"

"Coming back to Mr. Huntley, I believe he is a true gentleman. Don't you?"

"You're still too naive."

"How so? He said he lost everything when his ship sank, except for the clothes on his back and that bag."

"I see things my white sister doesn't," Mara observed sagely, but she declined to elaborate.

☙

When Shiloh reentered the house, she was startled to hear Clay's voice slightly raised. "Are you saying that California won't be admitted as a state?"

"As I told you," Jared replied a little sharply, "Southerners don't want any free territory west of Missouri. The Missouri Compromise of 1820 . . ."

"But California has got to be a state!" Clay interrupted. "Most of the people who are pouring in here from the East expect that."

"I suspect there will be a terrible fight in Congress, but in the end, you won't get your statehood."

Jared's tone changed when Shiloh entered the room. He stood, smiled, and said, "Clay and I have just been having a stimulating conversation."

"So I gathered," Shiloh replied, glancing at Clay. She could see angry little lights in his eyes. She had never known him to show much emotion about politics.

Suddenly Jared excused himself with, "If you two don't

mind, I'm rather exhausted from the day's events. I think I'll retire for a while."

∞

Mara heard Jared enter his bedroom at the far end of the cookhouse. She paid no attention but continued her dinner preparations. A moment later she heard the door to the kitchen open from the small sitting room that connected the two ends of the building.

He leaned against the doorjamb and studied her for a silent moment. After a quick glance at him, Mara bent and picked up a piece of wood to put in the stove.

"Mara," Jared said softly, causing her to look up again, "come to my quarters tonight after Clay's gone and Shiloh is asleep." He tossed a gold coin toward her.

She watched it land on the stove and roll off onto the floor at her feet; she recognized it as an eagle, or ten dollars.

"I'm no slave," she said coldly, fixing him with hard black eyes.

He raised his eyebrows and smiled. "There will be another coin just like it waiting."

"Get out of here!"

Obviously startled at the blunt reply, his eyes narrowed. "Now see here."

"No, you see here!" She turned to face him, a heavy ladle in her hand. "I am not for sale at any price!"

He hesitated a second, then shrugged and started toward the coin in the middle of the floor.

As he bent to pick it up, she said softly, "Leave it."

He straightened up, grinning. "Changed your mind?"

"No. That's the price of your mistake."

"I don't pay for what I don't get!" He again reached for the coin.

She smacked his hand with the ladle. "That's your second mistake," she assured him in a barely audible voice. "Don't ever take me for granted again."

Rubbing the back of his hand where the ladle had hit, he considered her in silence before smiling. "I like a little fire in a woman," he said and reached out. He grabbed her so fast that she dropped the ladle and threw her hands up to his chest. She could feel many round, flat, hard pieces in Jared's vest. She realized the vest was filled with coins. They had to be gold coins.

"I always get what I want," he said huskily, looking down into her beautiful face.

"So do I," she replied, shoving both hands against his chest. There was no fear in her dark eyes, just a cold calmness as she raised her right shoe and scraped it hard down his shin. When she felt his foot, she threw all her weight onto it, grinding her heel into what she hoped were his toes.

With a yelp of pain, he released her and stepped back, breathing hard and watching her.

She reached behind her to the pegs that protruded from the wall. She removed a heavy wooden mallet used to tenderize meat and faced him in silence.

He warned, "This isn't over."

She watched him leave. Her hands could still feel the strange vest that she was now sure contained gold coins.

"No," she whispered, "it's not over, but not for the reason you think."

∽ CHAPTER IV ∽

S HILOH WAS pensive the next morning when Clay arrived with the wagon. She definitely did not feel up to facing the office this morning.

Clay, riding beside her on the single front seat, sensed her feelings and drove in silence, content to glance at her and admire the way the sun enhanced her red-gold curls and lovely face.

Upon arising, Shiloh had as usual prayed for patience and wisdom in dealing with the various problems facing the company. Yet as the wagon moved across the sandy hill, she couldn't see any answers to those prayers.

Finally she sighed deeply and turned to Clay. "Am I being selfish? I know we have to deal with all these business problems, but I keep thinking about my baby. I can't help but wish I could stay home, make baby clothes, and plan how to convert Mara's room into a nursery."

"I wish you could do that too."

His sympathetic tone almost made the tears start. None of this was Clay's fault, but she found herself directing all her frustrations at him.

"I know you do, but instead I have to make this daily trip to the office then spend all day doing things done only by men in the rest of this city. I have to act as if there is no expected child. On top of that, I have to deal with male merchants who act polite but obviously wish they didn't have to work with a woman in my condition. All I want is to be an expectant mother!"

"We could probably hire someone."

"No!" She hadn't meant to respond so sharply, but her emotions were raw and her tolerance almost nonexistent. "You know we can't afford that."

Clay hesitated before answering. He recalled how his wife, Elizabeth, had been during her pregnancy. He had been younger then and not too understanding. But now both Elizabeth and their son, Mark, were long in their graves, and Clay had learned patience. Finally he replied quietly, "Neither can we afford to have you jeopardize your health, or your baby's."

Shiloh nodded. "I guess this takes us back to our drive yesterday when we started to make some decisions. They've got to be made, no matter how difficult."

Clay absently slapped the reins along the mare's back. "I agree. But first, there's something new that you should know."

Something about his voice made Shiloh look up. She studied his face intently, but he stared straight ahead and didn't meet her eyes.

"Well?" she prompted.

"Remember what Jefferson Locke said when we met him on the road?"

"He said several things." She instantly regretted the impatient edge to her words.

"I mean, what Locke said about there being three basic reasons why the movement failed for California to become a separate nation instead of a state. You remember what those reasons were?"

Shiloh shifted on the hard wooden seat, trying to ease her aching back. "Yes." She softened her reply. "He said they needed a newspaper to carry the movement's message and that they needed to raise an army. Oh, and there was something about no organized staging system."

Clay turned to face her as she continued. "But that's what you and I are trying to do: give California an . . ." She stopped as another thought hit her. "You don't think he wants *our* stage line?"

"I ran into him last night at supper," Clay replied. "He said he and Denby Gladwin want to meet with you and me first thing this morning at our office."

"Did he say why?"

"No, but I think we can both guess."

"He probably wants to buy us out. But what if we don't sell?"

"He could wait for us to go broke and then buy our line for next to nothing."

"Locke might do something like that, but not Gladwin. He helped me survive after Aldar died."

Clay didn't answer but looked at her the same way Mara did when she accused Shiloh of being naive.

Shiloh reviewed her impressions of Denby Gladwin and

confirmed her own naivete. Aldar had introduced her to Gladwin at one of his two canvas-tent hotels. He was a stout man with a bulging middle and hairy forearms. He exuded power. Aldar had told her that's what Gladwin wanted: power and money. A lot of people in California wanted the same thing, and many were willing to do anything necessary to get it.

Instead of seeing California become a state, Gladwin preferred to form a separate nation, the Empire of Pacifica. Gladwin wanted Aldar to join the Pacifica movement, but he had refused, causing Gladwin's short temper to erupt.

One of the last things he had said to Aldar shortly before Aldar died had sounded ominous. "This world belongs to those who know what they want and are willing to reach out and take it."

Riding beside Clay and recalling Gladwin's words made Shiloh fear that this morning, which had started off badly, had suddenly gotten worse. Shiloh's emotions piled up so rapidly that she had to caution herself to be careful. *Don't jump to any conclusions. Listen to what they have to say.*

But she was in no mood to obey herself when she saw Locke's horse and buggy outside the frame building where Shiloh and Clay had their office. They climbed the stairs to find the two men waiting outside their second-story office.

Gladwin was a man of considerable bulk. He was not a handsome man, and the sight of the usual dead stub of a cigar in his mouth did not enhance his image. He removed the cigar with a flourish and bent to kiss Shiloh's hand. She resisted the temptation to draw back while Clay spoke to Locke and opened the office door.

"Like I told Aldar the first time I ever laid eyes on you, Shiloh," Gladwin said, straightening up, "you're a mighty pretty woman."

She tried to make a light reply. "Thank you, but I assure you that right now I feel anything but pretty." The faint odor of stale cigar lingered on her hand, making her slightly queasy.

Shiloh had made some changes in the office since coming to work there. The counter ran along the front, just inside the door. A swivel chair and rolltop desk still sat prominently. But around it, three straight-backed wooden chairs had replaced the upturned empty barrels that had sufficed before.

The two visitors waited until Shiloh had chosen one of the chairs. Clay leaned on the counter.

"We'll come straight to the point," Locke began, showing crooked teeth in what was probably meant to be a pleasant smile.

"I'll handle this, Jefferson," Gladwin said, shifting positions on his chair and looking quickly from Shiloh to Clay.

She caught a momentary flash of anger in Locke's face, but he caught himself and forced the smile back.

"It's no secret," Gladwin continued, "that your one-vehicle stage line is having some financial trouble."

"Nothing we can't handle," Clay said quickly.

Shiloh nodded although she knew that certainly wasn't true.

Gladwin continued around the dead cigar. "Locke and I aren't here to disagree with you two. We've come to make you a fair business proposition."

"That's right," Locke added. "Best deal you'll ever get."

Gladwin shot him a disapproving look, then turned back to Shiloh and Clay. "How would you like to have the financial resources to expand your business? I mean, a first-class office on the ground floor in a choice location. You could buy the finest stagecoaches and the best horses. Plus you could erect way stations and hire drivers and other help to expand this stage line, not only in California but also to the Missouri River, as Aldar had planned."

Shiloh wanted to stop Gladwin and his tempting words, but the picture he painted so closely matched what Aldar had envisioned that she sat without replying.

She wondered briefly how Gladwin knew so much about Aldar's plans. Then she glanced at Clay, trying to understand what he was thinking. His eyes were half closed but steadily fixed on the speaker.

"Sound wonderful?" Gladwin asked, waving the cigar in a broad circle. "Everything any stage company could ask. Right?"

"Right," his partner echoed, then flinched as Gladwin's gray eyes fastened onto his.

Clay inquired quietly, "Why don't you start your own stage line?"

Gladwin shook his head. "We've got too much to do in other areas, so we don't have time to do anything else."

Clay was thoughtfully silent. He was sure the real reason was that the U.S. government would not grant a mail franchise to men who advocated creating a separate nation of California.

Finally, Clay asked, "What's your proposition?"

"Not that we're interested," Shiloh hastily added.

"Of course." Gladwin popped the cigar stub back in the corner of his mouth and turned to his partner. "Locke, you used to be a lawyer. Lay it out for them."

Clearing his throat, Locke explained, "It's simple, really. Gladwin and I will put up the money for everything you need to expand your stage line in California. You two will ostensibly be the sole owners, so no one can know Gladwin and I have anything to do with the line. For that, you'll be well paid and have the honor of being successful stage operators. So what do you say?"

Shiloh and Clay exchanged knowing glances. They couldn't say it, but both knew that there was more to the proposal than met the eye.

Clay said, "Shiloh and I will talk it over."

As Gladwin and Locke left, the business day was beginning. Clay left in search of short-haul passengers at the hotels while Shiloh dealt with merchants who came in to make transportation arrangements.

Finally, the day ended. Shiloh wearily closed the office door and let Clay assist her into the wagon for the ride home. She was in no mood to discuss Locke and Gladwin's offer, but she knew it had to be done.

She asked Clay, "Have you had a chance to think about what they said?"

"Some." He clucked to the mare, who kicked up sand from the road. "It seems logical." he explained. "We could carry out Aldar's dream, pretty much the way he and I had planned. I'd head up the field work. An experienced man would run the office, and you could stay home and do what you want to prepare for the baby."

"That's not the way it would actually be, and we both know it," she replied vehemently. "We would really be a front for people whose ideas I totally disagree with. It *wouldn't* be Aldar's dream come true. And once those men had us under their thumbs, who knows what they would do?"

"I agree with you, but let's look at everything, point by point, and then decide."

☙

After a hot bath and full restaurant meal, Brakken's stolen gold dust was gone, but he felt great. He could always steal from another miner, and he still had the gold double eagle coin.

He began whistling cheerfully as sunset approached, and he guided the mules through the last of the foothill gold country. They had left the manzanita, chaparral, and pines behind. Oaks dotted the smaller hills that blocked his view of Johnson's ranch.

Brakken had inquired at the hotel and had learned that this ranch was the only civilized spot he would see until he reached Sutter's Fort farther down in the valley. There he could begin his search in earnest.

He had no doubt that eventually he would find both the

man and the woman. The anticipation made him kick his heels against the mule, but the nearly exhausted animal had no extra speed to give.

Brakken had turned to look back, tugging on the pack mule's lead rope, when his mount suddenly swerved.

"What the?" Brakken cried, whirling around to face forward again.

A young man with as wild a beard and uncut hair as Brakken's own had stepped from behind a huge valley oak that had lost most of its leaves. He pointed a rifle at Brakken's chest.

"Evening, mister," the rifleman said pleasantly. "Seen you top that ridge a while back and figured it'd be neighborly for me to wait up for you."

Brakken didn't scare easily. His skinny mules and the thin pack the second one carried showed he had little of value. He was more annoyed than anything else.

"That thing you're holding on me doesn't look too neighborly."

"Oh that." The stranger cast a quick glance at the percussion rifle, then back to the rider. "I won't need this when you dismount and I ride off with your mules."

Brakken stared, not having expected that.

"Tell you what," the rifleman said in a friendly way, "I'll trade you. My horse for your mules." He jerked his head toward a huge boulder behind him.

Brakken saw a horse lying on its side, all four feet thrust out stiffly in rigor mortis.

"Now see here," Brakken began, temper suddenly showing. "You can't leave a man on foot out here in this country! There's not another living person between here and Johnson's ranch!"

"Easy, mister." The rifle didn't move from where it was aimed at Brakken's chest. "Now, you just step down, nice and . . . hey! Don't I know you?"

Brakken didn't reply. Neither did he move.

"Sure I do!" The gunman stepped a little closer and squinted up at the rider. "Underneath all that wild hair and beard, you're one of the Brakken twins from Texas!"

Brakken replied coldly, "My name is Yancy Tate."

"Maybe that's what you're calling yourself, but that wasn't your name back in the states. I recognize your voice. Sounds like you're talking with a craw full of pebbles."

Brakken searched his memory but couldn't place the other man's voice or what little of his face he could see under the beard. "I told you my name."

"It's Alvin Brakken!" the rifleman interrupted. "Some *hombre* hanged your twin brother some years back! Yeah! Now it all comes back to me! You looked alike as two peas in a pod, but Alvin, *you* had the funny voice."

Brakken started to protest again while wondering if he dared reach for his pistol. But it was a percussion weapon, and he had carefully removed the cap so it wouldn't accidentally discharge. The way it was, the gun was only good for a bluff, and Brakken didn't think that would work with this adversary.

"Now," the stranger continued, "I'll take your rifle and pistol." Sticking Brakken's handgun in his belt and easing the rifle to the ground, the robber said, "Now you can step down, nice and easy, then empty your pockets."

As Brakken obeyed, he tried to palm the gold coin, but the other man warned, "I want that too."

"You got to leave me something!"

"There's water in the creeks, and you can walk to Johnson's by this time tomorrow. Now, step away and start walking west."

Controlling his rising anger with difficulty, Brakken obeyed, cursing softly under his breath.

"Watch your language," the stranger advised. "I got tender ears."

Brakken stared hard, vainly trying to recognize the man who had known him in Texas. "I'll remember you," Brakken said quietly. "I'll catch up with you, and I'll kill you!"

"You shouldn't have said that, Alvin," the man replied, tilting the rifle barrel toward Brakken's head. "I'm beginning to think that there's only one sure way to keep you from doing that."

Too late, Brakken realized his error, but he tried to bluff it out. "Forget it." He deliberately turned and started walking, his skin puckering with the expectation of being shot in the back. When that didn't happen after a few steps, he stopped and looked back. The rifleman was about to mount the lead mule.

"Can I at least have my rope?" Brakken asked.

"Rope? You're here in this wilderness, penniless and unarmed. There's not another soul within miles, and you want me to leave your rope?"

"It's tied on the outside of the pack. I can get it easy."

The rifleman examined the rope, shrugged, and began working it free with one hand while he kept the gun on Brakken. "Looks just like any old rope, so I guess you may as well have it."

He tossed the coil toward Brakken who deftly caught it. "Alvin, why do you want this particular rope?"

"It's Tate. I'm going to hang somebody with it," he replied and again started walking west.

⌒

Dusk slipped over San Francisco's hills with the same quietness as its famous fog when Clay stopped the wagon in front of Shiloh's house. For a moment, neither moved. They sat silently on the high wagon seat, each sensing that this was a momentous time.

Then Clay looked down at her and commented, "From what you've said, it sounds as though you've made up your mind."

Shiloh considered his words, then slowly nodded. "Yes, I guess I have. How about you?"

He managed a faint smile. "I'm with you. We don't want to be associated with Gladwin and Locke."

Shiloh returned the smile, but inside, she fought down a frightening sense of panic. That decision not only meant that they had all their original obstacles to overcome, but now they would also surely face new threats from Gladwin and Locke.

"We need a plan," Clay said, stepping on the front wagon spokes and onto the ground. He reached up to help her down. "I've been thinking about some men who might help us with the money we need. Have you ever heard of General Mariano Vallejo or Captain John Sutter?"

"Who hasn't? They're probably the two biggest land owners in this part of California."

"Maybe they could help us financially," Clay said.

Shiloh considered his idea for a moment then nodded. "Maybe they can."

∞

At Shiloh's insistence, Clay stayed for dinner. Jared Huntley did not join them but remained in his room. Shiloh guessed he had overdone things yesterday and was resting after his shipwreck ordeal. Mara didn't disagree. Neither did she mention her encounter with Jared.

When Clay left late that evening, he took with him a short list of prominent, wealthy men they had carefully compiled. Among them were Vallejo, a native *Californio* who owned vast acres of land in the Napa area to the north, and Sutter. A native of Switzerland, Sutter had become a naturalized Mexican citizen and now owned leagues of land around Sacramento. The well-known generosity of both men made Clay hopeful that they would loan Laird and Patton Stage Lines the money they needed.

That required Clay to personally call on the prospective lenders. But first he and Shiloh would work out a business proposal to make the men see the benefits of backing the stagecoach venture.

Shiloh said good night to Mara and retired, exhausted but hopeful, to her bedroom.

Mara remained before the fireplace, staring thoughtfully into the flames. When she no longer heard Shiloh moving about in her room, Mara silently rose from her chair. Leaving the candle behind, she walked into her darkened bedroom and eased up to the window.

Through it, she could see Jared sitting by the small box stove in the center room, reading by the light of three candles. Satisfied, Mara returned to the living room and came back with the candle.

She set it on the washstand, then walked around the end of her bed in front of the window. Without looking out the window, she began undoing the back of her dress. She started to pull it over her head, then stopped.

She walked slowly back around the end of the bed. Without turning her head, she saw that Jared had blown out his candles. Only a little bit of the fire in the stove glowed in the darkness.

Smiling with satisfaction, Mara reached into her armoire and removed her long nightgown. She slowly undressed down to her chemise. Then she walked back around the end of the bed and turned the covers down.

She heard Shiloh's bare feet at the doorway. "You know, Mara, I just thought of some . . . Mara! The window!"

Mara straightened slowly and glanced at the window. "Oh, the shade," she said.

Shiloh hurried across the room and pulled the shades closed. "You forget we're not alone anymore! With the light on the other side of the room, Jared could see right through your chemise!"

Mara suppressed a smile. "Yes, I suppose he could."

∞ CHAPTER V ∞

CLAY LEFT Shiloh at the office before going to meet Gladwin. Saturday was less hectic than weekdays, giving Shiloh an opportunity to bring the ledger up to date. But when she sat down before the untidy rolltop desk and opened the books, she felt disheartened. She was also concerned about how the short-tempered Gladwin would react to Clay's news that he and Shiloh were declining his offer.

Glancing at the ledger, Shiloh sighed because the income column was woefully smaller than the expenses. She wondered if it was a mistake to reject Gladwin and Locke's offer.

She didn't feel like doing the books and slammed the ledger shut. She needed to do something active to work off her tensions and fears. A look around the office convinced her that she could turn her attention to cleaning. Stacks of barrels, boxes, and crates still remained against the back wall. Most were empty, but some were nailed shut. Many had been left by the express business that had previously occupied this office.

Shiloh decided she could safely handle some of the smaller containers without injury to herself or the baby. She walked back, debating where to start. She would need help in getting some of the higher ones down.

The door opened. She turned around to see a burly bear of a man squeeze through. "Brother Sledger!" Shiloh exclaimed and hurried toward him. "I'm glad to see you."

"Same here," he answered in a low, rumbling voice. He studied her with eyes that were such a strange blue that Shiloh couldn't accurately describe them.

"What brings you here?" she asked, going to the end of the counter and raising it so he could enter.

He continued to study her thoughtfully before answering. "Looks like the good Lord did. Something wrong, Sister?"

She returned to her chair at the desk and motioned for him

to take one of the straight-backed ones. She was embarrassed that her inner struggles had registered outwardly. She asked, "Is it that obvious?"

He gingerly lowered his three-hundred-pound, six-foot-six-inch frame onto the chair, automatically testing if it would hold him. "When I was a little shaver in the backwoods, one of the first things I learned was how to read signs. Your face, especially your eyes, tell me something's troubling you."

She hesitated, absently letting her gaze drift around the room. The preacher had given her an obvious opportunity to share her concerns, but she wasn't certain it would be proper to say anything of a confidential nature without asking Clay.

"It's all right if you don't want to say," Sledger assured her, and changed the subject. "Will I see you at church tomorrow?"

"I'll be there." She needed soothing assurance in this time of fear and doubt.

Sledger nodded approvingly. "Good!" He hoisted himself to his feet and asked, "Is there anything I can do for you while I'm here?"

Shiloh didn't want him to go. She hurriedly sought an excuse to keep him there. "Why, yes, thank you. I was just going to see what was in some of those containers back there." She motioned toward the far wall. "But some are up too high . . ."

"I'll get them down for you," he broke in, leaving the counter and walking heavily across the wooden floor. "Those barrels are not as big as some of the men I've rassled to make them see the errors of their ways so they'd get right with the Lord."

Shiloh smiled and followed him to the stack. "When are you going to give up standing on empty whiskey barrels and preaching on street corners? Why not just pastor the church?"

"Lots of folks never enter a church, so I take God's message to them, wherever they are." He studied the stack before him. "You want me to start any special place?"

"No, just wherever you want." As he began lowering the

highest boxes, she explained, "Except for routine sweeping and hasty tidying up, this place is pretty much as it was when Aldar died and his partner, MacAdams, sold out to Clay. Those crates and barrels obviously didn't belong to MacAdams, or he would have taken them when he left."

Sledger finished setting the last container in a row on the floor. "You want me to open these?"

"Thank you. That would be a big help." She wished she could tell him what troubled her. But she stood silently as he began opening the boxes.

⬡

Mara had just finished making her bed when she heard Jared's footsteps coming down the hallway. She smiled to herself and looked up at he stopped in the doorway.

His hungry eyes swept over her briefly, then met her dark ones. "What do you want?" he asked bluntly.

"First, I want to sit in the parlor where it's proper." She moved toward him.

He stepped back and let her pass. "After what you did last night, I thought you were expecting me."

"I was," she replied matter-of-factly and led the way into the sitting room. She walked past the sofa to sit in a chair, motioning for him to take the other.

He looked at her with such uncertainty that she gave a low, throaty laugh.

He complained, "You're the most exasperating colored woman I've ever met." He hastily added, "But you certainly are some woman."

Mara smiled. "I knew you were a smart man. So tell me, why did you come to San Francisco?"

He wasn't in the mood for talking, but he was experienced enough not to rush things. "To get rich," he answered, leaning back in the chair. "Isn't that why everyone comes here?"

"So I hear. But I also hear that most men expect to make their 'pile' and return to their eastern homes. Is that your plan, Jared?"

He was jarred by the familiarity of a colored person addressing him by his first name, but he tried not to show his displeasure. "No. I plan to stay."

"So do I."

"Why?"

"Everything I've always wanted is here."

"And what is that?"

She leaned forward and met his eyes squarely. "To be everything that any woman of my looks and ability could be if she were all white."

He squirmed at the thought of a colored woman speaking so candidly. "You're a strange one," he observed. "Strong willed, blunt, and reaching for things that can never be."

"That's where you're wrong, Jared."

He flinched at the second use of his name and started to rebuke her, but his ultimate goal made him keep quiet. He waited until she continued.

"A while ago, you asked what I wanted. Well, first I want to own a lot downtown where I'll build a first-class boarding-house. From there, I'll move on up."

"You want to borrow some money for that?"

She laughed softly. "No. I have the money. What I need is someone to buy the land, then give it to me as a gift. That will avoid problems with some of the bigots and the obstructions I'm running into by trying to buy in my own name."

Jared's eyes opened in appreciation. "You're not only beautiful, but you can also think."

She gave him a little smile but didn't reply.

"All right," he said. "What are you willing to do for someone who might give you what you want?"

She leaned forward again. "What do you think would be an adequate exchange, Jared?"

This time, he did not even notice the familiarity. He abruptly reached out to her, but she stood suddenly.

She whispered, "Let me know when you decide." She walked out of the room.

Clay tied his horse outside of a new brick building with a ornate sign over the door: New York Hotel. It was a marked improvement over the board-and-canvas structure that had stood here when he had taken Shiloh and Aldar to breakfast back in June. Then there had been only a rough, hand-painted sign in front of rough cut framing timbers over which an ancient piece of canvas had been stretched. They had once been sails, salvaged from an abandoned ship in the harbor.

Six months ago, Denby Gladwin's office had been nothing more than a corner separated from the hotel's restaurant with other pieces of old sail. Now Clay knocked at a door apparently made of teak removed from another dead ship.

Gladwin opened the door, revealing an elegantly paneled room with a conference table and chairs.

"Clay! Good to see you!" Gladwin cried heartily, shaking hands and motioning for the visitor to enter. He rolled the ever-present cigar stub in the corner of his mouth before adding, "Grab a seat."

Clay remained standing. "Thanks, but this won't take long."

Gladwin's face clouded, the friendliness of his greeting replaced by a hard, flat tone. "I take that to mean you two have decided not to accept our offer?"

"We appreciate it, but that's the way it is."

"You realize what this means?"

Clay nodded. "We do." The chances of success for Laird and Patton Stage Lines had not only just decreased, but Clay also knew that Gladwin and Locke could be vindictive. However, that was a risk Shiloh and Clay had decided to accept.

Having delivered his message, Clay was ready to leave but didn't want to be rude. It would be bad enough having Gladwin and Locke against them without making the short-tempered Gladwin angry.

He removed the cigar stub from his mouth and used it to point at Clay. "You know we can ruin you?"

Clay shrugged. "That could happen without your help, as I'm sure you know."

"But why are you doing this?" Gladwin's features darkened, and a hint of temper sounded in his words.

"You really want to know?"

"I asked, didn't I?" he snapped.

Clay thought for a moment on how to best explain it. "You know that Aldar Laird had a kind of dream about stagecoaches running all over California."

"Get to the point."

"I was to be a part of that with Aldar. Of course, Shiloh shared her husband's vision. It was hers too. Now he's gone, and all she's got left is his dream. If we sold out to you and Locke, we'd simply be employees. But mostly, we would be fronting for the Pacifica movement. We want California to be a state, not a separate nation."

Clay paused before adding firmly, "We're going to do all we can to make Aldar's dream come true."

Gladwin's features relaxed. "I like Shiloh, and I always liked Aldar," he said quietly. "I would have given anything to have him with us in the Empire of the Pacific movement. But he was stubborn. I guess that stubbornness carries over to Shiloh and to you."

"I'm glad you understand." Clay turned to leave.

"I do, but Locke won't."

Clay turned back to look down on Gladwin. "Shiloh and I don't want any trouble with either of you."

"Try to understand his viewpoint, Clay. He wanted California to be admitted to the Union as a slave-holding state. The Monterey delegates voted against that, as you know. Naturally, Locke is very angry."

Gladwin rolled the cigar stub with his tongue before continuing. "So he decided that if he can't have California as he wanted it, he will join the Pacifica movement. Even if Congress approves statehood for California, which is highly doubtful, there's still a possibility for a separate nation."

"You really think that will ever happen?"

"Absolutely! Locke told you and Shiloh what we need to succeed."

"Yes. One important thing was a stage line. But it's not going to be Laird and Patton's." Clay put on his hat and started to leave.

"Hold on." Gladwin motioned for Clay to come back. When he did, Gladwin said, "I don't have many soft spots in my life, but I do for Shiloh. In anticipation of getting your stage line, I bought a used mud wagon. Paid for it with my money, not Locke's. It's a gift for your stage line."

Clay wasn't comfortable with the offer. "I can't speak for Shiloh, but under the circumstances, I don't want to be obligated to you."

"Then consider it a gift to Shiloh."

Clay briefly considered that. "Maybe I'm speaking out of turn, but I know her pretty well. I don't think she'll accept it, either."

"Tell her it's part of Aldar's estate; something I owe him."

Clay couldn't argue with that. "I'll tell her." He turned to leave.

"I sent it over to your place a while ago."

Annoyed, Clay asked, "My place?"

"Where you live over in Cow Hollow near the stables. You're still there, aren't you?"

Clay nodded, marveling at how sure Gladwin had been about the mud wagon. Clay stood with his hand on the door handle and confessed, "I don't understand you."

"You don't have to. It's something I want to do."

As Clay walked out, he knew that there was now another very real and direct threat to Shiloh and him.

☙

Alvin Brakken raged against the darkness that had fallen since the rifleman had ridden off with everything Brakken owned except the hanging rope.

Unable to see, with no flint to start a fire and not even a blanket to protect him from the crisp autumn night, Brakken hunkered downwind behind the great boulder near the dead horse. He had already examined the animal in hopes of finding a saddle blanket or some food or water. He found only the bridle and the saddle, which the rifleman had been unable to remove.

Coyotes yipped in the distance, making Brakken aware they could catch the dead animal's scent and come to investigate. He doubted they would bother him, but without a weapon, he couldn't feel comfortable. He felt about for rocks and limbs, but found nothing heavy enough to be of use.

The rising moon sent shadows slipping silently from the valley oaks. It was too cold for rattlesnakes to be out, but Brakken wondered if there were bears down this low, away from the mountains. Could be panthers. He might hear a bear approaching but not a big cat.

Something screeched off to his right, sending little tingles of fear along his shoulders and down his arms. After a tense moment of listening, he decided it was a small creature—nothing bigger than a wildcat. He had never heard of one attacking a person. Of course, this was California, and maybe the cats were different, but he doubted it.

Brakken's stomach constricted inside him, sending hunger pangs that seemed to pierce his body. He told himself that a man could go days without food, so he forced the stomach pains out of his mind. In the morning, he would find creek water to drink. Then he would start walking, knowing that Johnson's ranch couldn't be too far ahead. Beyond that was Sacramento and what he considered the logical place to pick up a warm trail.

I'll make it, he told himself as the cold night winds began.

He drew his knees under his chin and made himself into as tight a ball as possible so the cold wouldn't be so bad. *When I do, they'll pay extra for putting me in this fix.*

His anger seemed to insulate him against the chill, so he let his mind wander, concentrating on his revenge. It had driven him for seven years; now it would taste even sweeter when he extracted it.

෴

The preacher held up a small wooden box for Shiloh.

"This is the last one, but it's nailed tight. You got something I can use to pry it open?"

"There's a closet back there where I keep the broom. I'll take a look."

"I'll do it. You just sit."

He found a hammer and began using it on the box.

Shiloh watched him before deciding to say something about what troubled her. "Brother Sledger," she said, "a while ago you asked if something was wrong."

He broke off a small section of the wooden lid with his bare hands. "Preachers are good listeners, Shiloh."

"It's about a mighty important decision."

"They're sometimes hard to make."

"Actually, the decision has already been made. The hard part is planning how to carry it out."

"You mean about the stagecoach business?"

"Yes. Aldar had all these big ideas, which I always thought were wonderful. So did Clay. Except for getting a contract to carry the mail, Aldar never told either of us the details of how he planned to make it all happen. But I know he not only had plans for extending stage service all over California, but overland to the Missouri River too. Getting a government contract to carry the mail to all those places was very important."

"He was a real man of vision."

Shiloh nodded and continued. "At the time, I wasn't concerned because I certainly never expected his death."

"You never found any information in his personal belongings?"

She shook her head. "He didn't even leave a will. Later we found a document he and his partner, MacAdams, had signed. It gave me half of this business." She was tempted to add something Mara had said about why she hadn't liked Aldar. *He keeps secrets.*

"On top of all this, Denby Gladwin and Jefferson Locke have offered to fund our efforts to see Aldar's dream come true. But I don't like what they stand for. Clay and I have decided to try to do this alone, so now we need more than ever to find Aldar's plans."

Sledger looked at the scattered containers that had held some old receipts and other papers of the now defunct express company. "Maybe we'll find them in here someplace."

"We haven't found anything so far."

"Well, let's take a look in this last box." He ripped away the remaining top boards. "When I've finished with this, if there's nothing else I can do for you, I'll be on my way. And Shiloh . . . I'll pray for you."

"Thank you."

Both of them turned as the door opened and a pretty young blond woman entered.

"Good morning," Shiloh greeted her, coming to the counter.

"Morning." The blue-eyed woman smiled pleasantly. "I'm afraid I'm lost," she began, glancing from Shiloh to Sledger. "I'm looking for the offices of Laird and MacAdams Express Company. I was told it used to be in this building."

"It was," Shiloh explained, "but it sold out and is now Laird and Patton Stage Lines."

"Yes, I noticed the sign, so I'm hopeful that my trip isn't in vain."

From behind her, Sledger said, "Excuse me, Shiloh, but I found something you should see."

"Just put it on my desk, please," she said, still looking at the woman. "How may I help you?"

The long golden curls bounced as the woman shook her head. "I'm looking for Aldar Laird." When Shiloh looked surprised, the visitor added, "It's a business matter."

It was still hard for Shiloh to say it, but she replied, "Aldar is dead."

"Oh, I'm so sorry! That's dreadful! What happened?"

"He was killed last June." Shiloh didn't want to mention that he was murdered because that would open up a painful explanation. She said simply, "I'm Mrs. Laird. Is there something I can do for you?"

The woman's eyes widened. "You're his widow?"

When Shiloh nodded, the woman's hands fluttered nervously. "Oh, my! This is so unexpected." She paused then added, "I'm a widow too. My husband and Aldar owned some property together."

"What?" Shiloh was so startled the word popped out.

"Yes. I've come to ask for a settlement on my share."

ᗧ CHAPTER VI ᗧ

SHILOH STARED in disbelief. "Your share?"

"Yes," the blond woman replied. She hesitated before adding, "You obviously didn't know." She extended her right hand. "I'm Victoria Barclay."

Still in shock, Shiloh automatically identified herself. "I'm Shiloh Laird." She heard the preacher's heavy step behind her on the wooden floor. "Oh and this is Brother John Sledger. He's pastor at our church."

"Mrs. Barclay," he said, accepting the small hand she held out to him, "I'm sorry about your husband."

"Thank you." Victoria looked from Sledger to Shiloh. "May I come in?"

"Of course." Still stunned, Shiloh moved down the counter and raised the far end. "Please have a seat."

Sledger cleared his throat. "Shiloh, you must take a look at that box. I left it on your desk."

"I will after a while. Thanks for coming, Brother Sledger. I appreciate your help and the prayer."

"See you tomorrow," he replied and left.

Shiloh returned to her chair in front of the desk and turned to face Victoria, who had seated herself. "Forgive me, Mrs. Barclay," Shiloh said, "but I don't know what property you're talking about."

She fumbled with the drawstrings on her purse and urged, "Please call me Victoria."

Shiloh didn't want to do that. She didn't want to know this woman who had just made an outrageous claim.

"Mrs. Barclay," she said deliberately being formal, "I'm sure there's some mistake."

"I brought the deed," Victoria broke in without rancor, "in case Aldar and I needed to review some details and he didn't have his copy handy."

"I mean," Shiloh explained, "he did not own any property. All he had was a half-interest in an express company."

Victoria extended the document to Shiloh. "He also had a half-ownership in the Mount Saint Helena property described in this deed."

Accepting the document without looking at it, Shiloh replied, "I don't recognize that name."

"Henry, my late husband, told me that many people think Mount Saint Helena is an extinct volcano, but it's not really. It's northwest of Sonoma, if you know where that is."

"Yes, General Vallejo lives there," Shiloh replied, "but now I know there's some mistake about Mount Saint Helena because Aldar never mentioned being up there."

Victoria pointed to the document. "Is that your husband's signature at the bottom?"

Shiloh carefully examined it, expecting to see something totally unfamiliar to her. Reluctantly, she said, "It does look like his handwriting."

"I assure you that's what it is, along with Henry's. Now, please read the deed."

Trying to keep her emotions under control, Shiloh skimmed the contents. She finished, looking up uncertainly. "I'm not very good at understanding legal documents."

"I assure you that it's genuine, but I expect you would feel more comfortable if an attorney examined this. Do you know one?"

Jefferson Locke had been an attorney, Shiloh recalled, but she certainly didn't want to ask his advice about anything. "No, I don't . . . wait!" She thought quickly. "A lawyer newly arrived from the East is a guest in my home. Could he look at this?"

"Of course," Victoria said, returning the document to her purse and standing. "I'll be glad to show him. When shall we do that?"

"Someone is coming to take me home soon. Could you wait a bit? We can ride together."

"I have to return to my hotel, but I'll be back."

After Victoria had gone, Shiloh sat at her desk staring at the door. She still could not believe what she had just seen and heard. How could Aldar have failed to mention such an important matter? It was true that he hadn't always told her everything, but if he owned half-interest in some real estate, surely he would have told her. Or would he?

If Shiloh had read the deed correctly, then she and Victoria Barclay, as surviving widows, jointly owned a piece of property north of San Francisco. But a mountain? What kind of property was it? What was it worth? Why hadn't Aldar ever mentioned it?

Shiloh's eyes narrowed in concentration. What was it Victoria Barclay had said at the beginning? Something about coming to ask for a settlement on her share. That sounded as if she wanted to sell her part. Shiloh certainly couldn't buy it, and she already had enough problems without this one. She wished Clay would return.

∽

An hour after leaving Gladwin's office, Clay had hitched a team to the mud wagon, more properly called a passenger hack. The square, boxlike conveyance had three seats under the roof but no sides. Much lighter than a coach, the mud wagon had earned its familiar name because of its ability to go through terrain where heavier carriages mired down. From having lived in hilly San Francisco through the winter, Clay knew that the sandy streets could become impassable when the rains came. It was even worse in Sacramento, where the land was flat and had two big rivers for neighbors.

There had already been some indications of an early rainy season. Miners and other men, desperate to get to their destinations in places where spare horses and mules were almost nonexistent, would pay to ride in a carriage with a top. The open wagon that Clay had been using would be their last choice in rain or summer sun.

He decided to get the feel of the new conveyance and headed toward the Old Plaza surrounded by Washington, Clay, Kearney, and Dupont Streets. New structures around the square included the city hall, post office, hotels and some mercantile establishments.

Driving along, Clay enjoyed the jingle of chains and creak of harness leather. The team had no trouble with the light mud wagon, which handled well on the hills. He wasn't sure how Shiloh would react to Gladwin's gift, but for the time being, Clay appreciated the way it handled. This was certainly a lot more enjoyable than driving a vehicle with no pretense of springs. At least the mud wagon, weighing about five hundred pounds, had rounded irons that rested on thoroughbraces. These were not equal to the Concord's suspension system but certainly made easier riding than most carriages.

Clay's thoughts turned to the beautiful Concord that had sunk on the clipper just offshore. Clay wondered about Jared Huntley. The survivor said he had recently lost his wife. The pain of losing his own wife cut through Clay like a knife.

He shut his eyes, but the images were still there. They were as vivid as they were when he rode home one afternoon seven years ago on the west Texas plains, a handkerchief over his mouth against the blowing sand.

The door knocked off its leather hinges had first alerted him. He leaped from his horse and dashed toward the house calling, "Elizabeth! Mark!"

He found them inside the one-room structure he and Elizabeth had built together. Elizabeth was sprawled out on the floor, her long blond hair plastered across her crumpled and bloody body. She had vainly tried to shield their three-year-old son behind her.

Clay was alone in his anguish, while the wind moaned around the house. He vainly tried to deny that his family was dead. Then, when the truth penetrated, a terrible fury seized him. In his frantic search for clues to the killer's identity he learned that a lone horseman was responsible. In a sheltered corner of the yard where the winds had not erased them, Clay found recognizable hoof prints. The Brakken twins made their own distinctive horseshoes.

One of the lawless twins had attacked a lone, defenseless woman and child. But which one: Alben or Alvin? Clay swore he would find out. But first, alone in the mournful wind, he dug a single grave in the little patch of garden Elizabeth had coaxed from the earth. While the wind-blown dust made muddy streaks where tears ran down his cheeks, Clay buried his family side by side.

Then in a quiet, seething rage, he mounted and rode out to avenge their deaths. Asking questions of remote neighbors brought Clay to a garrulous old woman. From her, Clay determined that Alben Brakken had killed his wife and child.

Clay's vengeance had been swift and sure. He caught Alben riding at night and brought him by gunpoint to the scene of the tragedy. Under the cold stars with coyotes howling nearby, Alben's fear of Clay's quiet, controlled anger caused him to confess to the murders. Then he warned that if he was harmed, his twin brother would hunt Clay down, no matter how long it took.

When dawn came and the wind died down, Clay forced Alben into the small barn behind his home. There Clay hanged Alben from a rafter. Clay was tempted to burn the barn down around the corpse. Instead, he tied the body on its horse and torched both house and barn.

Clay poured powder down the barrel of his percussion rifle. Inserting the ball, he rammed it down as far as it would go. Then he pulled the hammer back, very carefully set the nipple in place, and gently lowered the hammer. The weapon could then be fired by simply pulling back the hammer and squeezing the trigger.

With the rifle ready, and leading Alben's horse, Clay rode purposefully toward the Brakkens' place. In his fury, Clay would have not hesitated to shoot Alvin if necessary.

Clay reached the ramshackle house at dusk. There was no light in the window, no smoke from the chimney. He rode to the doorstep, hitched Alben's mount to a post, untied the body, and dropped it with the rope still around the neck.

Clay rode away, aware that the surviving twin could come looking for him, as Alben had warned. Clay aimlessly drifted east, ending up driving both express and stagecoaches outside of New York City. Eventually, he joined Stephen W. Kearney's dragoons and came with them to California.

He took a deep breath to shake off the haunting memories and turned the mules up Washington Street, heading toward San Francisco's Old Plaza. Seven years had passed, but Clay looked back over his shoulder and wondered where Brakken was.

A sharp, shrill cry made Brakken's eyes pop open. A yellow hammer regarded him from a dead oak stump. When he moved, the bird flew, gliding up and down in a series of shallow dips that ended just above the ground.

Brakken forced his aching muscles to move in spite of the cold that had made deep sleep impossible. Throughout the night, he had slept fitfully, awakened at times by unknown wild animals moving through the darkness. When he managed to doze, nightmares disturbed him. A wispy fragment lingered in his mind. He couldn't quite recall the details, but it had something to do with the rope.

He glanced down at the coil that rested on the damp ground near his right hand. It was all the robber had left him yesterday afternoon. In a strange way that he could not explain, Brakken was glad he had persuaded the man to leave the rope. It still gave him hope, the same hope that had made him keep it all these years.

His anger at the man who had robbed him had slacked off. Brakken could understand robbing a man. If the situation had been reversed yesterday, he would have done the same. Picking up the coil of rope with cold, stiff fingers, Brakken slapped it against his legs, remembering when he had first seen it.

He had been out all afternoon with a young girl he had known since she was little. Now she was sixteen and developing so rapidly that Brakken had to know her better. She had been reluctant, but before the afternoon was over, she had yielded.

But something went wrong, for Brakken had the terrible feeling he had known again at dawn today. It was as though something were drawn tight about his neck so he couldn't breathe. It had been so bad that he had suddenly ended his session with the girl. Even so, Brakken arrived home in the darkness.

Turning his horse into the long dirt lane leading to the house he shared with his twin, Alvin frowned. He wondered why Alben hadn't unsaddled and turned his horse into the corral, and why he hadn't lit the candles or started a fire. Then Brakken smiled. His brother was probably entertaining a girl.

Dismounting, Brakken removed the saddle and blanket and turned his horse into the corral. Then, intending to surprise his brother and his girl, Brakken quietly slipped toward the front door. In the darkness, he tripped over something and almost fell. Cursing under his breath, he reached down, feeling in the night until he found the rope.

He tried to throw it aside, blaming his brother for carelessness in leaving it out. But it jerked tight in his hands. Puzzled, Brakken knelt and traced the rope back to whatever had held it.

He recoiled when his fingers touched a human neck and face. Suddenly fearful, he dashed inside and lit a candle. Trembling with an awful sense of already knowing, he shielded the flame and bent over the still form.

Brakken didn't realize that his connection to his brother stemmed from their beginning as one egg. What had been the start of one person's life had become two people. But he knew of several times when he and Alben seemed to feel each other's pain. Now he understood why the moment with his girl had been ruined by a sudden choking sensation.

As then, his memories now made Brakken cry out, startling some mule deer nearby. They threw up their heads in alarm, then fled, black tails tightly tucked down.

Brakken watched the deer go, wishing he had his rifle so he could shoot one to ease his hunger. Thrusting that idea aside, he began walking toward Johnson's ranch. He hoped that he wouldn't miss it in this desolate country.

Brakken carried a grudge well. He lived for revenge, and

that powerful motive drove him on, even in his destitute condition.

He came to a small creek and drank, filling his stomach with more than he needed in hopes of easing the increasing hunger pangs. Then he turned southwest again, his step firm, his resolve steady. He absently slapped the coiled rope against his leg. It had been a long, long trail, but it was getting shorter.

❧

Victoria Barclay left her room in the Stuart House on the Plaza and crossed the hotel lobby. The clerk caught her eye and nodded politely. She gave him a smile and pushed through the door to the street.

Three drivers had been talking together near their carriages. As one man, they turned and hurried toward her. "Where to, Miss?" a burly, red-faced driver asked, tipping his dirty hat. Before she could answer, the red-faced man took her arm and steered her toward a light hotel coach.

Victoria had smiled at all three men, but as the aggressive driver helped her up into the vehicle, she caught a whiff of alcohol on his breath.

"Uh," she said hastily, "I believe I'll walk. Thank you just the same."

"Ah, you'll get sand in your shoes," he replied, giving her a push. "Besides, a pretty lady like you might not be safe walking around in a town mostly filled with men. Some ain't seen a pretty woman in a year or more."

"Really, sir," Victoria exclaimed, keeping her voice low while trying to step down. "I do not wish to engage your services!"

"That's mighty fancy talk." The driver turned to give his two companions a knowing wink. "Tell you what, Miss," he continued, again looking at her. "I'll give you a ride for half fare. Can't beat that."

Victoria didn't want to cause a scene although a few men

passing along the board sidewalk were looking at her curiously. The other two drivers didn't seem inclined to intervene. They looked uncomfortable, making Victoria suspect they were afraid of their big companion. While she hesitated, she was aware that a team was approaching with the usual sound of leather and metal. The burly driver suddenly put both hands on her waist and lifted her bodily into the carriage.

"Sir!" she cried at his unexpected familiarity. Anger replaced her concern for not attracting attention. "I said that I do not wish to engage your services!"

He grinned and hoisted himself into the carriage, sitting down beside her. "No need to get upset, Miss. I just want to talk . . ."

He was interrupted by a quiet, firm voice. "Let her out. Now!"

The driver whirled around. "Mister, mind your own business!"

Clay didn't say another word. He grabbed the carriage's handle and yanked so hard the entire door came loose. He dropped it in the street and reached in with both hands. They closed about the man's shirt front. In one continuous motion, he was violently pulled from the carriage and dropped on top of the broken door.

"Ain't no need to get all het up, mister!" the driver protested, scrambling to his feet.

"You'd better get out of my sight!"

The words were spoken quietly but the driver heard the threat behind them. He had already felt the power in the tall man's arms. "I'm going! I'm going!"

He scampered off to the laughter of his two driver friends and the verbal approval of passing men who had stopped to watch.

"I'm sorry, Miss," Clay said, looking at her for the first time. Her long blond hair and fair skin reminded him of Elizabeth. "Are you all right?" he asked.

"Yes, thank you."

He reached up to offer her help in descending. "I've got a team." He motioned toward the mud wagon and mules standing in the middle of the street, blocking traffic. "May I give you a ride?"

"That's very kind of you, but I don't want to be an imposition. I can engage another carriage."

"No imposition," he assured her. "Where are you headed?"

"To MacAdams and Laird Express Company; no, wait! The name is now Laird and Patton. You know where it is?"

"I should. I'm Clay Patton."

She let him take her elbow and guide her toward the mud wagon. "Don't tell me you're the same Patton?"

"The very same," he assured her. "What can our line do for you, Miss . . . ?"

"Mrs.," she finished for him. "Mrs. Victoria Barclay, lately of Missouri. I just arrived in California about a month ago. I spent most of that time in Sacramento City because I had heard Aldar Laird was there."

"Aldar?"

"Yes, but I've just learned that he died."

"That's true." Clay was suddenly very curious to know why this attractive young woman wanted to see Aldar. But Clay couldn't ask so personal a question. Instead, he glanced toward the hotel. "Is your husband coming?"

"Henry was killed when his rifle accidentally discharged just before we started across the prairies."

"I'm very sorry." Clay helped her into the mud wagon's middle seat, his curiosity rising another notch. "I'll have you at the office in a few minutes."

He turned and stepped on the front wagon wheel to take the high outside seat, his mind filled with intriguing questions.

☜ CHAPTER VII ☞

For a long time after Victoria left, Shiloh sat at her
desk, ignoring everything on it, including the wooden box
the preacher had opened for her. She was very puzzled over
Victoria's claim.

The door opened, and Victoria returned, accompanied by
Clay. Victoria explained how they had met. She concluded,
"On the drive over, Mr. Patton told me about Aldar's death,
and why you're now in the stagecoach business. Your husband
was a man of great vision."

"He was," Shiloh agreed. "Shall we go? I hope that the lawyer will be well enough to look at your papers and answer some
of our questions."

As the three descended the stairs, Shiloh was eager to learn
what Gladwin had said when Clay rejected his offer. Now
Shiloh had to wait until she and Clay could talk privately.

Downstairs, only the mud wagon and team stood in front
of the building. Shiloh looked questioningly at Clay, "Where's
your wagon?"

"Back at my place. This passenger hack replaces it. That is,
if you want. Gladwin gave it to you."

Shiloh wanted to know the details but couldn't discuss them
in front of Victoria. She held back her frustration at not being
able to talk freely. She thought some explanation to Victoria
was in order. "Mr. Gladwin was very kind in helping me after
my husband's death. He gave me a letter of introduction to
influential merchants whom I needed as clients for what was
then the express business."

Victoria commented, "It's nice to have friends, especially in
times of trouble."

Shiloh was distressed as she approached the mud wagon.
She didn't want to be obligated to Gladwin in any way, and she

regretted that Clay had accepted the gift. She planned to promptly return the coach.

Victoria said, "I told Mr. Patton about my reason for being here. I thought you wouldn't mind, since you two are partners."

Shiloh sought a noncommittal answer. "Of course." Her frustration grew as she added pleasantly, "You said earlier that you had come overland by yourself. Surely it wasn't just to find Aldar and discuss this property situation?"

"Oh, no. My husband, Henry, had long planned to migrate here and to settle. He had once been a miner but was a farmer when I met him—a very successful one."

Shiloh had many questions to ask Victoria, but she waited until they had climbed into the mud wagon and Clay had taken his seat outside. He could not hear the women's conversation.

"Did your husband ever say how he and Aldar met?" Shiloh asked as the wagon started moving.

"Of course. Henry always told me everything."

The casual remark rankled Shiloh. She had loved Aldar with all of her being, and she was sure he had loved her, yet he had not shared everything with her.

Mara's familiar lament echoed in Shiloh's mind: "I don't like your husband. He keeps secrets."

Victoria explained, "Henry had come to California once before, prior to the war with Mexico. He met Aldar on that trip, and they bought the property."

Shiloh wondered where Aldar got the money for that purchase. What else had he not told her?

"Henry returned East," Victoria continued, "and we were married."

Shiloh looked at her with new interest. "Then you had only been married a short time before his death?"

"A little over a year. It was Henry's second marriage, but my first. He lost his wife three years before he came to California the first time. They had a grown son."

Shiloh estimated Victoria to be in her early twenties. Her late husband must have been at least in his midforties if his son was grown.

As though reading Shiloh's mind, Victoria said, "He was fifty-one when he died."

Shiloh was becoming more and more intrigued with Victoria. She asked, "Did your husband tell you what kind of property he and Aldar bought up north, and what they planned to do with it?"

"Why, farm it, I assume. Come to think of it, Henry never said that specifically. But why else would he own land? He loved farming."

Shiloh frowned. Farming had not been Aldar's background or interest. So why would he have gone in with someone on farm land? It just didn't make sense.

She asked, "Did your husband say how long he and Aldar knew each other?"

"No, but it had to have been a relatively short time. Now, enough about me. Tell me about yourself and Aldar. When did you come to California?"

Shiloh didn't want to discuss such matters, but neither did she want to seem to pry too much into Victoria's background. Not yet, anyway. So Shiloh somewhat reluctantly explained about meeting Aldar when he was east on business and coming together to California across the Isthmus of Panama.

When Clay stopped the team at Shiloh's house, she was pleased that Jared came out of his quarters to greet them. He was obviously recovering well from the trauma of the sinking ship.

After introductions, Shiloh drew Mara aside and asked if she had enough food to invite everyone for lunch. In the strange way she sometimes had of anticipating things, Mara replied that she had already prepared for unexpected guests.

Shiloh announced that she expected everyone to stay for lunch. In the meantime, she invited them to be seated in the parlor. After a few minutes of casual conversation, Shiloh briefly explained to Jared about the deed. "Would you mind looking at it?" she concluded.

"My pleasure." He accepted it from Victoria and studied it. Shiloh made small talk with Victoria and Clay, eager for Jared to finish.

When he looked up from the document, Shiloh spoke quickly. "What's your opinion, Jared? Is it valid?"

He replied, "I'm not familiar with the laws in California, but I've been reading the local newspapers about the decisions reached by delegates to Monterey this month."

"Yes?" Shiloh prompted, trying to not sound overly anxious. "Does that seem like a legal deed to you?"

"It does."

Shiloh had hoped it was spurious. If it were, she could put another perplexing problem behind her. But the attorney's words dashed that hope.

"Clay, correct me if I'm wrong," Jared said, glancing at the tall man, "but from what I've read, the delegates pretty much accepted previous Mexican law as the basis for what will be in effect under American law."

"That's right. The plan is also to have everything accepted by the U.S. Congress, if California becomes a state as expected."

Victoria shook her head, making the long golden strands dance. "Since we women can't vote, would you explain what that means to us, as widows of men who jointly owned property?"

Shiloh's head bobbed in agreement. She was very anxious to understand this problem now that it seemed to be dumped on her and Victoria.

Jared lightly tapped the document. "The newspapers report that the delegates agreed that all the wife's property, both real and personal, owned by her before marriage or afterward acquired by gift, device, or descent, shall be her separate property."

"I don't understand," Victoria said.

"Nor I," Shiloh admitted.

"It's a community-property law." Jared handed the deed back to Victoria. "In the case of you two ladies, it means that whatever your late husbands owned in California passed to you upon their deaths. In other words, both of you now possess a half-interest in the property described in this document."

Shiloh wanted to have time alone to think about this complication or to discuss it with Mara. Instead, she tried to participate in the conversation until Mara announced lunch was almost ready, then she offered to set the table while the men went to Jared's quarters to wash up. Victoria volunteered to help Mara carry the food from the separate cookhouse. When everyone except Mara was seated in the formal dining room, Shiloh glanced around the table.

She knew that Mara had deliberately chosen to remain standing and serve although she normally sat with Shiloh at every meal. Mara apparently was unsure of how a Texan like Clay might feel, and she certainly must have suspected that a Virginian like Jared would not be comfortable with anyone but whites sitting down to a meal together.

Shiloh bowed her head and offered a short, simple prayer before the meal. She expected the conversation would return to the deed and thought ahead to what she should do about it. Victoria had declared earlier that she had come to sell her share, but Shiloh couldn't buy it, even if she wanted to. She suspected that Victoria would not be interested in purchasing Shiloh's inherited share. She turned to Clay as she absently rearranged her flatware. "What are your thoughts on the deed?"

"It seems to me," Clay said thoughtfully, "that it would be wise to go up to Mount Saint Helena and see what kind of property you two ladies own. Then you'd both have a better idea of what it's worth or what to do with it."

Victoria exclaimed, "An excellent suggestion, Mr. Patton!" She turned to Shiloh. "Don't you think so?"

Shiloh was torn between wanting to see the property and her unwillingness to endure the trip. Along with feeling the baby's more active movement, Shiloh had recently begun to have leg cramps and mild swelling in her feet and ankles. She did not relish the thought of hours of uncomfortable travel.

She offered a lame excuse. "I'd love to go, but I'm needed in the office."

Victoria said, "Naturally, only you can make that decision, Shiloh. But I believe the property should be seen. So if you would rather stay here, and you have no objections, I'll go there and bring back a report."

Shiloh didn't feel comfortable with getting such information secondhand, so she stalled, trying to decide what to do. "It's getting late in the year for comfortable travel," she replied. "We've already had some rain, and winter is coming fast. Clay, what do you think of weather conditions?"

"Either go now or wait until spring. When it really starts raining this winter, mud will be so deep that even horses will have a hard time getting through."

Victoria declared, "I'm willing to go now. How's the best way to get there?"

"Because we're on a peninsula, there are only a couple of ways. One is to go overland down to San Jose, around the end of the bay and then north. But that's a mighty long way around. The fastest way is to take a boat across San Francisco Bay and up San Pablo Bay to the landings at Sonoma Creek."

Jared asked, "Victoria, are you subject to *mal de mer?*"

"I don't know, but I don't like water. There were some frightening experiences crossing all those rivers coming to California."

Shiloh recalled with revulsion getting violently seasick her first several days of sailing down the Atlantic. After she and Aldar had crossed Panama, she wasn't seasick coming north on the placid Pacific Ocean. However, unpleasant memories of morning sickness in her early pregnancy still lingered. She did not want to think about crossing the bay.

Victoria seemed willing to risk it. She added, "I suppose the best way is for me to go by boat to this landing you mentioned. Will I have any trouble getting a stage from there?"

"No stages have scheduled runs to Sonoma or anywhere else except in Sacramento," Clay explained. "Jim Birch's company makes regular runs from there to Coloma. That's where gold was discovered last year."

"Oh, my!" Victoria sounded distressed. "If there are no stages . . ."

"I didn't say that," Clay interrupted. "I said there are no regularly scheduled runs to the north. But anybody with the fare can hire some kind of vehicle at the landing. From there, you can go anywhere you want."

"That's no problem," she assured him. "But how safe is a woman traveling alone?"

"Women are not as rare as they were when Shiloh arrived," Clay pointed out, "but as you saw at the hotel, it's best to have a male escort."

Shiloh didn't want Victoria to be the sole judge of the Sonoma property. However, unless Shiloh went along, in spite of her misgivings, she would have to accept Victoria's report. Her mind spun with the possible ramifications.

The baby was her most important consideration, she told herself. She had lost Aldar, and she must not risk losing their child. But Shiloh had heard about women giving birth crossing the plains, so she didn't feel right using her condition as an excuse for not going to Mount Saint Helena. There was a more logical possibility.

"Clay," she said thoughtfully, "could you get a driver to take your runs for a couple of days?"

The way he looked at her before answering, she knew he was trying to understand why she had asked such a totally unexpected question.

"I suppose so," he said finally. "Why?"

Shiloh considered the revenue the company would lose

with her proposal, but she plunged ahead. "He could take the wagon on your runs while you drive the buggy down the peninsula and up the eastern shore to take Victoria to the property. You and I can't both go because of the stage line."

She paused, then met this eyes, hoping he would understand her next words. "While you're there, you could take care of some business for us."

Victoria protested, "That's very kind of you, but there's no need for Clay to escort me. I crossed two thousand miles of this country, walking and riding in a wagon. I can certainly take a boat from here and hire a carriage from the landing you mentioned."

Taking a quick breath, Shiloh declared, "I think Clay should go with you." She felt some doubt about the wisdom of what she had suggested, but it was too late to back out now. "Is that all right with you, Clay?"

He nodded but said nothing.

She intended to return the mud wagon to Gladwin while Clay traveled north, but she would have to wait to tell him so until they were alone.

Jared suggested, "Shiloh, perhaps I can be of some assistance in your office. I'm feeling much better every day, and I want to get acquainted with the business district so I'll know where to open my practice."

When nobody protested, Victoria cried, "Wonderful! How soon can we leave, Clay?"

"Probably Tuesday," he replied.

Victoria looked disappointed. "Why not tomorrow?"

"It's Sunday," Shiloh explained. "We always attend church."

Clay said, "It'll take a day to make arrangements."

"Of course," Victoria replied. "I wasn't thinking. Tuesday is fine."

Shiloh extended invitations for Jared and Victoria to join them at church. Both made excuses, which suited Shiloh. Since she had no transportation, Clay always picked her up in the buggy. During the ride, she would have time to discuss Clay's meeting with Gladwin and the other matters on her mind.

Clay had proposed approaching Mariano Vallejo for a loan to help develop the stage business. As the owner of vast acres of land, and a member of the recent Monterey Convention, he had both wealth and influence. Such a person would request a plan for assurance of a return on any loan. Shiloh and Clay would have to work something out before Clay left.

Shiloh looked forward to the church's atmosphere of comforting hymns and words of assurance. So many unexpected things had happened recently that Shiloh felt overwhelmed by forces that were stealing control of her life. She needed the rejuvenation that she found in worship services.

That evening after everyone else had gone, Mara sat on the edge of Shiloh's bed as she stood before the mirror, letting down her red-gold hair.

Shiloh caught her friend's eye in the mirror. "What do you think of Victoria Barclay?"

Mara parried, "What do you think of Jared?"

"He seems to be a real gentleman."

Mara smiled knowingly. "I think he's a man with a goal, and it's a big one."

"Oh? Like what?"

"I'm not sure yet, but I've seen enough to know that it will probably involve politics."

"Really? Why?"

"Because that's about the only way he can steal enough to get rich and still have people honor him."

"You have an interesting philosophy, Mara."

Mara shrugged, then asked abruptly, "When are you planning to give in and marry Clay?"

Shiloh tried to hide her feelings. "What are you talking about?"

"He'd like to marry you."

Shiloh spun around to face Mara. "Did he tell you that?"

"No, but I've been watching him for some time now. He follows you with his eyes when he thinks you're not looking. There's a softness and a longing in those looks that you've chosen not to notice. Has he ever said anything to you?"

Shiloh turned back to the mirror. She thought back to those terrible days after Aldar was killed. "When I was thinking about returning east after Aldar died, Clay told me he wanted me to stay. That's all. Now we're just friends and business partners."

"Glad to hear that." Mara rose and headed for the door. "That way you won't get hurt if anything happens between him and her."

Shiloh spun around again. "Between Clay and Victoria?" When Mara nodded, Shiloh asked, "Why would you think something like that?"

"I understand that woman, that's why. She's like me, only not as careful. When she wants something, she goes after it."

"Don't be silly!"

"Remember what I said, Shiloh," Mara said quietly and walked out of the room.

The warning jangled Shiloh's nerves. She had never known anyone with the discernment Mara possessed. It was often uncanny what she saw in people. Over the years, Shiloh had seen so many of Mara's pronouncements come true that Shiloh was tempted to believe her.

Sighing, Shiloh undressed and stood before the mirror. She gently ran her hands over her abdomen where a new life was developing.

Your father is gone, but nothing's going to happen to you. You are my reason for living. Whatever else happens, you come first.

Shiloh put on her nightgown and slid under the covers. She tried to forget her many concerns and finally fell asleep wondering what to name the baby.

⟶ CHAPTER VIII ⟵

IN MIDMORNING, as his empty stomach seemed to grind against his backbone, Alvin Brakken topped what he believed was the last small oak-covered hill. He had earlier reached Bear River, which he recognized from the description he had received when he had asked directions to Johnson's ranch. He expected to see that first outpost on the vast level plains stretching before him. Instead, he was surprised to see a flag pole in front of two log barracks and some military tents in the distance.

Cursing the unexpected development, and wondering if he could have become lost and missed Johnson's ranch, he hurried down the hill. He hoped that the men at the military post would not turn a hungry man away. Maybe he could even borrow a mule to take him on to Sacramento.

Coming around a curve in the river, he saw a lone cottonwood tree among slender willows. Some of its yellow autumn leaves still fluttered in the breeze. Near its base, Brakken spotted two mules switching their tails. They weren't tied, which was dangerous because free animals often ran off, leaving people stranded. Thinking the animals' owners might have some food to share, Brakken started to run toward them.

Then he stopped abruptly and took a closer look. "They're my mules!"

The discovery instantly made Brakken cautious. He stood dead still, searching the willows and the riverbank to locate the man who had stolen the mules. Not seeing anyone, Brakken looked around for some kind of weapon. The coil of rope he carried would be useless. Even if he could make a loop to lasso the man, it would be too slow against a gun.

Brakken quietly dropped the rope and picked up two rocks that fit nicely in his hands. He eased forward, keeping the cottonwood between him and the mules, hoping that he could surprise the robber before he could shoot the percussion rifle. There was a chance of that because most men didn't insert the nipple until they were ready to fire the weapon. This could give Brakken a few precious seconds to use his rocks.

Creeping stealthily on tiptoes and holding his breath, Brakken approached within twenty feet of the tree. He still saw no sign of the man he sought. Suddenly, one of the mules noticed him and broke the morning's stillness with a raucous bray.

Brakken froze, his right arm cocked to throw a rock, but he still found no sign of another human. After a few seconds, Brakken again cautiously started moving. He reached the tree and carefully peered around the trunk. He discovered both his pistol and rifle but not the man who had stolen them. Brakken rushed forward and snatched up the pistol. A groan behind him caused him to whirl, holding the weapon level.

The man reclined against a fallen log, his legs sticking straight out in front of him. He had a knife at his belt but no other weapon. Brakken took the knife.

"You got anything else worth having?" Without waiting for an answer, Brakken placed the revolver against the man's head and checked his pockets. There was nothing of value except the double eagle. "You won't mind if I take back what's mine, will you?" Brakken asked.

"I'm sure glad to see you, Mister. My ankle's broke bad. I need help."

Brakken casually glanced where the right boot had been cut away, showing the bloody ankle bone.

"Sure I'll help you," Brakken replied coldly. "Just like you helped me back up in those foothills."

The injured man studied him through pain-filled eyes. "Mister, I never laid eyes on you before."

"Don't try that on me. You were mighty cheerful when you robbed me. You said you knew me in Texas. What's your name?"

"Duggan; Arthur Duggan."

Brakken frowned. "I still can't place you. Maybe it's all those whiskers."

"Please! I'm bad hurt. If you'll just help me get on that mule . . ."

"Get on him yourself," Brakken interrupted.

"Every time I try, he runs away. I catch him, and he does it again. Been doing that since last night."

"You got anything to eat?"

"What?"

"Never mind. I'll look for myself."

Panic sounded in the man's voice. "If you won't help me get on the mule, at least ride to the post and tell them I'm here."

"I got no use for the army," Brakken replied, heading toward the pack mule.

"I ain't either, 'cause I deserted from there some time back, but they're my only hope."

Rummaging through the supply sack, Brakken said, "When you robbed me, you were miles away from here. If you deserted, why didn't you have sense enough to head away from here?" ·

"I never robbed you! Honest! You got me mixed up with somebody else!"

"Lying won't do you any good. These are my mules, and you're the one who took them from me at gunpoint. So why did you come back this way?"

"I had to after that fool mule pitched me off and busted my ankle. I finally got back on him and headed for the post to get help. That's the closest place with a doctor."

"You should have stayed in the saddle."

"I tried, but the mule shied at a rabbit that jumped up in front of us. I got bucked off again, and he won't let me get back on. I can't crawl all the way to the post. Please, Mister, help me."

Brakken found some strips of jerky and hungrily bit into one. "What post did you desert from?"

"Camp Far West, just down there. It was set up to protect miners and settlers from hostile Indians. They're no danger, but that camp is. Full of sickness and death, and we can't even get paid when it's due. Lots of us deserted. Please, Mister!"

Brakken ignored the plea. "Where's Johnson's ranch?"

"About a mile and a half downstream from the post."

Brakken nodded, looking beyond Camp Far West and seeing for the first time the low profile of farm buildings. Still chewing, he walked back to get his rope.

"Where you going?" the stricken man cried.

Without replying, Brakken carried the coil of rope to the pack mule and secured it. Gripping its lead, he mounted the riding mule.

Duggan's voice held panic. "Why don't you answer me? Where you going?"

"To Johnson's. I should be there by noon in time for a hot meal."

"Wait! Wait! You can't leave me here!"

Looking down, Brakken shook his head. "I told you when you stole everything I had except that rope that I'd find you and kill you. You should have believed me."

Ignoring the anguished cries behind him, Brakken rode off, drawn by memories of a blond woman and a tall man he had to find.

☞

Shiloh didn't like to discuss business on Sunday, but Tuesday Clay would head for Mount Saint Helena, and they had to arrange several things before then. She settled into the buggy beside Clay for the ride to church and tried to think how to express her thoughts.

"We still have to decide about moving to Sacramento and opening an office there. Last night, I thought a lot about it, and I think you're probably right. When you get back, we should pack up and move."

He frowned, thoughtfully studying her face. "That's a hard trip, even on a steamer. I wouldn't feel right about letting you do it now. You're my responsibility . . ."

"No, I'm not," she interjected, "and I'm not asking to be! I'm the only one responsible for myself and my child! Women in my condition crossed the prairies and sailed around the Horn, and that certainly was a lot harder than going from here upriver to Sacramento."

He replied quietly, "Yes, but those women had no choice. You do."

"Then I'm choosing."

Clay shook his head and smiled ruefully at her. "You sure have changed since I met you."

That wasn't what she expected to hear. "How so?"

"Then you were afraid to make any decision. Now you're coming up with big ones as if they were an everyday occurrence."

"When Aldar died, I had no alternative. I had to survive. Then I found out about the baby coming, so I've done what I had to do. Now, do you agree about us moving the business to Sacramento?"

Clay said, "I've been thinking about that too. It's important, but I'm not sure that it's a priority this late in the year. The way I see it, our real goal is to develop a major stage system along the lines Aldar wanted. To do that, we've got to have a complete plan, which includes qualifying for the government mail franchise. That's vital, but we won't get that unless we can show we're financially able to deliver the mail. That brings us back to the questions of where we are going to get the necessary money."

"Maybe I could sell my half of the property Victoria and I own, but I don't want to do that until I know what it is and why Aldar bought it. He must have thought it pretty valuable to have taken on a part-owner."

"That property may have enough value to help us. But I'm afraid we face an immediate threat from Gladwin and Locke.

If they just wanted somebody to front for them, they could surely find any number of struggling stage lines that would work with them. Why do Gladwin and Locke want *our* line so much?"

"I don't know, but I certainly don't want to be involved with them or their political activities. We need California as a state, not a separate nation."

Clay studied Shiloh before saying, "I have the feeling that something else is bothering you."

"Just some personal matters that I must work out by myself."

He raised an eyebrow but didn't reply.

She asked, "What ideas have you come up with about getting the money to develop the stage line?"

"I've been thinking about Mariano Vallejo. I've been around these parts long enough to know something about him. He's well thought of by both the *Californios* and Americans. He owns a forty-four-thousand-acre ranch called Rancho Petaluma."

"Forty-four *thousand* acres?"

"That's right. His headquarters are in a huge, two-story adobe building located between Petaluma and Sonoma Creeks. And he's building a home he calls *Lachryma Montis* in Sonoma."

"That name has a nice sound to it."

"It's Spanish for mountain of tears."

"I always liked the idea of giving a home a special name. Aldar often talked about us having a big house up on Fern Hill, but we never discussed a name for it."

"Vallejo's place is on the way to Mount Saint Helena. I could stop there and make our proposal to him. I assume that's why you wanted me to escort Victoria. He's certainly wealthy enough that he could loan us the money we need. The question is: Will he?"

"He might if we show him a well-thought-out plan on how we intend to use the money and, more important, pay it back." She rummaged in her purse. "I got up early this morning and wrote out the main points. Read it when you get a chance and see if it'll be helpful when you call on Vallejo."

Clay accepted the two sheets of paper and glanced at the top one. "I'll do that. If we could just be sure of getting that mail franchise, I think Vallejo would go along with us."

"Even if he won't, we can still try John Sutter when we get to Sacramento. I've heard that he's one of the most generous men in California. He helped lots of people who came overland, including those in the Donner party who survived that awful ordeal." Shiloh couldn't bring herself to mention the cannibalism that the ill-fated immigrants were forced to resort to during the winter of 1846 and '47 when early snows in the Sierra Nevada Mountains trapped them.

Shiloh broached the second problem. "How do you think we should deal with Gladwin and Locke?"

"That's political, and I don't know much about those things."

She reminded him, "You used to talk politics with Aldar and seemed to know a lot about such matters."

"I have information because I listen and read a little, but that's different from knowing how to deal with people like that. I don't understand them, always wanting power."

"Neither do I, and I have seen and heard enough to make me want to avoid any involvement with them. I wish I had told you to take the mud wagon back right away. But I'll take it back myself."

Clay nodded and guided the mare around a corner. The newly built church came into sight. It was a simple white wooden structure with a steeple on top. John Sledger had started preaching in a large tent that, except for two hours on Sunday, served as a saloon. His first congregation had gathered from San Francisco's then almost exclusively male population. Shiloh had been the first woman to attend. Since then, however, many women and children had arrived.

A bell, removed from one of the hundreds of abandoned ships in the harbor, sounded the worship call. That stirred old memories of Shiloh's childhood in Pennsylvania, a time of no real problems and lots of opportunities for fun with other people her age.

Shiloh suppressed a sigh and turned back to Clay.

"I'd like to settle this matter of moving to Sacramento. Although it makes sense to go and I'm willing to move, I would prefer to stay here in San Francisco where Mara can help with the baby."

"I've thought of that. So I've got an idea. We really need to be in Sacramento. But we can't afford to lose the business we've built up here in San Francisco. I think we could run both offices for a time."

"We can't afford that!"

"Maybe we can. A small office could serve the companies headquartered here. But we would do most of our business out of Sacramento, which is where most people need a stagecoach."

"You want me to maintain this office while you open up in Sacramento?"

"You need to be near Mara, but maybe Jared would like to use our office to get his law practice started. While he's building that up, he could represent us."

The idea had possibilities. Shiloh asked, "What makes you think he would consider such an arrangement?"

"Yesterday, while we were washing up for lunch, I felt him out on the subject. Naturally, I wouldn't make him an offer without consulting you. I just asked if he might be interested. And he was."

"But you decided to talk to him without asking me, just as you chose to accept that mud wagon from Gladwin."

The reproof in her tone caused Clay to study her in silence

for a few seconds before replying. "Let's not get off on something like that," he said finally. "We've got too many serious problems."

"We're partners!" she reminded him crisply. "Neither of us planned it, but we are, and that means we should be equal."

Her voice rose with anger that surprised even her. "All my life, someone else has made decisions for me. First it was my father, then Aldar. Well, there was a time when I was glad of that, but circumstances have changed all that."

"I didn't mean to upset you," Clay said, turning the mare into the wagon lot behind the church. Other arriving parishioners waved in greeting.

Shiloh forced a smile and waved back. In a low voice she said to Clay, "I think we had better finish this conversation after services."

"Maybe we'd better." He said the words quietly, but they somehow further agitated her. She was tempted to step down by herself, but the buggy always tipped sharply with weight shifted to the outside step. So Shiloh waited for Clay to come around the buggy.

He offered her his hand when what he really wanted to do was hold her. But he could feel her tension. "You go on in if you want," he told her. "I'll see to the mare and follow."

She turned away without answering and saw Jefferson Locke approaching, crooked teeth showing in a smile.

"Mrs. Laird! How nice to see you."

"Thank you."

"You going to wait for Clay, or may I have the privilege of escorting you inside?"

She wanted to avoid Locke, but Clay had turned his back to lead the horse toward three men in their Sunday best. They had tied their horses to the long horizontal limb that served as a hitching rail.

When she didn't answer, Locke glanced at Clay's back and then lightly took Shiloh's elbow. "I'm glad we have this moment to speak," he said, slowing his steps and causing her to do the same. "That nigra woman . . ." He caught Shiloh's sudden pointed look and corrected himself. "That friend of yours came to me this week, wanting to buy real estate."

"She has the money."

"It's not that simple, Mrs. Laird. She's uh . . ."

"Negro," Shiloh replied sharply, "although that's something over which she had no control, any more than you and I had any choice about being born white."

"I didn't mean to offend you, Mrs. Laird. I just thought you should know what she's trying to do."

Shiloh stopped, ignoring other nearby parishioners. "Mara is a free woman, with the right to do whatever she wishes! She wants real estate, and I'm sure that she will have it. I'm absolutely sure of that. Please excuse me."

She walked rapidly toward the front door to the church, trying to force a smile and friendly nod to other worshipers. She severely castigated herself. *That's the one man in the world I should not have offended!*

She abruptly felt very uncomfortable about going in to worship when her heart and mind were so full of un-Christian turmoil. For a moment, she thought of walking right on by, but John Sledger saw her.

"Shiloh!" he called, leaving the church steps where he had been greeting parishioners. "Do you have a moment?"

Taking a deep breath to conceal her thoughts, she replied, "Of course."

Sledger guided Shiloh away from the other people. "Did you go through that box I opened for you yesterday?"

She shook her head. "As you know, we got interrupted by Victoria Barclay. I never got back to it."

"At the time, I mentioned that there was something in there you needed to look at."

"I'm sorry. I forgot all about it. Anyway, they were probably just more old receipts or something left over from the express company days."

"I don't think so." He glanced around, making sure nobody stood close, then lowered his voice. "I only had a glimpse, but . . ."

When he hesitated, she prompted, "Yes?"

"It was a quick glance, and it didn't really register on me until later. But I saw Aldar's name on it, and a single line."

"What did it say?"

"It was something like: 'The Mount Saint Helena property will pay for the stage line expansion.'" Sledger hesitated, then asked, "Does that mean anything to you?"

Her pulse sped up as she replied, "No, but I'm going to find out what it means!"

∽ CHAPTER IX ∽

S HILOH SEARCHED for Clay and spotted him near the horses, still conversing with several men. Forgetting herself, she nearly ran toward him.

Startled by her demeanor, Clay quickly met her halfway. "You all right?" he inquired anxiously.

"Yes! No! Oh, I'm so mixed up!" she cried. Drawing him away from everyone else, she briefly related what Sledger had said.

"Do you want to stay for services?"

"I don't know. I need the comfort of church, but there's so much on my mind. I probably couldn't think of anything but those papers and what they mean. How could that property pay for the stage line?"

Briefly closing her eyes, she decided. "Let's go to the office."

∽

Through her bedroom window, Mara watched Jared in the small room between his bedroom and the kitchen. She clearly

91

remembered feeling the gold coins in his vest when he had grabbed her after she rejected his first advance. Since then, she had not seen the vest or his carpetbag.

Neither had she allowed herself, clad only in a thin nightgown, to cast her shapely silhouette where he could again see it. She had given him no further encouragement, satisfied to let him wait. It would make him more eager and pliable for the next step in her strategy.

Hearing a knock at the back door, she wrapped a white shawl from the armoire around her and opened the door. A six-foot-tall runaway slave stood on the step. Ten months earlier, along with the rest of the crew, he had jumped ship when the master, not knowing about the California gold strike, had dropped anchor to take on supplies.

"Morning, Miss Mara," he greeted her with a pleased grin as he removed his cap with one hand. He held a shovel in the other. "I come to dig them postholes you wanted."

"Thank you, Samuel." She stepped outside, drawing the shawl closer about her shoulders. "I'll show you where I want them."

She deliberately walked past the cookhouse windows where she knew Jared Huntley was discreetly watching. "Samuel," she asked, "have you been thinking about what I told you?"

He nodded, his black hair glistening in the sunlight. "Yes'm."

He treated her with the deference he had given his white Louisiana mistress from whom he had run away. But Samuel had different reasons for his behavior toward Mara. He wanted Mara to join with him. He had asked her to "jump over the broom with him," a form of marriage ceremony. Although she had refused, he still held hope for the future.

"I'm glad to hear it," Mara said as she walked beside the big man. "What have you decided?"

"I'se gwine . . ." He checked himself, recalling Mara's instructions on how to improve his speech habits. "I mean," he continued, "I'm goin' to buy my freedom."

She gave him a warm glance and lightly touched his strongly muscled biceps. "I'm so pleased. In the meantime, watch out for slave catchers and crimps."

"I'll be careful," he assured her, thinking of Joseph, another runaway slave with whom he had been friends. Both men had escaped the slave catchers so far, but Joseph had been shanghaied by the crimps last summer.

"Have you been asking your other friends to do what I asked you?"

"Yes'm. They glad to tell me what they hear."

"Good. You pass that information on to me, and I'll give you money to give to them, plus some for your own freedom papers, just as I promised."

"I'll remember, 'cause that's good; mighty good. But I gots . . . uh . . . I have one problem. I sometimes git a little drunk and spend every penny. Cain't buy no freedom papers that way."

"If you'd like, I'll keep your money for you, Samuel. And for your friends too. When they want it, they can have it. But if it's not in their pockets, they can't spend it. Right?"

He bobbed his head. "We all trust you, Miss Mara."

"Tell your friends that I'll also pay interest on the money I save for them. But if I ever hear of any one of them telling a white person about any of this, they will deeply regret it. Understand?"

He nodded without speaking. The veiled threat of a *houngan* was enough to convince Samuel. Some Negroes in California shared his French-Haitian origin and understood. White people had not yet learned about voodoo. But Samuel strongly suspected that Mara secretly practiced it.

Samuel had quietly convinced both free Negroes and runaway slaves that nobody should antagonize Mara or her suspected dark powers. He felt certain no white person would know that a slave or employee was gathering casual bits of information for the beautiful Mara.

"When I gits . . . get . . . my papers, like you, Miss Mara," Samuel said slowly and carefully, "will that make it different fuh you an' me?"

She did not tease him as she did Jared. Her relationship with each man was different because her needs from each were different. "I want to always be friends with you, Samuel," she replied gently.

He pondered that, wondering exactly what she meant. He hoped that when he had his freedom, it might mean rewards beyond his dreams.

Mara stopped at the back of Shiloh's property and drew an X in the sand with the toe of her shoe. "Start here," she instructed. "Dig down about four feet. I'll mark the other spots. Be sure they're in as straight a line as you can make them. Then haul in the posts and rails when you have time. All right?"

He nodded and removed his shirt, showing an impressive, muscled chest. He pretended not to notice Mara's admiring look, but bent to thrust the narrow, pointed shovel into the X she had marked.

When she returned from designating the other posthole spots, bright drops of perspiration already glistened through his shiny black hair.

"Samuel," she said softly, "stop by the house when you've finished."

She left him without looking back, aware that he followed her with his eyes. He wondered if there was something special implied in her invitation.

Mara walked across the field to the house and went back into her room. She and Shiloh had plans to convert it into a nursery. In time, Mara would move back to the bedroom that Jared now occupied. Through her window, she glimpsed him sitting beside the box stove, reading. Removing her shawl and replacing it in the armoire, Mara started contentedly humming to herself.

Brakken skirted Camp Far West, keeping far enough to the north to discourage any possible military challenge but close enough to see the log buildings and the tents. It had already rained enough to make Brakken sympathize with deserters. Mud on the post was ankle deep, and there was no high ground for the sagging tents. They offered little shelter to the troops.

Urging his bony, tired mules on toward Johnson's ranch and what he expected would be a solid meal, Brakken vainly tried to recall how Arthur Duggan knew his name. Brakken could not remember anyone by that name in west Texas. Of course, the man who had robbed him might have been just a kid back then. In between, Duggan could have changed a lot, especially with the whiskers hiding his facial features.

Brakken glanced skyward at the scream of a red-tailed hawk flying above some scattered valley oaks. Behind him, three black turkey vultures circled about over the spot where he had left Duggan to die.

Even the appearance of two more buzzards heading toward the first three did not completely comfort Brakken. He wondered if he had made a mistake in letting the man live. He had lost blood because of the compound ankle fracture, but the bleeding had stopped. Death would not come quickly from such an injury. What if a patrol from Camp Far West found him alive? Duggan would be locked up in the stockade and face desertion charges. But what if Duggan escaped? Or what if some immigrant train, coming down from the Sierras, found Duggan and nursed him back to health? Could he find Clay before Brakken did? He didn't want Clay to know that he was closing in on him.

"No," he told himself aloud, "that's not likely."

The last time he had talked with immigrants camped near where the Donner party had perished, Brakken heard a rumor that one hundred thousand people had entered California so far in 1849. It would take time to find Clay, even though Brakken knew the most likely places. Clay didn't have the temperament to be a miner. He loved working around horses or carriages, and that's where Brakken expected to find him. The chances of Duggan casually running across Clay were very slim.

"Yet Duggan and I met right after I barely got to California," Brakken mused. "What are the odds on that?"

That was not a comforting thought, for Brakken's plan included finding an unsuspecting Clay. The more he considered the matter, the more Brakken's anxiety grew. Should he take a chance and keep going or circle back and make sure that Duggan would never betray him?

Brakken took a deep breath and decided. He didn't want to waste the time to go back. The sooner he got to Sacramento, the sooner he could do what he had come to California to do.

⌒

At the office, Shiloh lifted the top paper from the wooden box, which Clay held for her. The torn sheet had a single line scrawled on it.

"That's Aldar's handwriting!" Shiloh declared. "Brother Sledger was right!" She held up the paper so he could see the words. "It says, 'The Mount Saint Helena property will pay for the stage line expansion.'"

Clay set the box with the remaining papers on the counter. "It looks like he just made a note and stuck it on top. Maybe the rest of these papers will explain what he meant."

Shiloh agreed and picked up the next document in the box. "Look, it's a copy of Victoria's deed."

Hurriedly, her anxiety rising, Shiloh skimmed the next paper as Clay lifted them from the box. "This is just a list of stations and related things."

She handed Clay the document and sat down, frustrated by the lack of details. Clay pulled out the next sheet of paper.

"Aldar used to tell me that the man who could think should leave the details to others."

That sounded like Aldar, Shiloh had to admit.

"Aldar probably kept it in his head, not figuring anything would happen to him." Clay rapidly thumbed through the rest of the papers. Some stuck together from the moisture in the air, but he tried to glance at each one. "I don't see anything else that looks interesting."

"This is maddening!" Shiloh's tone was heavy with disappointment. "Did he mean the land could be sold for enough money to carry out all his great plans?"

She spun around in her chair, facing the desk. "I remember he expected to be wealthy in three years, but we could be broke before then. We will never survive until then unless we get an investor and the government mail contract."

Pausing, she added, "I probably shouldn't give that mud wagon back just yet, but I will."

Clay didn't reply as he began returning the papers to their wooden container.

"I've got to find some answers about that property," she cried, getting up again to face Clay. "Maybe I'd better go see it for myself."

He cocked his head and looked disapprovingly at her.

"Earlier, you didn't want to go. I think your first decision was the right one. The trip could be risky for you and the baby."

"I know, but I made that decision before I knew that Aldar had a plan for the property. Maybe if I saw the place, I could understand what he had in mind."

"I still don't think you should go."

Shiloh felt her nerves fray further. She exclaimed, "Well, I'm going!" Until that moment, she had not made a firm decision, but once the words were out, she determined to stand by them.

Clay walked to the end of the counter and raised it. "I'm still against it," he said stiffly. She could be so aggravating!

Couldn't she understand he cared about her and only wanted to protect her?

After he slammed the door behind him, Shiloh wanted to call him back and apologize for her keen-edged words, but she did not. He was about the most considerate person she had ever met, and she couldn't have even tried to run the business without him. But, after what happened to Aldar, Shiloh couldn't give in to her feelings.

Surprising herself, she suddenly put her hands over her face and let the tears flow.

⟨∞⟩

Riding back from the office later, Shiloh kept her face turned away from Clay. Her questions tortured her, demanding answers.

"Clay," she began, still looking away, "I've been wondering. Is it possible that Aldar had something else in mind for that property?"

"I can't think what."

"Gold mining?"

"I don't think so. For some reason, gold seems to hide along a fairly narrow strip in the eastern foothills."

Shiloh turned toward Clay but kept her face lowered. "Victoria's husband was a farmer. Maybe he was going to raise crops up north and sell them. Fresh fruits and vegetables are so scarce that they might bring a big price if someone could supply them in quantity."

"On a mountain? Anyway, fruit trees would take years to produce after they were planted, so I think we can rule that out."

"I agree. Same with grapes. It would be a long time from planting to the first harvest, even if vines will grow in that area. But what about vegetables?"

"Not on the mountain itself, but maybe they could grow at its base. Even so, it's kind of far from the main markets at San Francisco and Stockton."

"What about wheat or barley?"

"I've never been up there, but I understand Mount Saint Helena is about four thousand feet high. The country around it is full of small hills and little valleys. Very pretty, I've heard, but not like the flat easy growing ground around Sacramento. Sutter gets a crop of wheat and barley and grows some potatoes using Indian labor. He also runs cattle."

"Could this property be good cattle country?"

"I'd have to see it before I could say for sure, but I sort of doubt it. Livestock likes the valleys around Sacramento and Stockton. Wild cattle roam those open lands by the thousands, along with antelope and wild horses. Of course, Vallejo raises some livestock on his acres, but I've never heard of any smaller operations trying to raise cattle up there."

"So if it's not farming, ranching, or gold mining," Shiloh summarized, "what else could it be?"

"Well, there's been some talk of silver being mined in that area, but the value doesn't compare with the gold that's being taken out of the Sierra foothills."

"Then what could Aldar have meant?"

Clay shook his head. "I guess we'll have to wait until we see the property."

Shiloh rode in thoughtful silence for a while, her mind in turmoil over the many problems facing her. Her thoughts jumped to the mud wagon and how she should try to return it to Gladwin tomorrow.

"Clay, I've been wondering why Locke teamed up with Gladwin. A few weeks ago, Locke wanted support to make the Monterey delegates vote to admit California to the union as a slave-holding state. When that failed, he joined Gladwin, who wants California to be a separate nation. Does it make sense to you?"

"It's my guess that Locke joined Gladwin because Locke wants slavery in what they call the Empire of Pacifica. If they can bring that about, and we don't become a state, countless thousands of slaves will be needed to work the fields all over California."

That thought revolted Shiloh, who remembered all the horror stories she had heard in the abolitionist home where she had grown up. "I remember hearing about the Missouri Compromise, which prohibited slavery in the Louisiana Purchase north of a certain parallel."

"Yes, but that wouldn't affect California if Gladwin, Locke, and their followers can manage to separate us from the Union."

"How awful that would be! Slavery is so terrible! It can't happen in California."

Clay didn't reply, causing her to look sharply at him. She was aware that as a Texan he had never talked of how he felt about slavery. She was tempted to ask, but feared his answer.

∽ CHAPTER X ∽

AFTER ARRANGING with Jared to look after their stage line office, Shiloh and Clay stood with Victoria on the deck of a scow headed north. Its flat bottom and broad square ends were not designed for speed or passengers. However, it was the only craft available to the three travelers.

They were limited to the narrow deck around the sides and brief shelter in the wheelhouse. An open sand-filled hold took up the rest of the vessel.

Captain Gannon, a stocky, middle-aged man, had a scraggly yellow beard that covered his red, weathered face. Once his slow craft was under way, he turned his attention to his passengers, who had squeezed into the cramped wheelhouse out of the morning cold.

"Sorry I can't offer you ladies something nicer," he apologized, removing his black knitted stocking cap and shifting a wad of chewing tobacco to his right cheek. "But your gentleman friend here told me you would take what you could get."

"That's true," Victoria replied with her usual friendly smile. "We have urgent matters waiting for us across the bay, and you apparently are the only one headed that way this morning."

Shiloh said nothing as she stared anxiously through the window streaked with white salt spray. She prayed that she wouldn't be seasick. Relatively calm water encouraged her.

After a brief glance that determined Clay was watching over Shiloh, Gannon focused his pale blue eyes on Victoria. "We should make it in record time for this old tub, Mrs. Barclay. We've got both the wind and the tide with us. Sometimes we get the tide going one way and the wind the other. Takes about all day that way. Today, maybe four, five hours is all."

Clay turned to the window and thoughtfully looked toward the area where the stricken clipper had sunk. "Captain, you ever do any salvage work on sunken ships?"

Gannon laughed, showing the wad of tobacco in his cheek. "No need to. There's about five hundred ships abandoned over there in the cove." He pointed back and to the right where a tall forest of masts jutted up from vessels whose crews had deserted them to search for gold. "Anything a seafaring man could want is above water, waiting for whoever wants to climb aboard for it."

Shiloh recalled that the bell hanging in the belfry of her new church had come from a such a dead ship. Many of the board walks placed on San Francisco's sandy soil had also been stripped from such vessels.

Intrigued by Clay's question, and feeling a little more confident that she wasn't going to be sick, Shiloh turned to look up at Clay. "Are you thinking about the clipper ship that sank under Jared Huntley?"

"Actually, I was thinking about that Concord that went down with her."

"I saw that happen," the captain said, taking a step to stand beside Clay and Shiloh. "Sank right over there."

Clay followed the stout, blunt finger on the man's gnarled hand. "Any chance that coach could be raised?"

"The coach, maybe. Not the ship's cargo," Gannon replied. "The master took her as close to shore as possible, knowing she was going down, but no man could work in these tricky currents where she now rests."

"Then how could the coach be raised?" Clay asked.

"Maybe with grappling hooks and a stout line from a derrick. I saw the coach break loose from where it was strapped down, but it only slid across the deck without going overboard. So it should be loose and sitting there for anybody who wants to try to raise her. You interested?"

"I might be," Clay answered casually.

From where she sat, Victoria protested, "Oh, but even if it could be lifted, wouldn't the seawater have ruined it?"

"Depends on how long it stays down," Clay said.

"Salvage rights would make it yours if you could raise it," Gannon explained. He wiped a fleck of tobacco juice from his lip and turned back to Victoria. "You interested in seeing the rest of this old tub?"

"Since we have a few hours, I think I would enjoy a tour."

"You two want to come?" Gannon asked Shiloh and Clay. When they shook their heads, he walked off with Victoria, explaining how the summer winds coming through the Golden Gate created rough water.

"Victoria is as friendly as a speckled pup," Clay commented to Shiloh.

"Very pretty too. And she has the clothes to go with her looks." Shiloh hadn't meant for her tone to have an edge, but she felt increasingly unattractive and still had several months before the baby was due.

Clay remembered how Elizabeth had been when she carried Mark and wanted to say he understood how Shiloh felt. But he hesitated to speak of such delicate matters, even though Shiloh was becoming increasingly special to him.

"What did Gladwin say when you returned the mud wagon to him?"

"He said it was a gift with no strings attached, but seemed to understand that I really couldn't accept it."

"He didn't get angry?"

"Not outwardly, but I could see it in his eyes. He had gotten that look once before, when he called Aldar pigheaded. Gladwin's got a temper. Yet I trust him more than Locke. He scares me."

"Well, if we can find out what Aldar meant about the Mount Saint Helena property paying for the stage line, neither of us will ever again have to deal with Gladwin or Locke."

"That would be wonderful," Shiloh said. "But we can't count on it; not yet, anyway." She let her thoughts wander, hoping that when she saw the property, the mystery of Aldar's cryptic note would be solved.

In San Francisco, Mara slipped her white shawl around her shoulders and strolled toward the back of Shiloh's property. She had only covered a hundred yards in the crisp autumn air when she heard Jared following her. She kept moving, seemingly unaware of him, until he called her name.

When she stopped and looked back, he smiled and waved in greeting, but she noticed that he looked around before hurrying toward her. Mara's face tightened, aware that he didn't want to chance anyone seeing them talking, even though it wasn't likely on this remote road with only one house. She waited for him to catch up.

"Good morning, Mara. Very pleasant out today."

She encouraged him with a brief smile. "Yes, it is."

"You headed anywhere special?"

"No. I'm just enjoying the outdoors."

"I was just on my way down to open the office for Shiloh and Clay, but that can wait awhile." Jared looked around nervously again before meeting Mara's eyes. "Have you been down to the beach?"

"No, I've been too busy helping Shiloh make baby clothes to have much free time. But I'm caught up for the present." She started walking again.

He fell into step beside her. "I admire your enterprising spirit in business," he said, looking up at a sea gull flying over. "You are to be highly commended."

"Thank you." She followed his eyes upward and lightly brushed against his right arm. She heard his sharp intake of breath.

However, he affected not to notice her closeness. "I have been thinking. In my capacity as an attorney-at-law, I may be in a position to be of some assistance to you."

She turned warm eyes on him. "That's very kind of you, Mr. Huntley."

"It's Jared—at least, when we're alone."

She tried not to cringe at the implication. "Jared." A faint smile touched her lips. "That's a good name."

"Mara also," he assured her. "I've heard it somewhere before." Underneath the smooth complexion, flawless face, and perfect body, Mara's name suited her. She explained, "It's Old Testament." She didn't mention that it meant "bitter."

He nodded. "I saw you supervising a big black buck in digging down this way."

It was an implied leading question, but he had not asked it. What was it she had heard Shiloh's father say one time? "A lawyer shouldn't ask a question unless he knows the answer." She wondered how much Jared had already quietly learned about her. He was obviously curious but cautious. That satisfied Mara. She was in no hurry.

"Yes. His name's Samuel," she replied.

"Friend of yours?"

She was tempted to reply sarcastically, "Of course he is," but instead, replied evasively, "I have many friends, Jared."

He took another approach. "I understand the pies and biscuits you made for the miners earned you a tidy profit before someone burned your bakery down some time back."

Mara recognized that this was also an indirect question. "I did well enough."

"I heard that you dealt only in gold."

"That's true. Only dust, nuggets, or U.S. minted coins. No Mexican money and none of those slugs that some Americans manufacture here with a claimed dollar value."

Jared cast an approving look at her. "Very astute of you, Mara. I assume you have invested profits wisely?"

The feeler delighted her. "They are quite safe."

"Ah, good! I understand that some banking houses that have sprung up here may not necessarily be financially sound. You are fortunate to have a bank in which you can feel complete confidence."

Mara suppressed a smile, glancing ahead to where three fence posts had been set in holes Samuel had dug. The other holes still had dirt piled beside them.

"Didn't Samuel do a good job?" she asked, indicating the fence posts and holes.

"He seems very competent."

Mara decided to satisfy a little of Jared's curiosity. "He's a runaway slave who jumped ship from a whaler in the harbor."

"I had assumed that." Jared hesitated, then added, "I'm sure you wouldn't want to appear to harbor a runaway. Under the Fugitive Slave Law, you could be in trouble."

"That law only applies in the states, as I'm sure you know."

"True, but if California becomes one, the law will apply here."

"You think it will become a state?"

"I don't think so, but if I'm wrong, you need to be careful. Before I left home, the Congress was moving to strengthen that law."

"I consider that an unjust act." Mara's tone took on a hard, flat sound. "Samuel, like many slaves, was very badly mistreated by his owner, worse than an animal. So when he got the chance, he ran away. Made his way north and signed on with a whaler. It's rough, smelly work, he told me, but the ship's master was a Quaker and treated him better than he had been treated on the plantation."

Jared noticed the intensity in her voice and decided to say nothing more. His plans would not work if he made her angry.

Mara also fell silent, thinking of Samuel. She knew that he would do anything for her. He had dug postholes although he could not understand why, telling her that there was nothing to keep in or out of the property except drifting sand. Only when he finished had she explained there would eventually be neighbors, and she wanted a split-rail fence to mark Shiloh's boundaries.

However, he had not realized that each post was discretely numbered. Only three were set, but the earth was not tamped down. In the night, alone and without a light, Mara had buried tins of gold and covered them with a foot of dirt. She had wrestled the posts down into the holes. Samuel would finish filling them tomorrow, tamping the soil down to hold the post firmly upright. Mara envisioned the time when every hole would have similar secret hoards.

"Mara?"

She looked up at him, seeing a change in Jared's eyes. She had seen similar looks in other men's eyes. None of them had interested her although she had carefully considered which might help achieve her ambitious goals. A lawyer, she reasoned, was a likely person to need what was politely referred to as a housekeeper or cook.

"Yes?" She turned and started strolling slowly back toward the house. He fell into step beside her.

"What is it you really want?"

She didn't reply, but her dark eyes seemed to laugh at him. Jared's desires overcame his discretion. He added hastily, "I can give you whatever it is. Maybe not right now, but eventually. I'm going to be a very rich and powerful man in California politics. Believe me."

She took her time, knowing that skill and patience were required to obtain her objectives. "I believe you."

"Then what do you want?"

"First and foremost, I don't want anything to happen to Shiloh."

"Why is she so important to you?"

"Why? Because from the time we met as little girls, we were closer than blood sisters, regardless of the color of our skins. Still are."

"I see. I'm still trying to learn what you want."

Mara took her time before answering. She wanted him to understand that she couldn't be hurried. "I want a lot near the Plaza on which to build a boardinghouse."

"I'm surprised you haven't bought it already. You must have enough money for that."

"I do, but I think of it as power, or leverage."

Jared stared at her. "You mean you don't want to spend your own money? How utterly unexpected—but delightful!"

"I will guarantee the loan to someone who'll buy the property and legally file it in my name."

Jared stopped and took her by both shoulders to look into her flawless face. "You are one shrewd woman."

She shrugged. "After that, I want the building erected and the deed in my name."

His voice dropped. "You're serious?"

"Very serious. I'm also serious about not wanting Shiloh or Clay to handle this. It has to be someone else."

He released her and they started walking again. "If I were advising a client who came to me asking counsel on the proposal you've just made, my first question would be, 'If Mara has gold but doesn't want to spend it, what does she offer as security to an investor?'"

A faint smile touched her lips. She stepped up on the porch and opened the front door before answering. "I'd suggest you tell your client that Mara is her own security."

She quickly closed the door, leaving him to reflect on exactly what she meant.

∽

Shiloh was nervous that afternoon as she, Clay, and Victoria approached Vallejo's headquarters. They had gotten here in a slow, rickety *caretta,* or oxcart, which an Indian had invited them onto, with gestures, for the ride up the long road to the largest adobe building ever constructed in California.

So much depended on this trip that Shiloh kept thinking anxiously about the outcome. If Vallejo loaned them the money she and Clay needed, the stage line could survive and grow. Even if he didn't, the Mount Saint Helena property might provide the financial backing they needed to assure the mail contract. It might, she reminded herself, *if we can figure out what Aldar meant in that single tantalizing sentence.*

"We're almost there," Shiloh commented, studying the adobe quadrangle grandly situated on a small hill.

When neither Clay nor Victoria replied, Shiloh glanced back to see that they were still in casual conversation. That had started on the long, tedious scow trip across San Francisco and San Pablo Bays.

The talking had continued after Gannon deposited them at Petaluma Landing. From there, they took a flat-bottomed boat up the slough. They landed a few miles south of Vallejo's famous Adobe *Petaluma* and faced the possibility of having to walk the last few miles along the road. However, the Indian with the *caretta* had insisted that they ride with him.

They had only traveled a short distance when one of Vallejo's *vaqueros,* obviously attracted by the two women, had galloped up with a flashing smile and an appreciative light in his dark eyes. He spoke little English, but quickly came to understand whom they wished to see.

Grandly sweeping off his sombrero, the young rider announced that he would inform the general of coming visitors. Then, in an obvious effort to impress the *Americanos,* and especially the blond woman who had smiled at him, the *vaquero* galloped away, displaying his superb riding skills.

Shiloh was annoyed with Clay and Victoria's long conversation and with the light laughter that seemed to be a part of Victoria's personality.

Shiloh tried to tell herself that she had no right to be bothered, but she still felt aggravated. She let her eyes sweep over the vast acres of unfenced land, dotted with Indian laborers on foot and horsemen herding cattle. When she again turned toward the front of the lurching cart, Clay and Victoria joined her in studying the general's adobe headquarters.

"It's huge," Victoria commented.

Clay explained, "I've heard it's about 250 by 145 feet. Notice how all the trees have been cleared from around it? That's the military part of Vallejo. Anyone approaching, especially an enemy, can be seen from that second-story veranda."

Shiloh didn't care. She was tired after the long trip and just wanted to meet with Vallejo. Clay had assured the women that the general would extend an invitation to spend the night. Tomorrow they could get a ride to see the Mount Saint Helena property. But Shiloh's deep concern centered on how Vallejo would react to her and Clay's private request for a loan. Shiloh was also tired of being pregnant, although happy that she would deliver Aldar's child. She felt certain that she carried a boy.

Vallejo, alerted by the horseman, came out to meet the visitors. At forty-two, he had a thick head of dark hair, wide forehead, alert brown eyes, and neither beard nor moustache. He wore a dark coat buttoned at the throat.

"Welcome! Welcome!" he said graciously greeting the women and shaking Clay's hand. "I am glad you have come."

After introductions, he led them across the broad open patio where Indian women baked bread in large beehive-shaped ovens while girls gathered firewood. Clay said, "I have heard much about you, General."

"I am sure much of it is exaggerated," he replied modestly, starting up the outside wooden stairs to the shaded balcony on the second floor.

"I don't think so," Clay said. "I know that you were once *commandante* of the presidio in San Francisco and that the Americans took you prisoner in what is now called the Bear Flag Revolt over at Sonoma. From all I know, that was unfair, since you have always been a friend to Americans."

"The bear flag incident was a misunderstanding," Vallejo replied, brushing it aside, "as evidenced by the fact that I was one of the delegates to the Monterey Convention."

He abruptly changed the subject and turned to the women. "You undoubtedly grew up in wood-frame houses. Mine is all adobe." He patted the three-foot thick walls. "Perhaps after you are refreshed, you would permit me to show you around. Of course, you will be our guests for dinner and the night."

"We'd be delighted," Victoria assured him.

Shiloh nodded in agreement, but her thoughts were stead-fastly fixed on how soon she and Clay could privately make their petition known to their host.

Their opportunity came a half-hour later when Victoria excused herself and entered the second-floor guest room. Shiloh and Clay rested with their host on homemade cowhide chairs in the sitting room at the far western end of the same floor. Clay broached the reason for their visit, offering their written plans for the stage line's expansion and speaking of their hope for a government mail contract. He was so intent in his explanation that he missed the frown that slowly slid over Vallejo's face.

Shiloh asked, "Is there something you don't understand, sir?"

Vallejo shook his head. "No, Mrs. Laird. I anticipated the reason for your visit as soon as I learned that you had been married to Aldar Laird."

"You knew him?" she asked, surprised that Vallejo had not mentioned it at their introduction.

"Yes. I regret his death, which I had heard about some months back. I met him here a few years ago when he convinced me of the validity of his mission."

Shiloh was puzzled by the contrast between Vallejo's words and his continuing frown. She asked, "If you are convinced of the stagecoach system's value . . ."

He interrupted. "Yes, he told me about that, but he asked for a loan to buy a piece of property on the eastern slope of Mount Saint Helena. I loaned it to him."

Shiloh exclaimed, "You loaned it to him?"

"Yes, but don't be alarmed, Mrs. Laird. There is no debt to you. Aldar repaid the loan, with interest."

That surprising news made Shiloh and Clay exchange puzzled glances. How could Aldar have done that?

Their host cleared his throat. "Please, let me make this as clear as possible. I would like to help you, but many problems have assaulted me recently so that I am not in the strong financial position I usually enjoy."

Shiloh's mouth had gone dry. "You mean, you can't loan us any money?"

"I'm sorry, Mrs. Laird. Believe me, it has nothing to do with the property. It is only because of my own restricted abilities at the present time."

Shiloh struggled to keep her voice steady as she asked, "Did Aldar say what he planned to do with that property?"

Vallejo slowly shook his head. "Not exactly, but I'm sure it had something to do with his stagecoach line. He was a very bright young man. Now, I believe there is time to show you around the *hacienda*."

The guests accepted and Victoria rejoined them. But Shiloh's attention turned more to how Aldar could have repaid a large loan than to the tour. More important, Vallejo's refusal, no matter how gracious and gentle, plunged Shiloh's hopes into an abyss of fear and doubt.

∞ CHAPTER XI ∞

THE NEXT MORNING, Vallejo sent Shiloh, Clay, and Victoria on their way to Sonoma with a driver and a celerity wagon. It somewhat resembled the two-seat mud wagon that Shiloh had returned to Gladwin, except that it was smaller and lighter. The canvas side curtains could be rolled up in good weather or dropped in poor.

Their driver, Pablo, a heavyset former *vaquero*, climbed to the outside seat and called in Spanish to the team of horses. The vehicle lurched away with a neck-snapping jerk. It did not speed down the wide road the visitors had arrived on the day before. Instead, Pablo sent the horses splashing across a small stream and headed north, following faint wagon tracks.

Clay, seated beside Shiloh, asked her, "Are you going to be all right?"

"I think so."

"I know enough Spanish to get him to slow down."

"Thank you, but no; unless Victoria . . . ?"

"Don't slow him down on my account," she interrupted from her seat directly across from Shiloh and Clay. "I'm anxious to see the property we own."

The passengers settled back for the trip, giving Shiloh an opportunity to ask Victoria some questions that had been running through her mind. "When did you decide to come to California?"

Victoria's face tensed ever so slightly, then her ready smile returned. "I didn't; Henry did. He was very prosperous but always looked for ways to do even more. When he first heard stories about all the land and opportunities out here, he decided to go see for himself. When he returned, he told me that we were going to sell everything except what we could get in our wagons and move here. He planned to farm in the Sacramento or San Joaquin valleys. I didn't want to go, but he was my husband, so of course, I did."

Shiloh agreed. "I did the same with Aldar."

Clay didn't say anything but remembered how Elizabeth had pioneered into west Texas with him early in their marriage.

Victoria continued, "I told you about the first time when he came alone, before the war."

Shiloh nodded. "I remember."

"After he got back, he started planning our crossing overland together. We were to leave this past May." She lapsed into momentary silence, remembering some things that she did not want to say aloud.

She was barely seventeen when she married Henry after seeing the large farmhouse he owned in Missouri and the prestige he enjoyed as the wealthiest man in the area. The great house was always full of important people who were served by Henry Barclay's small staff of slaves. Victoria loved the fine china and sparkling crystal that graced the long linen-covered table where she presided as Henry's young bride. Her loveliness brought constant attention from men of all ages. This made the other women somewhat uneasy and secretly delighted Victoria.

She had been bored with Henry's talks of grain, livestock, and cotton and of his interests in coal, zinc, and limestone mines. He tolerated her indifference because of her wit, charm, and beauty. She had enjoyed having him away so long in California, but that changed when he returned with plans to permanently relocate.

Victoria had vainly pleaded and cried. All that originally

attracted her to the man more than twice her age was ruined when he stubbornly sold everything except what could be squeezed into three wagons. By then, Victoria had become bitter and angry. She didn't want to give up her glamorous lifestyle for the rough frontier.

However, by the time she formulated the only alternative, the big house and most of their possessions had been sold. Victoria's anger had turned to quiet hatred by the time she realized there was no way to keep from heading west.

That's when she took an action so secret that only she and one other person knew about it.

Victoria forcibly put those memories aside and continued her explanation to Shiloh and Clay. "The day before our company of wagons was to leave, Henry was found dead of a gunshot wound. Some of the men figured out how it had happened. He had been alone, they said, when he reached into the wagon and took his rifle by the barrel to pull it toward him. He had apparently forgotten that he had already put on what the men called 'the nipple.' I understand this makes the gun fire when the hammer hits it."

"Happens too often," Clay said.

"I guess so," Victoria said. "Anyway, they figure that the hammer apparently caught on something, pulling it back. It must have been jarred because the hammer fell, sending the ball into Henry's heart."

Shiloh and Clay expressed their sympathy, then all three fell silent, lost in their own thoughts.

Newly widowed Victoria quietly decided that San Francisco would more likely offer the exciting lifestyle she preferred, so she had made the trek to California. The key to entering the San Francisco society she envisioned was the right man: handsome, successful, and wealthy.

She had been very cautious in projecting the image she wanted prospects to have of her while she hoarded Henry's money and looked for substantial new sources.

Shiloh's thoughts were on birth and death. There was so much of the latter and so little of birth. She had observed that hardly anyone grew to an old age. Long before then, most succumbed to accidents, disease, or murder, as in Aldar's case. Yet a part of him lived on in the new life within her body.

Clay gazed absently over the passing countryside of small, oak-studded hills, but his mind remained on his two companions. He found it pleasant that Victoria paid him a great deal of attention. However, Shiloh had become a vital part of his life. He had not meant to care so deeply for her, but she had stirred something in him that he had missed since losing Elizabeth. He hoped that Shiloh considered him as more than a business partner.

☙

About midmorning, Mara answered a knock at the front door. John Sledger's bulk filled it.

"Good morning, Preacher," she greeted him. "That was a gentle knock for a man of your size." She invited him into the parlor and gave him a cynical smile. "Did Shiloh send you to save my soul?"

"That takes more than my doing, you know." He settled gingerly onto the chair Mara indicated. "I came to check on Shiloh because she left church so abruptly, but I also wanted a chance to talk to you."

"Shiloh's fine," Mara replied and briefly explained about the trip she, Clay, and Victoria had taken to check on the Mount Saint Helena property.

"I trust that she finds the answers," Sledger said then looked quizzically at Mara. "You're an interesting combination."

"How so?"

"You have demonstrated great love for Shiloh, for which I am grateful. But I'm also concerned about the rumors of your so-called powers. That sort of thing comes from evil, you know."

"You should not take rumors seriously."

"I must at least investigate charges as serious as this." He paused while she seated herself opposite him, then asked her bluntly, "Are they true?"

"You get right to the point, don't you?"

"It seems to work best."

She considered him in thoughtful silence, then shrugged. "When I was little, I heard the Bible stories along with Shiloh. I believed the way you do although I had to attend a church for coloreds. That went on until I was about thirteen years old."

She paused and closed her eyes tightly while her mind leaped back to one terrifying day when her world was shattered.

Sledger leaned forward and asked gently, "Do you want to tell me about it, Mara?"

She opened her eyes and looked straight at him. "Let's just say I lost my faith."

"We all have times of doubt, but . . ."

"Not doubt, Preacher," she interrupted angrily. "I lost my faith and all that I had been taught and believed! I was an innocent girl, all alone, when three white men grabbed me in broad daylight. You know what they did to me?"

"I can guess."

"They were brutal! To them, I wasn't a young girl, but a Negro, which meant that I was property, not a human being! They had their few minutes of depraved pleasure, but I've had years of pain that may never stop."

Her dark eyes misted as she plunged on with venom. "Nobody came to help. Shiloh would have, if she had known, but she wasn't there. So nobody helped me; not even . . ." she hesitated, then added softly, "what I had believed did not work for me when I needed it most."

"My words of regret will never erase your memory, Mara, but I am truly, truly sorry."

Her flawless face hardened and the mistiness disappeared from her eyes. With a barely perceptible nod, she said, "I know."

"So you turned from the God of your childhood to some form of ancient belief that comes from Africa?"

"I have said enough," she replied, standing. She had not intended to say that much. Except for Shiloh, she had never told any white person about the rapes.

Sledger also stood and held out both huge hands to take hers gently. "I only wanted to help, Mara. I did not mean to rip open old wounds."

She regarded him thoughtfully. "But you're too late to help."

"It is never too late, Mara."

She pulled her hands free and reached for the door handle. "You have your beliefs, and I have mine. It has to remain that way, but I am grateful for your concern."

Sledger stepped toward the door, then stopped and looked down on her with gentleness in his eyes. "My concern will continue, Mara."

A softness crept into her face. "I believe you."

"I see two sides of you, Mara. One disturbs me greatly. However, I see something else in you. You obviously have a great love for Shiloh and are very protective of her."

"She is closer than a sister to me." Her eyes locked on Sledger's. "As long as I am around, no one should ever try to harm her."

"I admire your loyalty, but don't be tempted to use the wrong methods to do something you feel is right."

Mara threw her head back and laughed. "Don't be concerned. Temptation is something I handle very well."

⚭

Listening to the drumming hoofbeats and creaking coach, Clay mentally drifted back to the previous night with General Vallejo.

After seeing the *hacienda,* the visitors had explained Victoria's role in the Mount Saint Helena property, and Vallejo answered Shiloh's questions. No, he had no idea why Aldar wanted the property. Aldar had come alone, saying only that he wanted the land as an investment, Vallejo recalled. He had not seen the land, but he knew it was not far from Mount Saint Helena. He explained that it looked like a volcano but was really the remains of many volcanic rocks, with geysers and hot springs.

Clay, easily adjusting to the wagon's swaying motion, had not told Shiloh or Victoria what he had observed at the general's *hacienda*. Vallejo had been one of the most wealthy and influential men in California, but Clay had noticed signs of changing fortunes as the tide of inrushing Americans threatened to overrun the area.

After dinner, Vallejo had told briefly, how, as the Mexican *commandante,* he had been seized by a small group of Americans at Sonoma in the Bear Flag Revolt, and California prematurely declared independence from Mexico.

Shiloh roused from her reverie as the team slowed. Looking out of the carriage, she saw a small community in the middle of a large flat area.

Clay said, "That must be Sonoma. We'll stop for a while and then go on to the property."

"I hope we can find out what Aldar's note meant about the property paying for the stage line," Shiloh said wistfully.

"We'll probably know the answer when we see the land," Clay said. "Once we know what it is, you can stay in San Francisco and run that office, and I'll find someone in Sacramento to handle that one while I'm on the road."

"You two can buy my share of the property," Victoria added, "and we'll all be happy."

Pablo stopped the team at Sonoma, which was built around the typical Mexican plaza. Three cows grazed on the grass there, ignored by merchants and soldiers on the four facing streets.

"I'll go ask directions," Clay said after helping the women

down. Pablo led the tired team off to water them. "You ladies may want to refresh yourselves in the hotel. I'll join you at the restaurant in a few minutes."

Shiloh and Victoria, glad to be out of their confined space, strolled toward the Sonoma House. They were interested to see several soldiers who gave them surprised stares. Four young boys played mumblety-peg in the street.

"Quiet kind of a place," Victoria commented, holding her skirt out of the dirt. "Peaceful too. I guess having the soldiers here helps keep the Indians subdued."

"Before you joined us last night, Mr. Vallejo said that there haven't been any Indian problems, but I guess the U.S. Government wants to keep it that way."

The women approached the hotel's front door just as it opened and a middle-aged man stepped outside carrying a basket of eggs. He started to nod to the women, then took a quick closer look at Shiloh.

"Good Lord!" he exclaimed, dropping the basket and staring open-mouthed. Most of the eggs broke together with a soft crunch, but one hit the doorstep and splattered. Streaks of yellow landed on his boots and pants legs. Some of the gooey mess struck Shiloh's long skirt even though she automatically tried to jump out of the way. Victoria escaped without a single spot.

"Oh, I'm sorry!" the stranger apologized, bending to right the basket. His wide-brimmed hat fell off, but he didn't seem to notice. He looked up at Shiloh. "I thought for a moment . . . never mind! Wait! I'll get something to clean you up."

He turned, gave his leg a quick shake to dislodge broken eggshells, then opened the door and stepped inside. He called, "Quick, somebody give me some towels or rags or something!"

Shiloh wanted to tell him she was all right, but he had already gone inside the building as passing soldiers and civilians stopped to stare.

She whispered to Victoria, "I'm embarrassed with everyone

looking at me." Looking at her skirt again, Shiloh continued, "Let's go inside where I can have some privacy and attend to these spots."

She reached for the door just as it burst open and the man who had dropped the eggs reappeared with what looked like a tablecloth. For the first time, Shiloh got a good look at him. He was about six feet tall, very good looking with blue eyes and soft, wavy dark hair showing a few gray ones.

"I am very sorry!" he exclaimed, starting to kneel with the big cloth in his hands. Then he stopped, looked up awkwardly and extended the cloth. "Uh, maybe you should do this?"

She took the cloth and bent, quickly wiping off the runniest parts of the yolk while he continued to apologize.

"It's all right," she said, very anxious to go inside to avoid the increasing gathering of spectators.

Victoria commented with a light touch to her voice, "Sir, you looked as if you had seen a ghost."

"I thought I had." He looked awkwardly at Shiloh. "You reminded me of someone I knew long ago. For a moment, I . . . Well, never mind. Miss, if you have some other clothes, I'll see that these are . . ."

"Thank you," she interrupted hastily. "I can attend to this inside." Shiloh handed him the soiled cloth and rushed into the hotel after telling Victoria, "I'll meet you at the restaurant in a few minutes."

When she had cleaned up sufficiently, Shiloh made her way to the table where Clay and Victoria were seated. "Sorry to take so long," she apologized.

Victoria said, "I told Clay what happened."

"No harm done," Shiloh assured them. "Clay, did you get directions to the property?"

"Yes, but it's quite a ways north of here. We should probably take rooms here for the night and go on tomorrow."

"No!" Shiloh exclaimed firmly. "I want to see that place today. Victoria, do you agree?"

"If you're not too tired."

"I'm fine. Please, let's eat and be on our way."

Later, Shiloh regretted her words, for the trip was much longer than she expected. Pablo's wild driving soon took them through the last beautiful little valley where they glimpsed a spouting geyser and several puffs of steam escaping from underground.

Ahead loomed a massive mountain hidden by clouds at the top. Pablo headed toward it on the eastern slope, obviously having been instructed by his employer. Eventually, the team slowed under the labor of pulling a load up a narrow, twisting road where evergreens, madrone, and black oak made a canopy overhead.

Twice Pablo had to pull over when bells on teamsters' mules announced they were coming around one of the hairpin curves. Shiloh felt a little queasy when Pablo stopped the team under a great oak and motioned to the left. "*Aqui, Señor y señoras.*"

"That's it," Clay said, addressing both women but with his eyes on Shiloh. "That's going to be a very hard climb. I think you should stay here."

"I agree," Victoria said. "Don't risk your baby."

Eying the mountain, Shiloh reluctantly agreed to stay with Pablo.

"We'll be back shortly," Victoria said, gathering her skirts more tightly about her slender body.

"Be careful," Shiloh replied, anxious to learn the meaning behind her husband's note.

As they started across the unfenced land, Clay observed that Victoria easily stayed up with him. She had walked a couple thousand miles across the prairies and was obviously still in good physical condition.

As her companions disappeared into the undergrowth, Shiloh turned to look at Pablo. He bent over a section of road-bed that had been filled with bright vermilion rocks. He picked up a piece and studied it.

"*Muy bonito,*" he said, smiling and handing her a piece.

She knew no Spanish but guessed he had called the rock pretty. It certainly was, and it was surprisingly heavy. She walked over to the wagon, deposited the rock inside, then turned to watch the mountain's slope again. The two climbers were still out of sight.

Shiloh focused on possible reasons why Aldar and Henry Barclay had bought this piece of land. As a farm girl, Shiloh knew the hill was too steep for plowing and planting. The ever-present oak trees, which thrived in dry or well-drained terrain, showed that there wasn't much water available. The grass did not appear to be something on which cattle could thrive.

It just doesn't make sense, Shiloh silently confessed, *but two smart men must have thought otherwise. So what did they know that we don't?*

‫ᴄᴏ‬

After a rest that Clay had suggested, he and Victoria again climbed up the hillside. Early rains had softened the dry grass so that it yielded readily underfoot. The ground was slippery in spots, but not bad.

The top was still lost in the clouds when Victoria asked, "Clay, what's that in the side of the hill?"

"A coyote hole."

They went to examine the excavation, which was much too large for a small coyote to have made. "Looks more like a bear made it," Victoria commented.

"It's man-made," Clay explained. "'Coyote hole' is what miners call a prospect hole. Somebody's been digging for gold or silver. I've seen a couple of others off to the side."

"You mean there might be something valuable in the ground that made my husband invest in this huge mountain?"

"Maybe, but the fact that there's no sign of any extensive digging shows that the holes didn't produce much of value." Clay checked the deed that he had brought along. "The way I read this, that little stream off to the right marks the northern boundary. That huge old oak where lightning struck the top is the southern one. Have you seen anything of value so far, or do you want to climb clear up into those clouds?"

"I don't know what I'm looking for, but I certainly don't see anything that seems remotely valuable."

"Then let's rest a minute and start back."

Looking in all directions, Victoria remarked, "This is a magnificent view. Breathtaking, in fact. But that's not why my husband and Aldar Laird bought this land. So what are we overlooking?"

Clay slowly shook his head. "I could take some samples from the coyote holes to be assayed. But I prospected for gold awhile when the rush started. I don't see anything to make me believe there's gold here."

"How about silver?" Victoria asked.

"I never mined for that, so I don't know what the ground should look like. Anyway, Vallejo obviously doesn't think there's anything really special about this place."

"Let's ask Pablo anyway."

"I don't speak enough Spanish. I know that *oro* means gold, but I don't remember the word for silver."

"Wouldn't hurt to try," Victoria said. "There's certainly nothing we can learn by ourselves."

"I think I see an easier way down," Clay said. "Let's try that."

Victoria followed him down a narrow path that Clay said had been made by deer.

About halfway down, they stepped over some bright red rocks that lay exposed on the path. Clay picked up a piece. It was porous and yet surprisingly heavy.

"What is it?" Victoria asked.

"I don't know. I've never seen anything like it."

Clay stuck it in his pocket. "I'll show it to Pablo."

When they reached the driver, Clay asked, "*Que es esta?*" and pointed to a piece of vermilion rock.

Pablo shrugged. "*Quien sabe?*" he replied, offering a piece he had picked up, then pointing to the countless pieces that workmen had paved the road with.

"I think that means he doesn't know," Clay explained, walking the women toward their vehicle.

Shiloh said, "Even though it's used to make the road, I'm taking a piece home."

Clay asked, "You want this one too?"

"No, thanks. Victoria, how about you?"

"There's not much room in my hotel room for rocks."

Victoria took a last look at the mountain's slope and said sadly, "Shiloh, I have absolutely no idea how your husband thought this land would pay for a stage line."

Shiloh admitted, "Neither do I."

When they were seated, Pablo turned the team around and headed back toward Sonoma.

Clay observed, "I didn't know your husband, Victoria, but you said he was successful."

"He certainly was."

"I knew Aldar very well," Clay continued, "and I know that he believed what he wrote in that note. There's something valuable on that property that made him risk borrowing from General Vallejo. Aldar was a man of honor, so I'm sure he believed he could repay that loan, which he did. But how?"

Victoria said carefully, "Please don't be upset, Shiloh, but could he have sold half interest to my husband for enough to repay the entire loan?"

Shiloh hesitated, thinking. If Aldar had done that, then Henry Barclay must have thought it was a good deal or he wouldn't have joined Aldar in the venture.

"I don't know," Shiloh confessed, "but I suppose it's possible."

"Anyway," Victoria said, "whatever it was those men saw in that mountain now means nothing. That property is useless to me, Shiloh, but I guess I can't expect you to buy my share because it's also worthless to you. Right?"

"Looks that way," she admitted sadly. Sick with disappointment, Shiloh cast a final glance at the hillside property. "Well," she added sadly, "that puts Clay and me even farther back than where we started. How are we going to finance our stage line in time to be eligible for the mail contract?"

⊙⊙ CHAPTER XII ⊙⊙

THE MORNING following their return to San Francisco, Shiloh awoke with such heaviness in her heart that she didn't want to get up. In a restless night, she had grappled with many problems that seemed to have no answers.

With a deep sigh, Shiloh sat up in bed and reached for her small white leather-bound New Testament on the nightstand. Her arm brushed across the vermilion rock she had brought back.

The rock seemed to mock her, silently reminding her that the trip had been in vain. Vallejo had declined to loan them money to develop the stage line. The taunting mystery of how Aldar had expected the land to pay for development of the stage line was still unsolved.

The deadline to submit a proposal for the government mail contract was now only weeks away, and it seemed Shiloh and Clay were worse off than when they had started.

She impatiently shoved the rock aside and picked up the testament. Shiloh kept the volume, in spite of its well-worn and loose pages, because it was the only clue to her birth parents. Whoever had abandoned her as an infant had tucked the Scriptures into the blankets with her. There was no writing on the book except a single word inside the front cover: *Shiloh.* She had no idea what it meant, but when Mara started calling her that, Shiloh accepted it.

Gently, she opened the pages and tenderly touched the two locks of hair that had always been there. One was short, dark, and curly, the other was long and red-gold. As she had countless times over the years, she fingered the locks before beginning to read, seeking comfort and guidance for the day ahead.

Mara quietly opened the door and peeked in. "I thought you were going to sleep all day," she said, stepping to the windows and opening the shades.

"It was a long, hard trip."

Mara sat on the edge of the high bed, her legs dangling well off the floor. "You feel like talking?"

"We pretty well covered everything last night when Clay and Victoria dropped me off."

"I understood all the words I heard, but I'm not so sure about the looks I saw."

Shiloh frowned. "What's that mean?"

"I saw Clay looking at you with soft eyes, but you ignored him. That wasn't true of Victoria. I wonder what's going on under all her fine yellow hair?"

"That doesn't concern me. I'm trying to figure out how to keep this stage line going and especially how to qualify for the mail contract."

"You know you're welcome to what I have."

"Thanks, but I can't do that. You've earned your money and should be able to do what you want with it."

"It's still yours if you want it."

"Clay and I need investment money from someone who won't be hurt financially if it's somehow lost. I guess our next move is to go to Sacramento and talk to John Sutter. We'll probably move the office there too."

"I thought you didn't want to move to Sacramento."

"I don't, but I may have to in order to make this stage line successful."

"Move permanently to Sacramento?" Mara got up and turned to face Shiloh. "You plan to move away from me, the one person you're going to need as the baby's birth approaches? You're going to risk being alone in Sacramento where you don't know a soul except Clay? Oh, sure, he'd do anything in the world for you, but there are some times when a woman will be of more importance than any man, except maybe a doctor."

Shiloh regarded her friend with surprise. "You don't have to raise your voice."

"Would you listen if I didn't?"

Shiloh briefly turned her face to the wall, then back toward Mara. "I don't know if I can explain this to you," she began, "but I came to California with a new husband, great expectations, and high hopes. I thought that Aldar would take care of me and protect me, provide love and security. I know he wanted to, that he expected to. Instead, I've had nothing but sorrow, disappointments and frustrations. So I've got to take care of myself and work out my own problems, personal and business. The trouble is: I have no experience, only my faith in God and my determination to work things out."

Mara brushed a strand of red-gold hair back from Shiloh's face. "I know," she said softly, "but in your determination to be strong, don't overlook those who want to help."

Shiloh took Mara's hand. "I never want you to be left out."

"I meant Clay."

"He's a very special man, but I don't dare let him get too close to me. I'm afraid to let myself love anyone, to trust in any man to always be there. I couldn't stand to be left alone again."

"Clay's in no danger."

"We didn't think Aldar was either."

"There's no point in thinking that way," Mara said reprovingly. "Your whole life is ahead of you. Don't let fear spoil the future. Grab another chance at happiness, and don't let her get Clay."

It took Shiloh a moment to realize whom Mara meant, but by then, she had left the bedroom.

∽

Three days before, Alvin Brakken had arrived at Johnson's ranch some forty miles northeast of Sacramento. In his semi-starved condition, he was discouraged at what he saw. The ranch had fallen into decay. Stalks of poor corn stood forlornly in the fields near acres of wheat that had been harvested. There were no fences, although Brakken guessed that some trenches with dirt thrown up along the sides served to keep the wandering stock away from the house, which was constructed of logs on one end and sun-dried adobe bricks on the other. Under nearby oak trees, pens made of poles held a few cows and calves, while some beef cattle roamed freely on the land.

The thought of a juicy beefsteak started Brakken's empty stomach churning. He hoped there was a woman at the house, knowing that his gaunt appearance would cause her to at least offer him a meal, and maybe enough food to make it to Sacramento.

A man might turn down his request for food or ask him to perform some chores in exchange. Brakken had no desire to work or do anything else that would delay him. Cautiously approaching the ranch, trying to appear at ease, Brakken decided that he might have to steal what he needed. However, that was risky, for his mules would easily be outrun if someone chased after them. He didn't want to be held as a thief after traveling all this way on his mission.

He would have liked to trade his mules for fresh stock but doubted that anyone would do that without asking for something extra. Brakken had nothing of value to give except his last twenty-dollar gold piece, but he didn't want to spend that. It was his link to the pretty blond woman who had given it to him. When he found her, he expected there would be many more, and more than gold.

Brakken approached the ranch house with hat in hand, a forced smile, and polite words for Mrs. Johnson. He introduced himself as Yancy Tate. After one glance at the pitiful condition of Brakken and his animals, Mrs. Johnson was very hospitable. She hastily treated him to fresh meat and milk right from the cow. The Indian workmen fed and watered Brakken's mules. Then Brakken took a bath in the river and washed his filthy clothes.

That evening, greatly refreshed, he ate two huge beefsteaks and learned about William Johnson. A former English seaman, he had located here north of Bear Creek, a tributary of the Feather River. Almost all travelers coming over the Sierra Nevadas heading for Sutter's Fort had known that Johnson's was the first civilized outpost before the fort.

John C. Fremont and his scout, Kit Carson, had camped at Johnson's about the time of the Bear Flag incident. Attempts to rescue the surviving members of the Donner party had been launched from Johnson's after seven forlorn survivors from the ill-fated party had staggered to the ranch with news of their tragedy.

After an evening of stories, Brakken slept outside under a big oak, thinking how nice it would be to laze around for a few days. But there was a chance that Duggan or someone who knew him might show up. So he rose early in the morning, planning to steal supplies and be on his way before the ranch people stirred. Before he could carry out his plan, Mrs. Johnson approached him with an offer of breakfast. She stuffed him with cornbread, ham, eggs, venison, and coffee, then gave him supplies for the rest of the way to Sacramento.

Before noon, Brakken saw sunlight reflecting off the confluence of two large rivers. From directions he had gotten at Johnson's, he knew that he was seeing the American River join the greater Sacramento River. The tents and buildings marked Sacramento City itself. It was larger than he expected, spreading out across the vast, flat land in all directions.

Brakken reined in his skinny mount and eased out of the saddle to stretch. He dropped the pack mule's lead rope, knowing that both animals were too weak to wander off. They had been fed and rested at Johnson's, but it would take more than a few days to restore them to health.

Brakken still regretted that he had not killed Duggan after he recognized him above Camp Far West. An uneasy feeling still gnawed at Brakken's insides even though he had tried hard to convince himself that even if Duggan lived, he had almost no chance of ever alerting Clay Patton before Brakken could catch up with him.

With a final glance over his shoulder to determine that no one was following, Brakken turned, seized the pack mule's lead rope and swung into the saddle of the first mule. He kicked it in the ribs and hurried on to Sacramento. It had been a long, long search, but now the end of the hunt was in sight.

〇〇

Shiloh had forced herself to get dressed and have breakfast, so she was ready when Clay came to take her to the office.

In the carriage, he asked, "You get enough rest after the trip?"

She waited until he took his seat beside her before answering, "I'm fine, thanks."

There was no point in telling him that she had spent a restless night or that, after her conversation with Mara, she had been quietly concerned about the coming birth. The uncertainty of how much pain and discomfort she faced didn't trouble her as much as the possibility of Clay being away on a stage run when the birth started. What would she do without Mara?

Clay broke into her musings. He slapped the lines across the horse's back but looked straight ahead as he bluntly declared, "I don't want you to go to Sacramento."

He wanted to explain that he wanted very much to have her near him, now and always, but she would be much better off with Mara to watch over her in the remaining months before the baby's birth. That would be a hard, lonely time for Clay, but a few months was nothing compared to the years of heartache he had known since losing Elizabeth and Mark.

When Shiloh didn't answer, Clay looked down at her to see various emotions flitting across her face.

She asked, "Why don't you want me to go?"

"I've told you. I'm concerned for your health, and the baby's. You need to be near Mara."

"That's what she told me this morning."

"Then you'll stay here?"

Shiloh's face hardened with determination. "No, I can't. I am a partner in this business, and I have an equal responsibility with you to make it succeed. It was Aldar's dream, and he had a plan to finance it. Just because we haven't been able to figure his plan out doesn't mean that we can't. We just need to know more."

"I didn't mean to upset you."

"I'm not upset! Everybody has problems, but I'm still learning how to deal with some of mine, like the business and the baby. But this stage line is going to succeed, and I'm going to rear a healthy child."

Clay was uncomfortable with the tension between them. Shiloh had slipped into his heart and mind as no one else had in the years since Elizabeth's death. But he had other pressing problems that he needed to discuss with Shiloh.

Clay shifted the conversation to a less stressful topic by asking, "How do you feel now about Victoria owning half-interest in the Mount Saint Helena property?"

"If I had the money, I would buy her out."

"Then you would own 100 percent of nothing; at least, that's the way it now looks."

"I want to find out why Aldar and Victoria's husband bought that property. I just hope I do in time." She also wanted to end the relationship with Victoria. There was no special reason, Shiloh told herself. Things would just be less complicated with only Clay and herself.

"We'll make it," Clay assured her. "Even if we don't get the mail contract, we could run a profitable business out of

Sacramento where we'll be in the middle of all the staging activity."

"Aldar's dream wasn't just to be profitable. He said California's future depended on transportation. That's why he dreamed of a system that covered all of California and the overland route to the Missouri River." She looked up pleadingly to meet Clay's eyes and added, "We can't let him down now, can we?"

"No, of course not," he replied. To himself he added with grudging admiration, *She's pretty—but stubborn!*

⌇

There was little time to think about solving the enigma of the northern property in the rush to make all the arrangements necessary for the move to Sacramento.

Sledger stuck his head in the office late the next afternoon. "Am I interrupting?" he asked Shiloh.

"No, of course not. I'm about to close up because Clay should be here to pick me up in a few minutes. Please come in and sit down."

He squeezed through the opening at the end of the counter and sat on the chair she indicated.

"I was concerned Sunday when you rushed off after I told you what I had seen here. I came by here and learned from Jared that he was minding the office while you three had gone up north."

"Mara told me you also came by the house. Thanks, Pastor. I appreciate your concern."

"How did the trip go?"

"It was a disappointment," she admitted, and quickly related the pertinent details. She concluded, "So we still don't know what Aldar meant."

"You'll figure it out."

"I hope so. In the meantime, we're planning on moving to Sacramento because that's where all the other major stage lines are headquartered."

"I'll be sorry to lose you, Shiloh."

"I've no choice," she replied and briefly outlined her reasoning. She finished by saying that Jared had done a good job in managing the office while she and Clay were away. He had also agreed to represent Laird and Patton Stage Lines in the city while developing his law practice out of the office.

As an afterthought, Shiloh said, "Mara suggested to Jared that he hire her friend, Samuel, to clean up the office in exchange for a small salary. Sweeping out this place is a job I won't miss. I just hope that I don't have to do it in Sacramento. Incidentally, Samuel told Jared that he's lined up several other offices to clean. He's got a sort of business of his own going."

"He sounds like a mighty hard worker."

"I suspect he's trying to make a good impression on Mara. But that's going to be hard for a runaway slave because Mara's ambitions are quite high."

Sledger considered that before asking, "What's Victoria going to do?"

"She told me that she loves San Francisco, so she'll stay here. I suspect her husband left her rather well off."

Aldar hadn't been able to do that for her. Not that Shiloh blamed him. He was much younger than Henry Barclay had been. If Aldar had lived to be Henry's age, Shiloh was sure she would have been very well off financially. But there was no sense thinking about that.

Sledger observed, "It's good that she's comfortably fixed."

"Anyone as pretty and vivacious as Victoria will have many opportunities to remarry. But in the meantime, she's apparently got enough money for all the fancy clothes she will need to attend dress balls and other social activities."

"They're becoming very popular as more women arrive. Shiloh, you should be enjoying them yourself."

"Maybe someday," she said wistfully, gently folding her hands across her middle. "You see, part of me will always belong to San Francisco. My husband is buried here, and one day I expect to have the home on Fern Hill that he promised me."

She caught a slight raising of Sledger's eyebrows. She added quickly, "Aldar won't be here to share it with me in person, but he will always be with me in memory, and the stagecoach system he planned will make it possible for our child and me to live up there."

The preacher hoisted his big body from the chair and said fervently, "As I said, I'll hate to see you go. You've been a faithful member and helped get our Sunday school department going. I will always be grateful, and our little church and I will miss you, Shiloh."

"And I'll miss you and the wonderful people too. But someday I'll be back. Every time you drive by Fern Hill, think about that."

☞

Shiloh's thoughts were still on her conversation with Sledger when Clay came by to take her home. She did not feel like talking, but Clay didn't seem to notice.

After he was seated beside her, he said, "I ran into Jefferson Locke today. He was furious."

Shiloh's reflections on her remarks to Sledger vanished with her sudden prick of alarm. She tried to tell herself that she had returned the mud wagon to Denby Gladwin; she actually owed nothing to Locke just because they were associated.

Still, she was curious. "Why was he furious, Clay?"

"It seems that Mara now owns a lot near the plaza where she's going to construct her boardinghouse."

Shiloh frowned. "What's that got to do with Locke?"

"He said that she had come to him some time ago, wanting to buy the land, but he wouldn't sell it to her."

"Because of her color!" Shiloh's voice rose angrily.

"He's upset that apparently someone bought it for her as a gift."

"Really? Who did that? And why?"

"You honestly don't know?"

Shiloh knew it had to be a male Caucasian admirer, but

Mara hadn't recently said anything about any well-to-do man who might have made such an expensive gift.

Stumped, Shiloh said, "Clay, tell me what you know."

"Maybe Mara would rather tell you herself."

Shiloh sighed. "That's probably true." She started to settle back in the seat, resigned to wait until she got home. Then she jerked upright as the thought hit her.

"Not Jared?" She gripped Clay's arm. "Jared?"

"You'd better ask Mara."

Stunned, Shiloh exclaimed, "But he recently lost his wife! Remember? He said she died at sea shortly before the ship went down in the harbor! How could he?"

"Now, Shiloh, don't jump to . . ."

"He's a Southerner!" she interrupted. "He would never treat Mara as an equal! That can only mean one thing. But I don't want to believe that! I won't believe it!"

Clay didn't reply, and Shiloh fell silent. She did not want to accept the obvious answer that sprang to mind. She stormed mentally, *Right under my own nose too! How could Mara have done that? She knows how I feel about such things. And Jared! I thought he was a real gentleman!*

"Clay," Shiloh said through suddenly tense lips, "Get me home—fast!"

~~ CHAPTER XIII ~~

SHILOH WAS STILL very upset after Clay dropped her off at home. She followed the fragrance of Mara's cooking out to the separate cookhouse.

The shades were open on the small parlor and the tiny bedroom, and she could see Jared wasn't in. Shiloh sighed with relief and opened the kitchen door.

Mara turned from the wood-burning stove with a long-handled fork in her hand. "Smells delicious, doesn't it?" she asked. "Fresh fish. I bought it from a fisherman just getting out of his boat."

Shiloh stopped by the small preparation table inside the door. "I just heard about the gift you received near the plaza."

"My boardinghouse will soon be a reality." Mara set the fork down and crossed the small room. She cocked her head slightly to look at Shiloh. "I thought you would be happy for me, but you're wearing a mighty long face."

"Did Jared buy that lot and give it to you?"

Mara stiffened at Shiloh's cool tone. "I have my own money. You know that. But since I couldn't buy it in my own name, Jared purchased, then transferred, title to me."

Shiloh searched for words that would not betray her anger. "I know you and I don't hold to the same moral standards, but do you know what this looks like to me?"

Mara lifted an eyebrow. "You're wondering what I gave him in exchange, aren't you?"

Shiloh's words popped out in cold fury. "You and I both know what he expected. You're a grown woman, and you can do what you want. But not in my home!"

"You know me better than that. I respect you too much to do something that I know would upset you."

Shiloh wanted to believe her, but she wasn't quite ready to accept that. "Really?"

"Really." Mara reached over and took Shiloh's hand. "In fact, nothing has happened between Jared and me."

"Nothing?"

"Not a thing. Oh, it's not his fault. He's made his wishes plain enough. But I know enough to get what I want before I consider giving anything in return. And don't worry; when and if it happens, it won't be in your house."

Relief and shame swept over Shiloh in a rush. "I should have known. I'm sorry, Mara."

"It's all right. I may be many things that you don't approve of, but I love you too much to hurt you. Now, how about giving me a hand with dinner?"

∽

Alvin Brakken arrived in Sacramento shortly before noon. Intent on beginning his search, he rode by Sutter's famous fort and barely gave it a glance. His eyes skimmed the newly laid out town, taking in the ships tied up at the embarcadero, the ceaseless traffic of teams and wagons in streets still muddy from the recent rain, and the low-lying main section of town where gambling tents, saloons, and other businesses thrived.

Somewhere in Sacramento, Brakken fully expected to either find Clay Patton or get a solid lead on his location. He no longer intended to simply find Clay and hang him with the same rope that had taken his twin's life. After waiting seven years for vengeance, he wanted Clay to suffer in every way possible before his life ended.

Brakken also hoped to pick up the blond woman's trail. Riding down the streets still muddy from the recent early rains, Brakken rolled the gold coin in his palm, recalling all the others she had paid him for the job. But it wasn't just the double eagles that stirred his memory. She had slipped away from the caravan marshaling area beyond the Missouri River without making the final, personal payment he expected. The thought of soon collecting that made him squirm in the saddle. "In due time," he said softly.

At Johnson's, Brakken had picked up some rudimentary information about Sacramento and Sutter, whose generosity to earlier-arriving immigrants was well known.

Eight years earlier, the Mexican government had granted Sutter eleven leagues of land near the confluence of the Sacramento and American rivers. There the Swiss-born, naturalized Mexican citizen had built the most imposing fort in the West. With the help of Indians, he raised wheat and cattle and became the undisputed land baron of the area.

One of his employees, James Marshall, had discovered gold

on the American River in January 1848. That proved to be Sutter's ruin. The vast influx of gold seekers had overrun Sutter's lands, killing his cattle, and trampling his crops while ignoring his protests.

Now between two and five thousand people lived where there had been only two log cabins and the fort less than two years earlier. The incoming Americans expected to homestead as had been done in the Midwest and Oregon. They refused to recognize property rights set up under the Mexicans, who had been defeated in war just nineteen months before. Sutter, already seriously in debt, turned his holdings over to his son, but that didn't stop the Americans from claiming rights to the land.

Brakken's musings were interrupted by hearing the ring of hammer on steel. He followed the sound down a side street to a blacksmith shop. Tying the mules outside, he walked through the open barn door to where the smith worked.

In one hand, the smith held a glowing-red horseshoe with a pair of metal tongs. The other hand wielded a heavy hammer. After a couple more blows to shape the shoe, he plunged it into a wooden tub of water. Only when the hissing and steam subsided did the smith look at Brakken.

"No matter what you want, Mister, I can't help you until tomorrow. Come back then."

Rankling slightly, Brakken forced himself to smile. "I know these mules look a sight, but their shoes will last a spell longer."

The smith grunted and removed the cooled horseshoe from the water. "Looks to me like you should keep the shoes and get new mules."

Brakken tried to acknowledge the man's attempt at humor by giving a little laugh. "We've come a far piece, all right. Now that I'm here, maybe you can help me."

Bending to the forge, he worked a bellows on the glowing coals. "I got too much work to be helping anybody else, Mister."

Ignoring the insolent tone, Brakken explained, "I'm looking

for a friend I used to know back home. Told me that if I ever got to California, to look him up. His name's Clay Patton. Know him?"

"How would I know one man among thousands who arrived here so far this year?"

Brakken had never been known for keeping his temper, but he gritted his teeth and tried again. "This friend is a real tall man. Slender build but strong as rawhide. Always worked around horses. Maybe drives a team for someone around here."

The smith dropped the bellows and turned to scowl at Brakken. "Mister, I got work to do."

Brakken's hands curled into fists and his face blackened with anger. "All I want to know is if you've seen this friend of mine."

Alerted to the stranger's temper and not wanting to get into a fight with so much to do, the smith changed his tone. "Can't say as I have. But if I run into him, who shall I tell him was looking for him?"

"My name's Tate; Yancy Tate. I'll be staying at one of the hotels."

The smith snorted. "Ain't but one in town. Called the City Hotel. Frame building on Front Street between I and J. If I see your friend, I'll tell him."

"Much obliged." Brakken started to turn around, then asked, "I also have a lady friend. Blond hair and really good looking. You seen her?"

"Mister, you been out in the sun too long. Ain't seen a good-looking woman since I came west."

Brakken returned to his mules, fuming at how hard it had been to get simple questions answered. Maybe it wasn't going to be easy to find Clay or the woman, even after coming two thousand miles.

∽

Clay opened the office door, startling Shiloh. She jerked her head up and spun around, facing the door.

"Sorry," Clay apologized, coming around the end of the counter. "I didn't mean to frighten you."

"You didn't." She sounded as tired as she felt. "I was just deep in thought."

"Oh." He stopped beside her, fighting an urge to take her into his arms. Instead, he risked lightly touching her on her shoulder. "Things will work out."

Sighing, she pretended not to notice the pleasant feel of his strong fingers and the comfort that seemed to flow from them. "I know they will," she agreed. "But tearing up roots and moving from here, even after only a few months, is hard."

"I really wish you wouldn't try to move yet."

"We've been over that so many times that there's no use in doing it again."

"I know, but if anything happens to you . . ." He left his sentence hanging, aware of what he had started to say.

She gave him a tired smile. "Nothing's going to happen to me. Everything will work out fine."

He wanted to tell her that she had brought new life and hope to him after all these years. She had given him a reason to succeed in an impossible situation. But without her, the struggle wouldn't be worth tackling the obstacles that surrounded them.

To ease his discomfort, he glanced around the office, noting that wooden boxes had been filled with papers and other supplies. "Looks like you've got this under control."

"Brother Sledger helped first, and then Samuel finished up while we were up north."

Clay nodded and picked up the piece of vermilion rock that Shiloh had brought from home that morning.

Clay remarked, "What an unusual bright red."

"I don't know why I keep it." She took a deep breath and noisily exhaled. "Well, maybe because it's a reminder of Aldar's note that said the property would pay for developing the stage line. It's about the only tangible thing I've got."

"Want to leave it here or take it home?"

Shiloh pursed her lips. "I'll take it home and put it by my Bible on the nightstand. That will give me two mysteries to think about when the baby is restless and won't let me sleep."

Clay stuck the rock in his pocket and offered Shiloh his hand. As she arose under his gentle pull, it took all his willpower to keep from drawing her into his arms and holding her close.

⁓

Returning from another stealthy late night visit to deposit gold under a fence post, Mara was startled when a figure silently stepped from the deep shadows of the house. She wasn't afraid but bent quickly and laid her shovel on the ground as quietly as possible. When she stood again, she had reached into her jacket pocket and gripped the Remington derringer that Samuel had given her.

The click of the revolver being cocked was ominous in the darkness. "Who's there?" she called softly.

"Jared," he whispered back. "And ease that hammer back down before it goes off."

She obeyed. Leaving the shovel on the ground and lowering the weapon, she moved to meet him.

"Where have you been?" Jared asked in a low tone. "I saw you leave the house a while ago and tried to follow you, but lost you."

"I was just thinking."

He reached out and took her gently by the shoulders. "So was I." It was barely a whisper. "I've been thinking about what you said the other day about what reward a man could expect for helping you get what you want."

"I appreciate your putting that lot in my name, but remember, it was my money."

"That doesn't matter. You got what you wanted, now it's my turn." His arms slid about her waist to pull her close. "We can go to my quarters," he said huskily.

She delayed for just a moment to see whether he would kiss her. Satisfied that he would not, and thoroughly angered because she knew he couldn't bring himself to do so, Mara pulled away and started walking toward the house.

He caught up with her in a few quick strides. "What's the matter? What did I do?"

"You wouldn't understand," she replied coldly, still moving to keep out of his reach.

He caught up with her and swung her around. "I don't know what kind of game you think you're playing, but it won't work on me. I gave you what you want, and now it's my turn."

"No," she snapped, pushing against his chest as she had the day she had realized his fancy vest was filled with gold coins. "You have just shown me that you consider me no different from a common harlot! Now, leave me alone!"

He stood in the darkness, staring dumbfounded as her shadowy form hurried onto the porch. Fury and desire mused in him, stronger than his understanding. *You shouldn't have done that*, he thought angrily. *No colored woman can do that to me.*

☙

Victoria was preparing for bed the next night at her hotel when she heard a knock at her door. She turned from the closet where she had just hung up her outer clothes.

"Who is it?" she asked, standing in her chemise.

The man's voice sounded muffled. "Message for Mrs. Barclay."

"Slide it under the door."

"You've got to sign for it."

With an impatient gesture, she hastily drew a pale green dressing gown around herself and opened the door a couple of inches. "Jared! What are you doing here?"

"Delivering a message," he replied with an appreciative glance at the open neck of her dressing gown.

She looked at his empty hands. "What message?"

He tapped his head with a forefinger and grinned. "It's up here. I can deliver it better if I don't have to stand out here in this cold hallway."

"That could ruin my reputation."

Jared noticed that she didn't sound too concerned. "How about mine? I'm willing to take a chance on ruining my future in politics. On the other hand, my reputation might be greatly enhanced from being seen with you."

She laughed softly. "Come in. But only for a minute."

With a feeling of triumph, he stepped inside and closed the door behind him. She motioned for him to take the only chair. As he sat, she perched on the high bed and curled her long, slender legs so that her ankles showed demurely. Her loose, shoulder-length hair cascaded softly around her fair face. The light from the twin candles caressed her high cheekbones and small, straight nose.

She pretended not to see the hunger in his eyes. "What's your message?" she asked with a ghost of a smile.

He had to rouse himself from the emotions that gripped him. "I've been thinking about the property you and Shiloh inherited."

Delicately raising a hand in a casual motion, she prompted. "You have?"

"Yes. Since it has no known value, you will surely have a difficult time finding a purchaser for it."

"What makes you think I'll sell?"

"You're a practical woman, Victoria, but you like the nicer things in life that only cash can give you."

"My late husband provided generously for me."

"No doubt, but San Francisco is an expensive place to live." His eyes swept the room. "This is an example. So are your clothes hanging there." He motioned toward the open closet. "No matter how well your late husband provided for you, his money won't last forever. And while I've no doubt that soon many suitors will beg to take you to the finest restaurants, concerts, balls, and other expensive places, it will still cost you. You'll need new gowns and everything that goes with them."

"You want to buy my interest in the property I own with Shiloh?"

He shook his head. "I was thinking more along the lines of representing you in negotiations."

"This town is filled with men selling real estate."

He dismissed them with a word. "Opportunists."

"And you're not?" There was humor in her voice.

He pretended to be offended. "I was merely trying to be of service."

"Of course you were." She wanted to add that his actions proved it: coming here late at night instead of leaving a note downstairs asking to meet for lunch or something appropriate.

He sensed that she was teasing him. He hadn't expected her to be so discerning. He quickly changed tactics.

"Let's be frank, Victoria." Jared's tone became businesslike. "You want to sell that property, but you have no idea of what it's worth. You don't know what's on that hill, and you'd like to exchange the unknown for the known. Right?"

"Shiloh's husband believed that property would pay for developing the stage line. If he's right, then not only will she and Clay be wealthy someday, but so will I." Her tone had hardened with reserve. "Thank you, Jared, but I'm not going to even consider representation to sell until I find out what my husband and Aldar knew."

She slid off the bed, her dressing gown fluttering open to the knees. She seemed not to notice. "Thanks for coming."

He had hoped to not be dismissed so casually, but he followed her to the door. "Think about what I said."

She tossed her yellow hair, making it ripple seductively.

"And you think about why that property has value. When you have something to report, please let me know."

Smiling tauntingly, she closed the door with her challenge fresh in his mind.

Find out why that property has value, he repeated to himself. *She's not going to give in until then.*

Jared thoughtfully sauntered down the hall, feeling frustrated in his desires. He didn't understand why Mara had rebuffed him. Victoria had at least given him encouragement to return, but only when he knew why two dead men wanted a piece of property on the eastern slope of Mount Saint Helena. There wasn't a clue or even a hint of how to find out.

Or is there? The thought made him stop abruptly in the hallway. He rolled the possibility around in his mind. The idea was so wild, so unlikely, that it seemed foolish even to consider it. But he didn't have anything else, so why not investigate this? *As soon as I get a chance,* he told himself.

∞

The following night, Shiloh was so weary that she could hardly wait to get to bed. She had packed all of her belongings except what she would need between now and the time she and Clay left for Sacramento.

Sitting on the edge of the bed, Shiloh thought of omitting her usual Bible reading and going right to sleep. But old habits took over, so she reached for her New Testament on the nightstand. She opened it and started to lay back against the pillow. Then she frowned, sat up, and ran her hands over the marble-topped nightstand. "That's strange," she said.

She got out of bed, took the candle, and searched along the floor. She padded barefoot to Mara's room. The door stood open, and Shiloh watched her turn back the bedspread.

"Mara, have you seen my red rock?"

"It was on your nightstand this morning."

"I know." Scowling, Shiloh added, "It's not there now, and I can't find it anyplace."

"The doctor told you that being absent-minded is part of being pregnant. You probably misplaced it. We'll find it later."

Shiloh returned to her bedroom.

∽ CHAPTER XIV ∽

THE THREATENING skies the next morning warned of coming rain as Jared pushed open the door to the assayer's tiny office. It was cluttered with rock specimens of all shapes, sizes, and colors. There was a faint, unpleasant odor that Jared assumed must be from the chemicals used to test specimens hopeful miners brought in for evaluation.

Most men responding to the gold rush were young, so Jared was surprised when a bone-thin, gray-haired man with stooped shoulders emerged from the back room. His age-mottled skin was stretched tight over prominent cheekbones.

"Morning," he said, rubbing watery blue eyes with the back of his hand. "Looks like it's about to rain."

"Yes, it does." Jared produced the red rock. "Take a look at this, would you?" He had surreptitiously lifted it from Shiloh's room while Mara was drawing water at the well.

The assayer accepted the specimen but barely glanced at it. "Where did you find an Indian willing to trade this off?"

The question surprised Jared. "Indian?" he repeated.

"They use it for decoration; that is, when they wear clothes they can hang it from. Or they use it to make red paint for their bodies."

It was a big disappointment to Jared that the crumbly rock

was worthless except to Indians. He reached out and retrieved it. "I didn't get it from an Indian," he grumbled. "What's it called?"

"Cinnabar."

The word meant nothing to Jared. "Thanks," he said, and turned toward the door.

The old man followed him, warming to his subject. "It's been known since ancient times, maybe even since prehistoric times. The Romans used it in cosmetics. Called it minium back then. Aristotle and Pliny mentioned it. Maybe you saw some plains Indians with red marking the part in their hair when you came across?"

"I came by ship."

"No matter. Anyway, strange as it sounds, our country once shipped it to China where they manufactured vermilion. Then they sent it back across the ocean where the fur traders eventually got hold of it and swapped it to the Indians."

Jared opened the door, having lost all interest in the garrulous old man's words, who asked one last question. "Did you say you didn't get it from an Indian?"

"No." Jared stepped outside and started to pull the door after him.

"Then you had to get it from around the New Almaden."

Jared had never heard that name before, so it aroused his curiosity. "Why do you think that?"

"Because that's the only place in California I know about where it's mined in any quantity."

Mined? Jared repeated to himself, suddenly very alert to new possibilities. Aloud, he asked, "Do they make much off of the New Almaden?"

The assayer laughed. "Do they? Since the discovery of gold, the demand for cinnabar has been tremendous, but the New Almaden has a virtual monopoly because there's no other known source in California."

He stepped close and took hold of the door so it couldn't close. "The Mexicans have been mining it at New Almaden since 1824, near as I can recollect."

The mention of gold had fanned Jared's curiosity into a white-hot flame. "This New Almaden up north?"

"Nope. South, down by San Jose. The New Almaden Mine there was named after the big producer in Spain."

Jared recalled that Shiloh had said workmen had used the red rock as road fill near the Mount Saint Helena property, which was north. Jared decided to play a humble learner. "I've only been here a short time. What does cinnabar have to do with gold mining?"

"Everything! Absolutely everything, that's what! Close that door and don't be so blasted impatient. Come on back by the stove and have a seat."

Jared followed as the old man apologized. "No offense, Mister. I sometimes forget that most of you eastern boys get the gold fever and go scratching up the whole dern countryside without knowing a blasted thing about what you're doing."

Jared resisted the temptation to say he was a lawyer and not a miner. "How's this cinnabar used?" he asked.

"Cinnabar is the ore from which we get . . . sit down and I'll explain it to you."

Jared obeyed with alacrity, sensing that he had stumbled upon the answer to the enigma of the northern property.

∽

It was barely ten o'clock in the morning, and Shiloh already wished it was time to close the office and go home. She could hear the rain beginning to fall on the roof, and the wood-burning stove seemed unable to beat back the cold air that seeped in around her. Her one consolation was that everything was packed for the move.

All that remained on the rolltop desk and in the drawers were the items Jared would need to process orders that came in. *There wouldn't be many of those,* Shiloh thought ruefully, *judging by how slow business had been the last few weeks.* Older residents had told her that with the onset of the rainy season, mud would be so deep that soon only the lightest vehicles could get around.

She didn't really mind that there had been almost no counter traffic this morning. Her pregnancy made her uneasy about the future, and this was aggravated by her increasing discomfort.

She leaned back in her chair, facing the desk, and let her mind drift. *At least the baby will know who his mother is,* she thought, *even though he'll never see his father. I just wish I knew the truth about my birth parents.*

She closed her eyes, trying to imagine what they must have looked like. She was sure, from the two locks left in the New Testament, that her mother's hair was just the same red gold as her own. But what had she looked like? Suddenly, Shiloh opened her eyes, recalling the man in Sonoma.

He had come through the hotel door, seen her, and dropped the eggs. Victoria had remarked that he looked as if he had seen a ghost. Shiloh remembered his reply "I thought I did."

She concentrated, trying to remember what else he had said. Something about my reminding him of someone he had known long ago. Shiloh's pulse sped up. *A woman, a young woman who must have looked then much as I do now. A woman who . . .*

Shiloh abruptly checked her thoughts. Aloud, she scolded, "No! Not a woman who could have been my mother! There's no sense in tormenting myself like that. I don't dare hope for that after all these years. Still, if I could see that egg man again and maybe ask . . ."

"What egg man?"

The man's voice behind her made Shiloh jump and whirl around, her heart leaping.

"It's just me," Jefferson Locke said from across the counter, showing his crooked teeth in a smile. His hat and clothes were wet from the rain. "I didn't mean to startle you."

Shiloh got up, embarrassed at having been overheard talking to herself. "It's all right," she said. "I was just thinking about something."

"I hear you're moving the office to Sacramento," Locke said, shifting subjects. "From the looks of this place, you're about gone."

"A lawyer friend will develop his practice in this office and handle what business there is for the stage line. Now, what can I do for you?"

"Since you're moving away, I thought you might like me to sell your house."

"I'm not going to sell it. Mara's going to stay on and take care of things there."

"Ah, yes! Mara! The most ambitious nigra I ever met."

Shiloh decided to cut the conversation short. "Thanks for coming in, Mr. Locke."

He didn't take the hint. "I also hear that you and another woman have some property to sell up in the Sonoma area."

"You heard wrong." Shiloh tried to keep her dislike of the man from showing. "That property is not for sale."

"I see. May I ask what you plan to do with it?"

She was tempted to snap, "No, because it's none of your business." But she managed to answer politely, "Those plans are confidential."

"Of course. Forgive me for asking." He started to leave the counter, then hesitated. "What did you say the woman's name was?"

"I didn't say." Her tone was distinctly frosty. She did not want this obnoxious man talking to Victoria.

"I see." Locke reluctantly turned from the counter but stopped with his hand on the doorknob. "Gladwin tells me that you returned the carriage he gave you."

"Yes, I did." Her impatience showed in the crisp reply.

"Mrs. Laird, you have pride, which is commendable, but it won't keep the stage line solvent. What you need for that is cash, if you don't mind my saying so."

She minded him saying so, but didn't answer. She just looked at him with cold eyes that said plainly that he should leave.

"I'm going to be impulsive, since I haven't mentioned this to Gladwin, but I'm willing to make you a final offer on the stage line."

She took a quick breath to reply, but he held up both hands to stop her. "Before you speak, let me assure you that you and Clay Patton will remain as the apparent owners. As I said before, everyone will think that is the case although Gladwin and I will run the operation behind the scenes. We'll guarantee the wages, the stock, and equipment."

"We have already been over this," she interrupted, her voice rising in spite of herself. "There is nothing more to say." She turned her back on him.

He stood for a moment longer before muttering angrily, "We shall see about that!" He slammed the door behind him.

Shiloh listened to his heavy footsteps on the stairs, then she sat down at her desk and closed her eyes, fighting back angry, frustrated tears.

∽

By noon in Sacramento, discouragement had begun to nibble at Brakken. He had repeated his story of looking for an old friend at livery stables, stage stations, and hay and feed lots. Not one person recalled a tall, slender driver named Clay Patton. Neither did anybody remember a pretty young blond woman although almost everyone assured Brakken that they would certainly have remembered such a woman.

The darkening sky hinted that rain was on the way in from the coast. Brakken had slept on the ground and been soaked countless times on the trip across the West, but now he had a strong desire to sleep in a real bed, a hotel bed. But that would take money, which he would have to steal. That might not be easy in daylight, even with the dark and gloomy skies.

His worn boots kicked up little pieces of mud as he walked along the business district, considering where to find a quarry with money. He passed a barber shop, caught a glimpse of himself in the mirror, and realized it would take more than money for a good hotel room. No one would let him in looking like a wild man.

A daytime robbery was so risky that he briefly considered breaking his precious double eagle. He could splurge for a shave, haircut, and bath, but would that leave enough for a good restaurant meal and hotel room? He had heard prices were high in Sacramento. Besides, he was reluctant to part with the gold coin. He had carried it all this way, and it reminded him of Victoria. No, he decided, it wouldn't do to part with it.

Brakken turned his attention to the only other solution, but he would have to choose his target carefully. It wouldn't be as easy as it had been on the trail, when few, if any, other people were around. Here, the principal streets were filled. Too many possible witnesses, Brakken decided. He would have to get away from all the activity. He could not afford to end up in some jail, losing valuable time from his search.

Not knowing the area put him at a distinct disadvantage. He would need to look around while he planned. He walked back toward the mules. It would be easier to ride around town than walk.

He found the animals where he had secured them in a thick growth of willows and cottonwood trees that rose out of the sandy riverbank. He slowed apprehensively when he caught a glimpse of a man through the trees.

A quick look around showed there was nobody else in sight. Brakken, surveying his possibilities, quietly approached the lone Negro, who fished unaware with a green willow pole.

As Brakken neared, the tip of the pole suddenly bent sharply. The fisherman jerked his pole and took a couple of quick steps back to keep the line tight. He almost tripped over an exposed willow root and glanced down at it. When he looked up again, he caught sight of Brakken and grinned.

"That's him," the fisherman announced, focusing his attention on the catch. The taut line cut the water, making a small ripple as the fish tried to escape the hook in its mouth.

Brakken casually swept his eyes in all directions, not seeing any potential witnesses. He didn't expect the fisherman to have much money, but whatever he had was better than nothing. He tried to sound casual as he got closer to the fisherman.

"What do you think it is?"

"I wisht it was a big ol' striped bass, but it more likely is a ol' carp, or maybe a fat catfish. Carp all full of bones, but cats is good eatin', you know."

"Keep your line tight," Brakken advised.

"I'm a'tryin' real hard." The fisherman asked over his shoulder, "You got a cold, Mister?"

The question annoyed Brakken. He had heard it countless times in his life because of his unusual voice.

"No," he replied shortly.

When the catch was pulled from the water, the fisherman announced happily, "Big ol' cat! Mus' weigh maybe five, six pounds, easy." He stooped and carefully placed his right hand in front of the sharp, upright dorsal fin. Slowly forcing it down, he said, "Suh, would you mind reachin' in that little can there and handin' me that stringer?"

Brakken could not see any sign that suggested the man even had any coins, so he bent down and reached for the container. It had once held the caps that ignite the powder to discharge a cap-and-ball gun. Raising the lid, Brakken retrieved the stringer. As he lifted it out, he heard the unmistakable sound of coins clinking together. A quick glance showed an old buckskin pouch at the bottom of the container.

He stole a glance at the fisherman and saw that he was preoccupied with keeping the slippery fish from wriggling free. Brakken's hand closed over the pouch. He straightened up and tried to shove it in his pocket while extending the stringer with the other.

But the fisherman looked up and exclaimed, "Suh, what you all doin' with muh money?"

Brakken started to turn away without replying, but the other man dropped the pole and rushed forward.

"Gimme back muh money, suh!"

"Take your black hands off me," Brakken snarled, jabbing his fist into the other man's stomach.

The breath exploded from him and he bent double as Brakken hurried toward the mules. He was surprised to hear the other man puffing after him.

"Please, suh! I'se a po'h man! Don't you all . . ."

Brakken drew his revolver and slapped the barrel against the fisherman's right ear, cutting it open. He staggered back, tripped over an exposed cottonwood root, and splashed into the water.

Brakken started toward the mules when he heard a man's excited cry from downstream. "Did you see that? He just killed a man."

Whirling about, Brakken saw two white men standing on the bank. One pointed at him. Brakken aimed the revolver at them, and they dove face first onto the ground.

Brakken hesitated a second, debating the wisdom of pressing his attack on them. Concluding they might be armed, he chose to run toward the mules.

He quickly untied them, seized the pack mule's lead rope, and mounted the other animal. The two witnesses had crawled behind a cottonwood log, keeping their heads down but peering at him. There was no sign of weapons.

Somewhat relieved, Brakken swiveled from the higher vantage point of the saddle to look at the river. Rain had started to fall, making little pockmarks on the surface. The fisherman was nowhere in sight.

Cursing his luck, he dug his heels into the mule's flanks and fled the scene, fearful that he could be identified as a murderer. He comforted himself with the knowledge that when he got a shave, a haircut, and clean clothes, the two witnesses couldn't identify him.

"But these mules," he muttered, "they could be recognized."

He would have to get rid of them, and fast, Brakken decided. If he didn't, his long search could be wasted, and all because of a few lousy coins.

☙

The rain's intensity had increased Saturday night when Shiloh sat at the dinner table with Clay and Jared. Shiloh had invited them to wrap up loose ends about the Sacramento move because she did not want to discuss business on a Sunday.

After Shiloh said grace, Jared surprised Shiloh and Clay by saying, "I know you two are packed to move, but would it inconvenience you very much if I didn't open the office until about midweek?"

Shiloh and Clay exchanged glances before he said, "I thought you were going to be ready Monday morning?"

"I was, but I have a new client here who has a pressing need for me to take a trip to San Jose on his behalf."

"There's only one stage going that way," Clay said, "and it doesn't run on a regular basis. John Whistman's got a French carryall that takes nine hours, even though it's only about fifty miles. So you can't be sure of when he's going or when he's coming back."

Shiloh suppressed her sudden exasperation. Surely Jared knew that she and Clay couldn't afford to lose any business, no matter how little was currently being done out of the San Francisco office.

Jared didn't seem to notice. "Well I guess that's how I'll have to travel." He added, "Shiloh, I am most grateful for your hospitality, but I've taken a room at a hotel near the Plaza. I'll move out tomorrow."

Shiloh suppressed a sigh of relief. Although she thought of Jared as a gentleman, she had fretted about the impropriety of leaving Mara and him alone here. She had dreaded having to ask him to move. Quietly she said, "I'm glad we could be of service to you, Jared."

The discussion returned to the San Jose trip. Shiloh and Clay agreed they would stay in San Francisco until Jared returned.

After everyone had gone, Shiloh retired to her bedchamber with mixed feelings. She set the candle down on the nightstand by her New Testament. Then she frowned.

My red rock, she thought, shaking her head and staring at it. *Right where I left it.* Sighing, she decided, *I really must be getting absent-minded.*

∽ CHAPTER XV ∽

WHILE MARA KEPT her company, Shiloh dressed for church with ambiguous feelings. She desperately longed for the comfort that the hymns and solid preaching would bring her, but she had some trepidation about the wisdom of going out in the unrelenting rain, even though she knew Clay would have lowered the canvas sides on the carriage. She resolved to brave the rain.

In chatting amicably with Mara, she mentioned Locke's visit to the office. Shiloh remarked, "I wish they would quit bothering us. Why don't they buy out somebody else? What's so special about our struggling line?"

"Maybe they know something you don't."

Shiloh stopped brushing her hair to ask, "Such as?"

"I don't know."

"Well, it troubles me. So did Jared's announcement last night about having to go to San Jose for a client. Did he say anything to you about having a new client?"

"I didn't know he had any clients."

"He hasn't mentioned any to me either." Shiloh turned back to the mirror and resumed brushing her hair. "His going delays our trip to Sacramento. There's a lot to be done in setting up an office there, and if what I hear about the rains shutting everything down until spring is true, we need to make as much progress as possible before it's too wet to travel."

Mara asked, "What do you really know about Jared?"

"Well, he's planning to enter politics, and he seems to be a gentleman."

Mara made an explosive sound, causing Shiloh to turn as Mara buried her face in her hands.

"What's the matter?" Shiloh asked.

Mara looked up, her dark eyes laughing. "Nothing, except I think it's time you knew more about Jared."

There was something in Mara's tone that made Shiloh cross the room to stand before her. "Meaning what?"

"You know I have many friends who hear things, and as a rule they come and tell me. Well, they overheard two people who had been on Jared's ship. There were no women aboard."

"Jared explained that his wife had been the only one, and she died at sea."

"I mean, there was never a woman on board. Jared didn't have a wife."

"Are you telling me he lied?"

"I believe my friends heard the truth."

Shiloh frowned. "But why would he lie about that?"

"Why don't you ask him?"

Shiloh considered that before nodding. "I will, just as soon as he gets back from San Jose."

⚭

Brakken set his first priority as getting rid of the mules. His own identity could be completely changed by a haircut and shave. Once those changes were made, no one could point him out to authorities.

It was not as easy to find a buyer for the mules with the rain starting to fall hard and fast. He slogged from one livery stable to the next and to various lots where horses and mules were offered for sale or trade. Nobody wanted to buy two footsore, skinny, and mangy-looking mules.

Late in the day, Brakken's luck changed. He rode up to a roughly constructed frame building at the edge of town. Through the dirty window of the small structure, Brakken saw the horse trader sitting on an upturned wooden crate, his run-over boots extended toward the box stove.

As Brakken opened the door, the trader studied him with calculating gray eyes. "Stomp some of that mud off your feet before you come in," he ordered, spitting tobacco on the hot stove.

It sizzled as Brakken obeyed, then knocked the rain off his hat before coming inside and closing the door.

Before he could speak, the trader squinted through the window at the mules and asked, "How much you give me to take them two bony critters off your hands?"

Brakken bristled, not being in the mood for any levity, but he kept his composure and even forced a smile. "They're top-grade animals," he declared. "Carried me all the way from Missouri with nothing wrong except they're a bit wore down."

"Completely broke down, you mean." The trader spat toward the stove again. "There ain't enough left of them two poor old jackasses to make a meal for a lone buzzard."

Anger showed in Brakken's face. "I didn't come in here to hear your smart remarks," he snapped, reaching for the door handle.

"Easy now," the trader admonished, working the wad in his cheek. "You sit here by the fire while I take a look at what they got."

"I been wet before," Brakken grumbled. "I'll go with you."

After briefly inspecting the animals for sound teeth, hooves, and bodies, the trader pulled the rifle from the riding mule's scabbard and glanced at the capital letters: J & S Hawken—St. Louis.

Brakken said hastily, "The rifle's not for sale."

The trader didn't say anything but replaced the weapon and walked back inside, trailed by Brakken.

The trader took his former position with muddy boots extended toward the stove. "Look at it this way," he explained, "them mules brought you a couple thousand miles. They done their job while lots of mules died on the trail, along with the oxen and plenty of horses. So you got your money's worth out of them jackasses the day you rode into town."

"I don't need your sales talk," Brakken growled. "What's your offer?"

"Give you a day's wages for each; six dollars apiece, as they stand; equipment and all."

"Six dol . . . ? That's robbery!"

"I know from the looks of you that you ain't seen twelve dollars in a spell. Fact is, I doubt you got two coins to rub together. Now, if you want to run up and down the streets in this rain lookin' for a better deal, go right ahead."

Seething inwardly, but aware that he was in no position to bargain, Brakken slowly nodded. "I'll get my rifle and rope. You get the money."

"I said, 'as they stand.' Rifle's in the scabbard on that riding mule. It stays, along with the saddle."

Brakken's fury exploded. "That's no ordinary rifle! That's a genuine Hawken!"

"I know. It's one made by two brothers, Jacob and Samuel Hawken. But you got past the plains Injuns safe enough and probably brought down a buffalo or antelope with it, so it's done the job, same's the mules. Rifle goes with the mules."

Brakken swore mightily. "Why, you thievin' skunk! You can have the saddle, but the rifle and the rope go with me! I ought to kick you from here to breakfast just for being so ornery!"

The trader spat on the stove again. "You might find that takes more doin' than talkin'." Now, since you're standing there hollerin' instead of walkin' out, I 'spect we got us a deal. Ain't that so?"

For a long moment, Brakken sputtered, but in the end, he calmed down. Maybe he could sneak back tonight and reclaim his rifle. He didn't care about the saddle.

"All right, but I keep the rope; you get the rest."

Eyebrows lifted over gray eyes. "Must be a mighty important rope to keep it over your saddle and rifle."

"I got a mighty important reason to keep it. Now, you going to talk me to death or pay up?"

With the equivalent of two days' hard physical labor in his pocket and the coil of rope in his hand, Brakken started to leave. Then he turned and asked his routine question about his old friend, Clay Patton.

"Saw him last summer," the trader replied.

"You did?" Brakken blurted. It was the first bit of good news he had heard.

"Yep. He was drivin' express for some outfit in San Francisco. MacAdams and something . . . Laird! Yeah, that was it. MacAdams and Laird Express Company."

"Where is he now?" Brakken tried to keep the excitement out of his voice.

"Who knows? I heard the company sold out. But if you ask around in San Francisco, somebody might tell you how to find your friend."

"Thanks," Brakken readjusted his wet hat prior to going out into the rain.

"Had a mighty purty young gal with him when he come through here last summer," the trader added.

That information intrigued Brakken. "Wife, maybe?"

Shrugging, the trader replied, "Don't know."

"Good looker, you say?"

"Sure was. Sort of red hair, as I recall."

"Sure it wasn't blond?"

"I can't remember for sure, but it seems to me it was more reddish, but not real red. Sort of a mix between red and blond. Why? Wasn't your friend married when you last saw him?"

"Widower, but he could have remarried."

"Hope you find him."

"So do I." Brakken stepped into the rain. Normally, he would have cursed the horse trader and the rain, but suddenly that wasn't too important. After seven years and thousands of miles of searching, he felt encouraged.

Maybe my luck has finally changed, Brakken told himself. He slapped the coil of rope against his wet pant leg and hurried toward the barber shop.

While getting a shave and haircut, Brakken learned that the barber didn't know anything about Clay Patton, or MacAdams and Laird, but Jim Birch or his friend, Frank Stevens, might. The barber said that Birch was first to offer regular scheduled stage service out of Sacramento. Almost as well known were Bob Crandall and Warren Hall. They had begun their stage line after Birch. In July, Sam Brannan had rented part of his store to Birch for office space. He had begun his stage line by driving an old springless wagon to Coloma where Marshall had discovered gold.

In spite of the weather, Brakken approached Birch's office. A slender, brown-eyed man who couldn't have been more than twenty looked up from behind the counter as Brakken entered. The room smelled of leather from pieces of harness piled near the back door. Boxes and small metal chests stood stacked along the walls.

"Evening," the younger man said. "What can I do for you?"

Brakken repeated his glib lie. "I'm looking for Clay Patton. The barber told me you might be able to help me find him. Clay and I are old friends, and he said to look him up if I got to California."

"Clay used to drive for Aldar Laird's express company before he got killed. I understand Clay and Aldar's widow sold the express business and started a stage line called Laird and Patton."

Brakken was pleased to have a second confirmation about Clay being in the express business. But he hadn't heard about the widow. "Laird's widow? A woman in business?"

"So I heard."

"I never heard of such a thing."

"Me either, but California's got a lot of things that are different from back east."

Brakken nodded. "Where's their office?"

"In San Francisco."

"You sure?"

Birch ignored the challenge in the question to say mildly, "Well, I'm sure it's not in Sacramento." He stuck out his hand. "I'm Jim Birch."

"Ah . . . uh . . . Yancy Tate." Brakken shook hands, silently cursing his near slip. He had the information he needed, so he shifted topics. "Will this weather hurt your business much?"

"It'll force me to shut down operations until spring, along with the other Sacramento stage operators. Hard rain like this makes it impossible for a stage or anything else with wheels to move through the mud."

Brakken thanked him and went back out into the dreary rain. He believed Birch. Patton was in San Francisco, but there was no way he could get there by stage while the rain continued.

That night, Brakken robbed a drunk in an alley.

He used part of that money for a solid meal and a hotel

room. He had his original gold coin, fifty dollars from his robberies, plus the paltry sum he had received for the mules. He would need all that and more for transportation to San Francisco, but he was tempted to try his luck at some of Sacramento's countless gambling establishments.

Brakken could see that many of them were already filled with men. The mixture of spirits and games of chance were designed to quickly separate miners from what few flakes or nuggets they might have scratched out of the ground to the east. Brakken loved to play but not with his own money. So Brakken cursed the weather and stayed in his room, while his stomach reminded him that he had not had breakfast.

The next morning, Brakken determined to catch the next available boat going downriver to the bay. He would find out where the MacAdams and Laird Express offices had been; someone there might know where Clay was now. His woman companion might make it easier to find him. Brakken had heard that, while more women had arrived in San Francisco, they were certainly not common. A pretty young one would easily be remembered.

It was only when Brakken looked out his hotel window that he had second thoughts.

He cursed the rain that still fell from the dark and glowering sky. There had been no thunder or lightning, just the steady downpour. The deep powdery dust of past days had become a thick, sticky mud. He could see men slogging through it, periodically stopping to scrape or kick off the thick clumps that clung to their boots. Brown puddles had formed where wagon wheels and hooves had punched deeper holes or ruts into the street.

His stomach reminded him that he had not had breakfast. The rain's delay angered him because he could sense that he was closing in on Clay and wanted to complete his mission.

He wondered if a steamer was at the embarcadero, thinking he could get inside the salon out of the weather. He decided that a prudent master would not risk his craft when there was debris in the river big enough to do damage. He had been told that when the rain stopped, there would be fog. He could do nothing except wait, but he was hungry and couldn't stand waiting in his room.

On his way downstairs, dressed and hungry, something happened to make him abruptly change his plans.

He had paid no attention to a man with crutches sitting in the lobby, his right leg thrust stiffly away.

As Brakken passed, the man suddenly called, "Hey, Alvin Brakken!"

Forgetting that he was supposed to be Yancy Tate, Brakken automatically turned around. Arthur Duggan, still bearded, was struggling to get to his feet with the aid of crutches.

"Surprised to see me, huh, Alvin?" Duggan managed to balance himself on the crutches and turned to the desk clerk. "This man tried to kill me. Get the law for me, and hurry!"

Brakken turned up his coat collar, pulled his hat down tighter and ran out into the rain. He paused a moment, debating which way to go. Then he remembered that the rope was in his room. Making his decision, Brakken darted down the street and into an alley before Duggan could hobble outside.

Slipping and sliding, Brakken raced around to the back of the hotel and climbed the wooden stairs. He trailed mud to his room, but he didn't notice that until he exited it with his meager possessions, including the rope. Avoiding the main streets, he circled wide through the rain and emerged at the embarcadero.

Choosing an unmanned boat, Brakken slipped on board and found shelter in its small cabin. He relaxed, satisfied that there had been no pursuit. As soon as he found a vessel preparing to cast off for the bay, Brakken determined that he would be aboard.

The rain was still falling early Thursday evening when Victoria entered her hotel's elegant dining room. She was conscious of the stares of open admiration from the male diners who had proceeded her. She had deliberately cultivated the habit of arriving about seven o'clock, knowing that word would spread and more men would choose to dine at the same time and place each evening.

Although more and more women and some children were arriving in San Francisco all the time, a pretty young woman with no escort was still a rarity. Respect and decorum were strictly observed in the fine hotel, so no man had ever even spoken to her except Elijah, her solicitous waiter.

He greeted her with a flash of white teeth in an ebony face, and, anticipating the usual generous tip, showed her to her favorite table by the window. There she could both look out on San Francisco's evening traffic and use the glass reflection to discreetly study the diners behind her.

They admired her trim, well-groomed figure and the golden cascade of soft hair that fell to her shoulders. She was confident that Elijah had been questioned by every man present. They soon all knew what little she had told Elijah: Her husband had died on the overland trip. She had no children and was just trying to get her life back together here in San Francisco.

When she occasionally made eye contact, she favored the man with a brief friendly smile, but not enough to offer any encouragement. So she dined alone, night after night, taking her time and lingering over dessert but never touching wine or any form of spirits. This, she was sure, was duly noted and approved even by those watchers who would have offered her a drink if they were alone.

So she was startled that evening to look into the rain-splattered window glass and see the reflection of a well-dressed man enter the dining room and head straight for her table. Then she recognized Jared Huntley.

"Good evening, Victoria," he said, smiling pleasantly and

touching the back of the vacant chair across the table from her. "May I?"

He was a handsome-enough man, a lawyer, and he obviously had some money, but she wasn't pleased to have him boldly approach her in the dining room. It spoiled her plans.

"You should have sent a message to my room," she replied under her breath and glanced around to see what kind of stir Jared had created.

"This couldn't wait." Ignoring the fact that she had not invited him to sit down and wasn't eager to see him, he pulled out the chair and hitched it close to the table. "I have big news for you, my lovely lady."

Trapped, she decided to play along with him "Oh?"

He leaned closer and lowered his voice. "I would prefer to discuss some business with you in private. How about my coming to your room in about an hour?"

"I told you the last time I saw you not to come around again unless . . ."

"I had something to report on your property," he broke in, grinning. "I have some real news. I'll tell you in your room in an hour."

"Not so fast!" She had no intention of being tricked into an unwanted encounter. "I want to know more, right now."

They both fell silent as Elijah approached politely. "Will the gentleman be having supper?"

Jared cast a questioning glance at Victoria, who replied, "No, Elijah, he will not be staying long."

When the waiter had gone, Jared commented, "I don't think that was appropriate; I'm about to do you an immense favor."

"You want to do me a favor by selling my property? Any number of men in this town would do that."

"You can be very exasperating," he exclaimed, his voice low but intense. "I'm trying to help you . . ."

"Correction!" she hissed, her eyes sharp. "You're trying to help yourself."

Jared had not expected the resistance, so he had to hide his disappointment. "I'm trying to help us both."

"Are you?" Her words took on an amused tone. "Do you want to tell me who the buyer is?"

"I wish I could tell you, but that's confidential."

"Of course." She began to play with him, mocking him. "But I can guess the buyer's identity."

"Impossible, my dear. I just got back from a miserable trip to San Jose, enduring all this rain to confer with my client who lives there."

She looked him squarely in the eyes and declared flatly, "Nonsense! You didn't go to San Jose; you went to see the New Almaden Mine, and you are the buyer for my share of the property."

She enjoyed watching the conflicting expressions that flickered across his face and eyes before he regained his composure.

"What makes you say that?" he asked, avoiding any indication on his part that she was right.

"After you left the other day, I started putting two and two together. I decided to call on an assayer named Homer, who turned out to be a garrulous old man."

She smiled at the expression on Jared's face. "He liked talking to a pretty young lady, as he told me. Especially when I described a certain red rock that a friend had found on a recent trip.

"Then this nice old gentleman told me about a man who had recently brought him a specimen of red rock. That man's description matched you perfectly." Victoria added triumphantly, "Interesting coincidence, don't you think, Mr. Huntley?"

The frost in her use of his surname rattled him, but he was used to courtrooms and quick recoveries. "Indeed, it is a most curious one. But such things do happen."

"Stop it!" She leaned toward him, her voice low but hard.

"You stole Shiloh's rock and found out that it's cinnabar, the most common ore from which quicksilver or mercury comes. This is used to—what was the assayer's term?—oh, yes, amalgamate gold. When you combine mercury and gold or silver the mercury picks up the metal so it's easy to handle. Later, it's processed, separating the mercury and leaving the gold.

"Ever since the gold rush started, the demand for quicksilver has gone sky high, and it will remain that way as long as the gold lasts. Now, tell me, Mr. Huntley, how many flasks of mercury does the New Almaden produce per day? And how many flasks of about seventy-six pounds each do you estimate my share of the Mount Saint Helena quicksilver mine will produce?"

She leaned back, her eyes bright, and asked quietly, "Enough to make me rich?"

Jared considered her with lidded eyes before trying another approach. "The assayer said that he couldn't tell the value of the cinnabar from the piece I brought him. He would need more of them, but I don't want to risk going up north in this weather."

He paused, then added, "Anyway, you only own half of that property. I could probably buy Shiloh's share, then you and I . . ."

Victoria's tinkling laughter stopped him. "Do you know that she considers you a gentleman?"

"It isn't important what she thinks."

"You're wrong," she snapped. "Shiloh thinks that her late husband meant what he wrote about that property funding the stage line. She has no idea of what you and I now know, but I still don't think she'll sell."

Jared replied, "Now that you know, what're you going to do?"

"I haven't decided. I would like to finish my dinner in private." Satisfied with her handling of the discussion, she watched him walk out.

Jared was annoyed with Victoria, but he got some satisfaction from the curious glances of the men diners he passed. They obviously envied him because he was the only man who had ever dared to approach the pretty but aloof blond woman. Jared expected to see her again, and soon.

By the time Victoria had finished the meal, she knew that she had to know how valuable the Mount Saint Helena property was. Clay was the only one who could get that information. Victoria realized that meant she would have no choice but to tell Clay and Shiloh what Jared had learned. Of course, Shiloh then certainly would not sell her share.

However, Shiloh would be a much better partner than Jared. Besides, if the property turned out to be rich in cinnabar, Victoria could later figure out a way to get control of Shiloh's half.

Victoria rose from the table, wanting time to rethink everything more thoroughly before she acted.

๑๐ CHAPTER XVI ๑๐

IT WAS STILL raining the morning of November 13, election day, when Shiloh and Clay headed for the office in the buggy. He had dropped the canvas side curtains, but only a heavy old buffalo robe over their knees kept them partially dry as the weather blew into the vehicle's open front.

Women could not vote, but Shiloh had a keen interest in statehood because her late husband's dream of a transportation system depended on California's admission to the Union. She plied Clay with questions as the mare slogged along San Francisco's hilly and thoroughly soaked sandy streets.

Her queries also helped to keep her mind off another concern. She had not told Clay of Mara's report that Jared had lied about being a widower. Mara had said last night that she'd heard Jared was back in town. Shiloh chose not to say anything to Clay until she could question Jared in private.

If it turned out to be true, they certainly could not trust Jared with the stage line's San Francisco office. That would greatly affect their move to Sacramento. Shiloh hoped Mara's information was wrong.

Shiloh asked, "Isn't it unusual to hold an election for governor and congressmen when California isn't even a state?"

"Yes, but Missouri and Michigan organized their governments before they were admitted as states, and Congress didn't object. Besides that, most people expect Congress to eventually admit California to the Union, so people here are getting ready."

"Who's going to win? Whigs or Democrats?"

"Actually," Clay explained, "there are no political parties in California. The terms *Whig* and *Democrat* are sometimes used because they are the two major national parties. I read in the *Alta California* that most of the candidates are not even known to most voters.

"Many of them are new to California, just as most voters are. The *Alta* reported about a hundred thousand men are eligible voters, but only about a 10 percent turnout is expected. The rain's not helping that, either."

Shiloh asked, "Did you read where on January first of this year, California's population was estimated at twenty-six thousand?"

"I saw that. Quite a jump in less than a year."

"Are you going to vote?"

"I plan to. I've heard some of the candidates' speeches, and I've read about each man in the paper. The results won't be announced until December 10.

"That's the deadline for us to file for the mail contract."

Clay nodded but didn't say anything. Shiloh also lapsed into silence without learning which men Clay planned to support with his ballot.

At the office, Clay was soon pacing like a caged animal. Everything was packed for the move to Sacramento, and the rain had discouraged possible counter traffic, so there was really no work for Shiloh. She kept busy with needle and thread, sewing a blanket for the layette.

Clay complained, "I would rather drive a team through a blizzard than sit around like this."

"You don't have to stay here; there's certainly no business today."

He didn't seem to hear. He said, "We should think about getting that mail contract. There's a little less than a month before it will be awarded."

"We've done everything we can without the money," she reminded him. "We've drawn up plans for which towns we'll start to serve, how many stations will have to be built, how many wells need to be dug . . ."

"It still boils down to being able to show the government that we're financially able to carry through our plans."

"Maybe when Jared returns and we get to Sacramento, Sutter will loan us what we need."

"I don't know. I've read that he's having some very hard times himself with people trampling over all his land, killing his stock, and ruining his crops."

"I've heard he's very wealthy, and he's certainly very generous. He might be able to loan us enough to get started."

"Maybe, but it will be a few days after the rains stop before we can go upriver. It will be full of half-submerged logs and other hazards being carried downstream by the swift current."

"Then let's drive."

"It's not practical. A team and carriage can get around town, but the mud will be too deep on rural roads. They'll also be full of muddy holes where a horse or mule could break a leg. Even if we were in Sacramento, all we could do is get ready for spring because men won't travel in this kind of weather unless it's absolutely necessary. Then they'll probably go on horseback or walk. Besides, waiting for the river to be safe will give you a few days to help Jared get acquainted with our office here."

Shiloh nodded, but more in agreement that they not leave Jared permanently in charge until she verified Mara's story about his wife.

Shiloh and Clay lapsed into silence. He looked out the rain-streaked window at the dreary skies and the deepening quagmire in the streets while Shiloh continued sewing.

Being close to her in the tiny office made it difficult for Clay not to show his feelings for her. He had originally decided that it would not be proper to do so until at least a year had passed. But that was still so many months away. He forced himself to talk about other matters.

"Sometimes I wonder if maybe we should have taken Gladwin and Locke up on their offer."

"You don't mean that!" She put down her needle and thread and stood up to face him.

He walked over and stood before her, not touching, but close enough that he could catch her fragrance. "No, I don't really. It's just at least I know you would have a steady income for when the baby comes."

Softening, Shiloh nodded. "Thank you." She hesitated before adding, "I keep thinking about Aldar's note regarding the Mount Saint Helena property. But for the life of me, I can't figure out what he meant."

Clay didn't answer because he had already expressed the same frustration.

She turned abruptly, brushing against him. "Oh! I'm sorry!" she exclaimed, stepping back.

The momentary contact was almost more than Clay could bear. He had to delay answering until he felt he could speak without his voice betraying the deep emotion that had engulfed him.

"My fault," he finally said, his voice low.

Shiloh moved to the window, hiding the flush that had

spread over her cheeks. She had been surprised at the warm sensation she experienced in that momentary contact.

Clay had become such a vital part of her life and yet, in many ways Shiloh felt she didn't know him. He said so little about the things that really mattered to him.

Clay walked up and stood behind her. "You know I'm not good with words, but you must know by now how very important you are to me." He gently touched her hand and added, "You are in my prayers every day of my life."

His few words were reinforced by the warm glow where his hand still touched hers.

Shiloh turned and looked up at him. "I've never really told you how grateful I am for everything you've done for me since Aldar was killed."

"You don't have to say anything. There's nothing I wouldn't do for you."

"You've taken care of everything for me. I know what a good, kind person you are . . . and yet . . ." She searched for the words. "There's so much I don't know about you." She smiled. "You keep your opinions to yourself. You're polite and considerate with Mara, but you're a southerner and I'm not sure how you feel about slavery."

He grinned at her. "Not all southerners think like Locke, you know. I saw a lot of mistreatment of Negroes when I was growing up. I never approved of it. I still don't."

Shiloh sighed. "I'm glad we had a chance to talk about this."

Clay looked into her eyes. "That's not all you're concerned about, is it?"

Shiloh nodded. "You see right through me, don't you? You've been so good about taking me to church because you know it means a lot to me, but I've never heard you indicate if it's also important to you. My faith is what gave me the strength to get through the horrible time right after Aldar was murdered. And, of course, your friendship and Mara's."

Clay shrugged. "You know by now that personal things are not easy for me to talk about. I grew up in a Christian family as you did and made my commitment when I was about ten. I drifted away in my teens and really lost my faith after burying Elizabeth and Mark. For a long time I didn't believe in anything. I felt so alone and without direction. Then about two years later, I was alone in a strange town on a Sunday morning. It was snowing hard, and I walked into a church to get out of the cold. I guess I needed it that day. I heard some comforting words that finally reached me, and I recommitted my life."

"I'm so glad," Shiloh said softly.

Clay's big hand gently closed over both of hers and her memory leaped back to when she was determined to return east after Aldar's death. That day last June, when Clay reached up to lift her out of a wagon, his arms closed tightly about her. She had thought he was going to kiss her.

Instead, he had said in a hoarse whisper, "Aldar was my good friend, and it's too soon to say anything to you, but if you stay, I'll be here for you. When it's time, I'll tell you what's on my heart."

She had stayed, but there had been no more tender moments with Clay. She hadn't realized until now how much she needed to be held. But, it was still too soon for Aldar's memory lived in her with his child.

She gave his hand a quick squeeze. "I'm so glad you told me."

He nodded and slowly released her. "The rain doesn't seem to be letting up, so I'd better go vote. Then I'll bring us back some lunch. You want anything special?"

"No, whatever you choose will be fine."

After he left, she turned back to the window and watched him running along the plank sidewalk, head down against the rain, until he turned the corner. She stayed at the window, trying to understand her reaction to the events of moments ago.

Clay had only been gone a few minutes when Shiloh looked up as the door opened and Jared entered.

"It's incredible," he greeted her, removing his wet coat and hat and hanging them on pegs behind the door. "I heard it rained in California, but I didn't expect anything like this, especially on election day."

She asked pleasantly, "How was your trip to San Jose?"

"Wet and uncomfortable, especially in that miserable old French carryall. Imagine, only five miles an hour in good weather."

"Clay says a good stage, like a Concord, should do about fifteen miles an hour, but most average around ten." Shiloh walked back to her desk and motioned for Jared to join her.

He sat facing her. "It's good to see you again," he said. "How have you been?"

"Fine, except that this rain has ruined what business we might have done on a nice day. Clay and I weren't expecting you until tomorrow, so you needn't have come in today. Not one customer has been in, and everything is packed for the move as soon as the weather breaks and you can take over here."

"I'm glad you mentioned that, Shiloh. My client has run into some unexpected complications. I'm sorry, but I won't be able to help in the office for several days."

Shiloh was both relieved and concerned. "It's all right," she assured him. "Clay says this rain will make it impossible for us to go for a few days, anyway."

Jared said, "Actually, I had another purpose in coming." He looked around the office. The emptiness made a slight echo. His eyes came back to Shiloh, knowing that she had no idea about the quicksilver possibilities in the property she owned with Victoria. Jared explained, "I would like to offer my services in helping you sell your share of the Mount Saint Helena property."

"You know I don't want to sell."

"I'm sure that's what you mean from an emotional standpoint," he said, taking care to sound reasonable. "After all, this was your late husband's project, and you're reluctant to give up anything that was his."

He paused, but when she didn't respond, he continued, "However, there's a practical aspect to this property situation. To carry out Aldar's vision, the stage line needs a monetary infusion. Selling your share of the property would give you at least enough to complete your application for the government mail contract. Then you can proceed in developing the business, as your late husband would have wanted."

Shiloh wondered if this was an answer to her many prayers. Yet the information Mara had brought about Jared made her cautious.

"That's possible," she replied. "However, we don't know the property's value. Aldar knew something that made him confident it would help to develop the stage line. I'm reluctant to sell until I find out what he knew."

"I understand. Perhaps I can be of some assistance to you. I can have a qualified person appraise . . ."

"No stranger can look at that property and see the real value because I certainly can't," she broke in, "and I know in my heart that Aldar bought that land to do exactly what his note said. The fact that he didn't have enough money made him take in Henry Barclay as a partner. Until I know more than I do now, I have to thank you for your offer, but the land isn't for sale."

Jared thoughtfully studied her before saying, "You've got less than a month before you have to submit your plan to the government. Without some documentation showing that the line is financially solvent, your chances of getting that mail contract are very poor."

"That property won't bring enough to impress the government. We need another investor."

"I have some resources, but unfortunately, not enough to

meet your needs. Perhaps we could work out something where I represented you to prospective investors?"

Still cautious, Shiloh shook her head. "Thanks, but Clay and I have plans along that line."

Jared sighed in disappointment. "Very well, but please don't lose out on at least applying for the mail contract."

Shiloh replied, "Even if I were willing to sell, it might take months to find a buyer. That's also complicated by Victoria owning the other half."

Jared arose and walked to the window before responding. Then he said over his shoulder, "You have been very kind to me, Shiloh. As I said, I have some funds available. If it would help you, I would be willing to buy your interest as soon as we can arrive at some value that is fair to both of us."

Shiloh didn't want to discuss the situation anymore, so she tried to think of a delicate way to bring up the subject of Jared's wife. She decided to pose a direct question. "How long were you married?"

She saw just a flicker of concern in his eyes, but he parried the question with his own.

"Why do you ask?"

Shiloh felt slightly embarrassed in bringing up a subject based on secondhand information, but she had to know. She tried to phrase her words so it didn't sound as if she was accusing him of lying. "I heard there were no women on board your ship."

He hesitated only momentarily before asking, "Did you personally talk to someone who had been aboard with me?"

There was a slight hint of steel in the question, and Shiloh was unprepared. "Well, no, not . . ."

"Then whose word would you rather take?" he broke in with a smile. "Some secondhand gossip, or mine?"

Trapped, Shiloh stammered. "Well, naturally, yours, of course."

"Thank you." His tone softened. "Now, please think over

what I said about the property. Let me know if you change your mind."

After his footsteps faded down the stairs, Shiloh sat frowning at the desk. Had he lied to her? Or had Mara's informants made a mistake? Should she accept his offer? She closed her eyes, seeking answers.

∽

The week passed while people speculated on who would be announced on December 10 as winner in California's first election. Peter Burnett, lately of Oregon, was considered the most likely candidate to become governor.

Voters had cast ballots for two new congressmen, but the full assembly would elect two senators on December 20.

John Fremont and William Gwin were considered most likely to be chosen senators by the forty-six delegates. Shiloh and Clay had met Gwin last spring, along with Fremont's wife, Jessie.

On the ride home that evening, Shiloh commented, "We still have two serious problems. The money, of course, and an impressive enough plan to convince the government to award us a mail contract."

"We've worked out a pretty good plan," Clay protested.

"Yes, but how does it compare to what some of the other stage line owners are going to submit? Jim Birch and Bob Crandall, for example. I wonder if our plans are going to be as impressive. Anyway, that won't matter unless we get the financial backing we need."

"I'm still hopeful that some of the men I've talked to will come through on that."

Shiloh added wistfully, "If we had that, and we knew what Aldar's plans were, we should have a very good chance of getting the mail contract."

"Are you sure you've looked everywhere? I know Aldar wasn't much for writing things down, but maybe . . ."

She interrupted. "I've looked everywhere I can think of. If there is such a plan, I can't find it."

"Maybe I'd better take some time Monday and help you. We can go through everything, even the stuff that's packed for shipment to Sacramento."

Shiloh didn't reply, but she was afraid it would be a waste of time.

∞

After talking with the mule trader and Jim Birch, Brakken's fortunes seemed to have changed. Satisfied that Clay was in San Francisco, Brakken caught the first available craft downriver, a cattle boat.

It had been one of the few vessels moving down the Sacramento. Most masters had not wanted to risk damage from submerged logs or other debris that might cost more to repair than the possible profit to be made from the sale of slaughter animals.

The stench of wet hides and excrement had been bad, but not as bad as Brakken's fear of facing a possible murder charge in Sacramento or dealing with the threat from the army deserter, Arthur Duggan.

At last the cattle boat reached San Francisco, and Brakken wandered across Kearney Street and along Washington Street of Portsmouth Square. It was barren of grass, trees, and shrubs. It held a flagpole, a speaker's platform, and a cow penned in the rain, but nothing else outside. Everyone had taken refuge from the rain inside the area's principal gambling houses and hotels.

He was again soaked to the skin and cold from the November air, but he couldn't afford San Francisco's high hotel prices. The money he had stolen in Sacramento and the price the mules had brought weren't enough for both a meal and bed. He briefly considered parting with the last gold coin he had carried these past months, then rejected the idea.

No, he told himself, *that's seed money from her. There will be plenty more when I find . . .* He broke off his thought and stared through a hotel window. He avoided the temptation to press his forehead to the glass and cup the side of his eyes to cut out all outside lights.

Instead, he simply stared at the sight of a shapely young blond sitting in the hotel dining room. "That's her!" he cried aloud.

Victoria could not see the man outside the window in the rain. She dabbed delicately at her mouth with her napkin and started to stand. Instantly, Elijah was there to pull her chair back. She smiled at him and left the table, unaware of the man watching her from outside.

⊙⊃ CHAPTER XVII ⊂⊙

VICTORIA HAD only been back in her hotel room a few minutes when there was a knock at the door. She opened it a crack and peeked out to see a rain-drenched man standing there. He held a coil of rope in his right hand and grinned at her while water puddled off his oilskin coat and slouch hat.

"Yes?" she said, imagining he was some drunk who had the wrong room.

"Don't you recognize me, Victoria?"

She stared, unable to recall the face, but the raspy voice stirred an old memory. Alvin Brakken was the one person in the world she had never expected to see again.

His appearance terrified her, and the sight of the rope he held added to her fear. "I don't know you, sir," she said coolly, and tried to close the door.

"None of that!" Brakken growled, putting his foot in the door and shoving it open with his shoulder. The grin slid from his face as he roughly pushed her aside and quickly closed the door behind him.

She kept her voice steady to threaten, "I'll scream if you don't leave right now!"

"Sure you will," he said easily, glancing around. "You got good taste, Victoria. Of course," he added, his eyes swinging back to her, "you've got the money to have things like this, and without old Henry to stop you."

"Get out!" She pointed with a long, slender finger. "I'll have you thrown in jail."

"Will you now?" he asked mockingly, tossing the coil of wet rope onto a chair. He reached under his drenched coat and pulled out the gold coin. He showed it to her in the palm of his hand. "Remember this?"

"It's a twenty-dollar gold piece."

"Not just any old twenty-dollar gold piece," he reminded her, holding it up so the candlelight reflected from it. "This is the last of those you gave me for arranging that little 'accident' for your husband back in Missouri."

She didn't reply, but stood still, desperately trying to think what to do.

"This one got lonely." He flipped it into the air and deftly caught it. "Remember you were supposed to give me a whole lot more of these last spring when I completed the job, plus you were going to meet me privately for a little fun. But you slipped away without paying." His tone turned ugly as he added, "That wasn't nice."

He hastily replaced the coin in his pocket, removed his hat and coat and threw them on the chair beside the rope before gripping her firmly by both shoulders. "I came to collect on both accounts, plus some extra for making me wait." He bent to kiss her, but she jerked her head aside.

"You are despicable!" She almost spat the words, her eyes suddenly glittering with hatred. "You are the most loathsome man . . ."

"I like a little fire in a woman," he interrupted with a half-smile on his lips. "But before you go calling me names, you'd better think what people around here will call you if they find out what you're really like under all those fancy clothes."

He let his gaze wander insolently over her slender form. "I been wondering that myself ever since I showed up for our little private meeting last spring that you never attended. Did you think I was a fool who would never find you?"

Logic replaced Victoria's initial alarm. She forced a smile and shook her head so that her mass of soft golden tresses tumbled teasingly about her face.

She said, "You can't threaten me and expect to get anywhere. So behave yourself and treat me right."

He considered that before nodding and releasing her. "You're right. You're so pretty it had me sidetracked, but I've got business to attend to, and I'll need money."

"I don't have very much with me," she explained, rubbing her shoulders where he had held her. "But I've got enough for you to get a room and a meal."

"I could stay here and save the price of a room."

She ignored his suggestion and reached for her purse on the marble-topped stand. Removing two coins, she said, "Here's a five- and a ten-dollar gold piece. That's all I've got."

"A half-eagle and an eagle isn't enough. I want double eagles, like the ones you gave me in Missouri."

"I'll need a couple of days to get some."

He shook his head. "You got until tomorrow."

She sighed. "All right. But don't come here. I'll meet you by the flagpole on the plaza about sunset."

He regarded her though half-closed eyelids. "You better show up this time."

"I'll be there." She watched him put on his hat and coat, then pick up the coil of rope. She tried to keep the fear from sounding in her voice as she asked, "What are you going to do with that?"

"Hang a man," he announced cheerfully and walked out the door.

∞

Shiloh waved good night to Clay and opened her front door. The questions raised by Jared's visit to the office still plagued her. Had he lied about being a widower, or had Mara's informants made a mistake?

Mara straightened from where she had been poking at the crumbling logs in the fireplace. "You look awful," she commented, anxiously coming over to inspect Shiloh's face. "Bad day?"

"Bad enough." Shiloh removed her coat. "Is Jared around?"

"No. He moved out this afternoon in the rain. Said he had taken quarters downtown. Why?"

"He came by the office today while Clay was out. Jared said he had a buyer for my half of the Sonoma property. When I said I didn't want to sell, he offered to buy it himself."

"I'm not surprised," Mara said quietly.

"Of course I wouldn't sell. I told him that I had heard some of his shipmates claim that he didn't have a wife on board the ship that sank. He denied it."

"What else would you expect?"

Shiloh ignored that question to continue. "Then he asked whether I was going to believe him or gossip."

"You can believe what my friends told me because I had Samuel recheck. Jared lied to us about a wife."

Shiloh wearily dropped her coat across the back of a chair. "That means we can't trust him to manage the office here while Clay and I open one in Sacramento."

"You can't trust him for another reason."

Shiloh shot a puzzled look at Mara before easing into a chair, trying to relieve the discomfort of the weight of her child. "I'm almost afraid to ask what you mean."

Mara moved behind Shiloh and gently began massaging her

shoulders. "One of my friends is a waiter at the Stuart House, where he overheard part of a conversation between Jared and Victoria. They both know why the Sonoma property is potentially valuable."

Shiloh shoved herself to her feet. "How could they know that?"

"Because of that red rock you brought back from your trip up north. Apparently Jared 'borrowed' it a few days ago."

"He was in my room?"

"Twice, it seems, because he later returned it."

Shiloh remembered that she had blamed herself for being absent-minded and misplacing the rock. Later, she had found it where she had originally left it. "What did he do with it?"

"Had it assayed. I guess he had a hunch. Anyway, it turned out to be cinnabar."

Frowning, Shiloh admitted, "I don't know the word."

"It's the ore from which quicksilver or mercury comes. It's used to recover gold and silver, and right now, quicksilver is more rare than gold. I don't know if the assayer could give a value from that one rock, but at least the potential is there. You own half of a quicksilver mine!"

"Are you sure?"

"Positive. Now you know why your husband thought that property would bring in enough to develop the stage line. You could be rich, Shiloh!"

⌒

Brakken hadn't felt so good in months as he walked out into the rainy night with the two gold coins Victoria had given him. They would barely meet his needs for the evening, but the prospect of endless others cheered him greatly.

He found a small hotel where his meager funds forced him to share a room with four other men. All strangers, they slept on tiered bunk beds in very tight quarters. Brakken didn't care. He turned his face to the wall, and ignored the snores around him in the darkness.

How much gold does Victoria have, and how can I get it all?
Brakken felt sure it was enough for all his needs while he looked for Clay Patton. He also expected more from her than money. She was as pretty a woman as he had ever seen, so it was only right that she pay extra for having made him look like a fool back at the Missouri River.

Brakken knew that Victoria was smart. She would try to find a way to keep from paying him. But she wouldn't dare try to get him arrested for murdering her husband because he would implicate her. He certainly couldn't trust Victoria, so he had to be alert.

In the meantime, he would continue his search for Clay Patton. After he was found and hanged, Brakken would have more time to appreciate Victoria and her money.

෨

The sun tried to break through the remaining rain clouds the next day when Clay picked Shiloh up for the short drive to the office. As the mare plodded through the mud, Shiloh quickly told Clay about Jared and Victoria's quicksilver discovery and about Mara's discovery that Jared had lied about having a wife.

Clay listened without interruption until she had finished telling him everything, including her confrontation with Jared in the office.

She concluded, "We certainly can't trust him to run the office. So who will take care of things here if we move to Sacramento? And what about Victoria? It seems we can't trust her, either, because she knows about the cinnabar but hasn't told me, even though I own half of that property."

"I'll talk to Jared because he's betrayed our trust, especially yours, while staying in your home," Clay said thoughtfully. "I'm not sure about Victoria. She may not have had time to tell us about the quicksilver mine yet. Let's wait a bit to see if she tells you."

"You may be right. She originally wanted to sell her half.

LEE RODDY

But now that she knows about the quicksilver, she may not want to sell."

"In that case, and since she's obviously well off, she may be willing to finance the development of the mine. You can repay her out of profits on your share."

"Will that leave enough for the stage business?"

"It depends on the value of the cinnabar. The assayer may need more samples to know its value. But since quicksilver is rarer than gold around here these days, I expect there will be enough to develop the stage line."

"Mara says that must be what Aldar meant, and I agree. So let's talk to Victoria as soon as possible."

"I'll leave a message at her hotel, but I want to talk to Jared face to face about why he lied about being married, and why he sneaked into your room and took your red rock."

Victoria was reluctant to eat breakfast in the hotel dining room for fear Brakken would return and destroy the moral image she had so carefully cultivated. She put on a hat and turned her collar up to hide her face, then slipped out a side door and walked down the street, alert to all the men she met or passed.

Victoria realized that Brakken was going to be a continuing problem. Any man angry enough to travel two thousand miles to seek vengeance was dangerous. She knew that the money she had given him last night, and what she would give him tonight, would only be the beginning.

He would want more and more, along with her personal favors. She was revolted at the thought of this rough-looking man touching her. Most of all, his presence was a constant threat of exposure about her miserly husband's death.

Victoria had suffered a bitter and lonely childhood with a drunken widower father. She had run away at age fifteen and had survived in the only way possible: by entertaining men

186

who relished her fresh, youthful beauty. Abandoned in Missouri by one of her temporary admirers, she had hidden her past after meeting Henry Barclay. She had easily manipulated him into marrying her.

He had provided her with a lovely home and beautiful furnishings with slaves to attend to her needs, so she had not missed Henry while he was away in California. She hadn't been lonely, for she had many fun-loving friends, most of whom were men her own age. They had scorned Henry because he was more than twice as old as she, and they were eager to offer her what they were sure Henry was unable to adequately provide.

That had changed drastically when Henry returned from California. He spoke enthusiastically of what she considered a wild scheme to sell out his substantial Missouri holdings to build a farming empire in California. There, he claimed, unlimited land was available for the taking. What he had now would be nothing compared to what California offered. He had mentioned some land he had bought with another man but refused to disclose his plans to Victoria.

She had tried everything from anger to seduction to get Henry to change his mind. He remained adamant. She had been forced to get rid of all her beautiful, beloved possessions except what would fit in the small, canvas-topped wagons pulled by yokes of oxen.

The drastic solution she settled upon depended upon finding a suitable partner to carry out her idea. When Henry interviewed drovers to handle the teams, Victoria noticed one whose eyes hungrily followed her as she helped load the wagons. She smiled at him and learned that his name was Alvin Brakken. Victoria had no trouble getting him to follow her to a quiet corner where she confirmed her suspicion that he would do anything for money. She also let him believe that there was a possibility that she would also be grateful beyond money if he helped achieve her husband's death.

She had given Brakken a token payment in gold and told

him about her plan that could lead to a fatal accident for Henry. Like some other immigrants, he kept his heavy percussion rifle loaded with powder and ball but capped for safety. He could quickly reach across the tailboard, grasp the barrel, and pull the weapon toward him. He had ignored stories in the papers about accidents to other immigrants when a loaded rifle was left uncapped. The hammer caught on something, cocking the weapon. It discharged when jarred. Brakken could cause such an accident by quietly uncapping and cocking Henry's rifle while Victoria distracted her husband and the other drover.

The plan had worked. At sunset, when Henry tried to remove his rifle, the half ounce lead ball struck him in the chest. He was dead before those who heard the report could reach him.

After Henry was buried, Victoria announced to friends that there was nothing to hold her in Missouri. Since everything she inherited was in the wagons or in a piece of California land, she would go to San Francisco. She had slipped away with the wagon train before Brakken received his final payment.

Now he was back, blackmailing her with threats of exposure. She doubted he would really say anything because of his greed, but his very presence was a danger to her plans. After he had gone, Victoria had concluded there was only one way to stop him. Now she just had to finesse the details.

Jared wasn't strong enough to help her. Clay was the most logical choice, but he could not be manipulated or bribed. *Maybe,* Victoria thought, *I can find someone else, but it's got to be someone who can't turn into another blackmailer.*

She had to work it out so that she would remain above suspicion, and she could continue developing the lifestyle she had planned in San Francisco. For now, she would have to wait.

Nodding in satisfaction, Victoria told herself that in the meantime, she'd better not arouse Shiloh or Clay's suspicions in any way. *After I pay Brakken this afternoon,* she mused, *I'd better tell Clay and Shiloh what Jared found out about the quicksilver.*

The sun was setting over the Pacific Ocean, casting shadows from San Francisco's hills when Clay returned to the office to pick Shiloh up.

"I confronted Jared about pretending to be a widower," Clay explained. "He denied it with a straight face. I realized that I didn't dare ask him about slipping into your room to take your rock to be assayed because I didn't want him to know that we had found out about the cinnabar. So I just told him that we were making other arrangements for the office and wouldn't need him to run it when we moved to Sacramento."

"How did he take it?"

"He just shrugged, but I could tell he was angry." Pausing, Clay added, "I left a message at Victoria's hotel. I asked her to meet us here at nine o'clock tomorrow, but didn't tell her why."

"That's good," she replied as Clay seated himself beside her and picked up the reins. She thought of asking how they could determine the value of the cinnabar, but Clay seemed so happy that she decided not to bring up the assay value just now.

Clay took a deep breath and observed, "It turned out to be a beautiful day after all the rain. The air's so clean and fresh, and there's not a cloud in the sky. Makes a man glad to be alive."

She smiled at him. "I'm glad you're feeling so happy."

"Aren't you? I mean, finally knowing the answer to Aldar's plans for the Mount Saint Helena property. That opens up the stage line possibilities, so things are looking up."

"I know, but I still have an uneasy feeling." Part of that uneasiness, she knew, was in never having found any trace of written plans Aldar might have for the stage line. The plans she and Clay had worked out would probably qualify them for the mail contract, especially if the cinnabar proved to be as valuable as was hoped. But still, Shiloh felt troubled.

She remembered how she and Mara used to hug each other

when they were growing up and either was troubled. But the very nicest times had been when Aldar held her. Once, when she was concerned about something, she had told him, "Being held is the nicest feeling in the world." She hadn't been held in a long, long time.

Clay seemed to sense her need. He looked down thoughtfully and spoke very tenderly. "You know that I'm not good with words, but I've been thinking about what I want to say. I hope you'll listen with your heart because what I want to say comes from mine."

Anticipating his meaning, she hastily tried to think how to stop him, but the words wouldn't come.

He continued, "I should be patient and wait awhile longer before saying anything to you, but these are not normal times. You must know that I love you, and I think you care for me too."

"It's too soon to talk of . . ."

"No, it's not," he interrupted firmly but gently.

"When I lost Elizabeth, I thought I'd never again care for another woman. Then, after all these years, you came along. I love you and want you to marry . . ."

"I'm going to have Aldar's child," she broke in quickly. "This is not the time to talk about us."

"This is exactly the time. You need someone to take care of you and the baby, to love you both."

She shook her head vigorously. "Right now I've got my whole heart set on trying to make Aldar's dream come true and to get my life back together."

"Let me help you put it together again, Shiloh." He took a long, shuddering breath. "I'm not trying to rush you, but we've already seen that too many things can happen that snatch away chances for happiness in life. I love you and want you to marry me. I'll always love and care for you, and I'll do the same for the baby, just as I would have for my own son."

Shiloh gently laid her hand on Clay's. "I know, and I do

care for you, very much. But please understand. It hasn't been a year since I lost Aldar. I just feel it's too soon."

Slowly, Clay nodded. "I accept that, but I wanted you to know where I stand. I'll wait. When you're ready, I'll be here. You'll never be alone again."

∽ CHAPTER XVIII ∽

WHEN SHILOH got home, Mara looked up from hemming a long white dress for the baby. "Something happen?" she asked.

"Why do you ask?"

"I can see it in your face. So what is it?"

Shiloh eased into the straight-backed chair in front of the couch where Mara sat, "Clay wants to marry me."

"That's no surprise. When are you going to do it?"

Shiloh hesitated, her excitement being replaced by doubts and fear. "I . . . don't know. I . . . didn't accept."

Mara shook her head in disapproval. "Why not? He's a good man, and they're rare."

"I know, but . . ."

"No 'buts' about it," Mara interrupted bluntly. She stuck the needle into a corner of the dress and reached across to take Shiloh's hands. "Maybe Clay accepted the excuses you handed him, whatever they were, but I won't. Grab a chance at happiness while you can."

Taking a deep breath, Shiloh said, "It isn't just that I'm not ready or this isn't the time. It's a lot of things that are hard to explain."

"Such as?"

"Well, my first concern is naturally for the baby. His father's dead, but at least I can tell the baby what his father was like."

She withdrew her hands from Mara's and continued. "I know it seems strange, but I envy him that because he'll have a mother, and I can tell him about his father. I have no idea who my father or mother were. That really concerns me, especially now, when Aldar's son will soon be born because they would be grandparents. Little Aldar shouldn't miss out on them."

"You can't help not knowing who your parents were, or why they didn't keep you, any more than I can help that my slave mother was raped by a young white man. I'm here because of that, yet I don't dwell on it because there's nothing I can do about it."

"I admire your strength, Mara, but I'm not you, and I have to do what seems right for me and my child."

She paused, thinking before continuing. "It's hard to explain, but I feel very strange because I never knew my birth parents, and I've never met Aldar's parents. I wrote them after we were married, and again after Aldar was killed, but they never answered. I'll try again after the baby comes, but my child may never know his paternal grandparents either. I can't tell you how all that distresses me."

Mara shrugged. "I never knew my grandparents because they were slaves. My maternal grandparents were sold like cattle to one master when my mother was a little girl, and I was sold like a puppy dog to another plantation owner when I was little. But that's past, Shiloh; my past. Forget your past too. Take the happiness that Clay offers. Do it while you can."

Shiloh stood up and walked around to the back of her chair. "I'm afraid and mixed up." She turned to look down at Mara. "There's something else." Hesitating, Shiloh added, "I've always told you everything, but something happened recently that I've kept to myself."

Mara said nothing while Shiloh paced for a few moments then stopped and gripped the back of a chair.

"Remember I told you about the man who was so startled when he saw me with Victoria at Sonoma?"

"You're wondering if he might know your mother."

Shiloh was startled. "How do you know that?"

"Since you've been back, I've seen you looking at those locks of hair in your New Testament almost every night, so it was easy to figure out."

"Do you think it's possible? I mean, all my life, I've wondered about my birth parents. I reminded that man of someone so much that he dropped the eggs he was carrying. I want desperately to believe he might have some information about my mother."

"It's possible, but don't get your hopes up."

Shiloh sighed heavily. "Anyway, I'd like to talk to him again."

"You're in no condition to go back to Sonoma, especially with the weather getting bad."

Shiloh took a quick, agitated turn around the room. "I may be foolish, but I've got to know!"

"Suppose he tells you something about this woman that shows she couldn't possibly be your mother?"

"Then I'm no worse off than before, am I?"

"You might be. You've had enough disappointments and problems this year. So you'd better be practical and marry Clay while you can." Mara stiffened, listening. "I just heard someone on the porch. Maybe Clay?"

Shiloh shook her head and stepped to the door as a knock sounded. She opened it to see Victoria standing there. Beyond her, a horse and carriage were faintly visible in the faint light that spilled from the open door.

"Sorry to bother you," Victoria said. "When I returned to my hotel a while ago, I found a note from Clay. I had wanted to talk to both of you anyway, and tomorrow seemed too long to wait."

Her lie was so smooth that there was no indication of the alarm she had felt upon reading Clay's message. She had guessed that somehow he knew about Jared's discovery of quicksilver near Mount Saint Helena and suspected Victoria was involved. She had taken a carriage to visit Shiloh, expecting she would be easier to handle without Clay.

Victoria asked innocently, "Is Clay here?"

"No, but I know about the note. Please come in. Let me take your coat."

"I'll only be a minute." Victoria stepped inside, adding, "I asked my hackney driver to wait for me. I wish Clay were here because I have some news that you both should hear."

"Sit down," Shiloh urged, wondering if she had been wrong about Victoria, and Clay had been right. "What news?" Shiloh asked.

Mara had started to leave the room but glanced back as Victoria's purse banged heavily against the back of a chair. Mara continued toward the bedrooms as Victoria seated herself on the sofa.

Straightening her long skirt, she said, "This is the first chance I've had to tell you. Jared Huntley somehow got hold of that red rock you brought back from Sonoma and had it assayed. It's loaded with cinnabar."

Shiloh suppressed a small sigh of relief. She was grateful that Clay had been right. Apparently Victoria had not yet had an opportunity to tell about her meeting with Jared where she learned about the cinnabar.

Shiloh quickly decided that she would give her guest as much latitude as possible to say what was on her mind.

Shiloh sat down facing Victoria and repeated, "Cinnabar?"

"It's the ore from which quicksilver or mercury is mined." Victoria paused, thoughtfully studying Shiloh. "I'm sure you know it's used to recover gold."

"I've heard something about it," Shiloh admitted.

Victoria leaned forward confidentially, "It looks as though the property we own together might have enough cinnabar to become a quicksilver-producing mine."

"Goodness." Shiloh tried to sound surprised. "That may be

what Aldar meant about the property paying for the stage line."

"That seems possible."

Thinking quickly, Shiloh asked, "What should we do about it? I mean, we're equal owners."

"I've had an offer to sell my share."

"To Jared," Shiloh guessed, "because he's the one who had the rock assayed. Are you going to sell?"

"I don't know."

"When we met, you offered to sell your half to me."

Victoria asked, "Are you saying you want to buy me out?"

"I'm not in a financial condition to do that."

"And now that you know there's quicksilver on that property, it wouldn't be wise for you to sell. Right?"

"I can't," Shiloh admitted.

"Then neither will I." Victoria replied, rising. "At least, not until we know its full value."

Shiloh was tempted to suggest they discuss that with Clay in the morning, but before she could speak, Victoria continued.

"Assuming the property has a high value, there's something else you should know. I am in a position to help finance its development—getting the legal work done, equipment and men lined up so that operations can begin as soon as weather . . ."

Shiloh interrupted, "Wait a minute. As equal owners, I have an obligation in that, but I'm not in a position to do so now."

"You won't have to put up anything now. Think of it as an investment on my part that you can repay out of future earnings from your share."

"I . . . I don't know. Anything that comes to me would go right into developing the stage line."

"There would be no hurry to repay me."

Shiloh hesitated. "I want to talk with Clay before I make any decision."

"Of course." Victoria reached for the door handle. "Clay's

note asked me to come tomorrow morning at nine. Why don't we discuss this then?"

"Fine. That will give me time to think about everything before then."

Victoria drew her coat about her shoulders and opened the door. "It's too bad that I couldn't tell Clay tonight, instead of having to wait for tomorrow."

"Yes, I suppose, but he lives at Cow Hollow on the north shore near our stables."

"Oh, yes. I've driven through that area and remember seeing the company sign. I could drive by there and leave a message for him."

Shiloh said, "That would be too much trouble."

"Not at all," Victoria declared. "It's the least I can do for my partner in a quicksilver mine."

After she was gone, Shiloh felt uneasy, wondering if she had played into Victoria's hands.

Mara reentered the room. "She's a clever one. I'm sure she just wanted to protect herself in case you or Clay found out on your own about the quicksilver. You didn't give her any indication that you already know."

"I wanted to hear what she would say if she thought she was bringing news that I didn't know about."

"She's also carrying a weapon."

"What?" Shiloh asked in surprise.

"Didn't you hear her purse hit the back of that chair?" When Shiloh shook her head, Mara explained, "It's small, like a derringer, but it'll kill the same as a heavy revolver."

Shiloh tried to shake off her concerns. "There's been a lot of crime lately. She probably feels safer with a weapon because she has no man to protect her."

"Maybe," Mara replied, as she picked up her needlework.

⌒

Brakken was impatient for his upcoming meeting with

Victoria, the money she would give him, and the possibility of getting together with her later in her hotel room. In the meantime, he planned to locate the offices of Laird and Patton Stage Lines.

Brakken enjoyed imagining the look on Clay's face when they met after all these years. It would be a complete surprise, unless somehow Duggan found Clay first and warned him.

Brakken scowled, still trying to remember why Duggan knew him, but he hadn't been able to place him. Then it came to Brakken. *He was Mrs. Anson's kid by her first marriage. He was just about fifteen, so no wonder I didn't recognize him with that beard. After seven years, I guess he's old enough to grow whiskers.*

Brakken wished now that he had carried out his threat to kill Duggan for robbing him of his mules.

Well, it was too late for that. Brakken wondered if Duggan was still in Sacramento, or had he reached San Francisco? If Duggan was here, Brakken warned himself, there was always a remote chance Duggan would run into Clay and warn him. But there was nothing he could do about that, Brakken decided, except to find Clay as quickly as possible. Knowing that he had a pretty women partner would make it fun.

Brakken started asking passersby where he could find the offices of Laird and Patton Stage Lines. The first two men didn't know, but the third did. Following directions, Brakken headed across town.

∽

A light fog lingered on the hills when Clay picked Shiloh up the next morning. As the carriage started moving, Shiloh asked, "Did Victoria find you last night?"

"Yes, while I was having dinner in the restaurant. She told me about your conversation. I followed your example, and didn't let on that I already knew about the cinnabar."

Shiloh asked, "What do you think we should do?"

"First, we need to know for sure how much mercury we can expect from the ore. So I'll go up and bring back enough samples for a proper assay."

"Of course!" Shiloh silently berated herself for not thinking of that practical aspect during her restless night. She also realized that the trip offered an opportunity to learn more about the man who had been so unsettled when he saw her. "I'll go with you."

Clay chuckled and smiled down at her. "You can't go, and neither can Victoria."

Shiloh didn't like being told she couldn't go, but she focused on his last word. "She wants to go too?"

"As a partner, she told me, she has a right to go."

"I'm also a partner!"

"Yes, but she's not going to soon have a child."

Shiloh forced herself to say nothing while she sought the right words.

Clay saved her the trouble. "I told Victoria that I'm going alone because of the uncertain weather and because I can travel a whole lot faster by myself."

More relieved than she cared to admit, Shiloh slowly agreed, "That makes sense." She leaned back against the leather seat, aware that she had unconsciously tensed. Then her thoughts jumped again. "I know you're going to be busy, but would you mind doing me a favor when you go through Sonoma?"

"Of course. What is it?"

"Will you find the man who dropped the eggs on me?"

"Yes, but why do you want me to find him?"

"I haven't thought it through, but the easiest thing would probably be for me to give you a note to deliver to him. Would you have time to do that?"

"I'll make time."

"Thank you. I'll explain it to you later," she replied as Clay reined in the mare in front of the office.

He commented, "It doesn't look like Victoria's here yet. I'll see you to the top of the stairs, then I need to speak to that man opening a new store down the street. Maybe we can get him to sign up for our services. I should be back by the time Victoria arrives."

Clay unlocked the office door for Shiloh, then hurried back down the stairs. She entered the room and removed her coat, occupied with what she should write in her note to the man in Sonoma. She could say that she was intrigued by whom he thought she resembled, and she would like to know more about this woman. Who was she? Where is she now? But Shiloh knew she couldn't ask the question uppermost in her mind: Could that woman have been her mother? Shiloh scolded herself, *The whole idea is probably silly, but I want to know for sure.*

Her thoughts were interrupted when the door opened.

"Morning, Mrs. Laird."

She turned to see a thin, slightly hunched-over man in the partially opened door. He was a bookkeeper who had recently moved into an office at the end of the second-story hallway.

"Good morning, Mr. Wilkins."

"I thought you had gone to Sacramento."

"We planned to, but there have been some delays. Won't you come in?"

"No, thanks. I've got a lot of work to catch up on before the end of the year. I'm sorry about things not working out."

"Thank you," she remarked as he turned away.

Then he stopped and faced her again. "That's what I told a friend of Mr. Patton's; I mean, that you'd gone to Sacramento."

Puzzled, she asked, "Someone was looking for Clay?"

"Yes. He said his name was Tate. Said that Clay had told him to look him up if he ever got to California."

"I don't remember Clay ever mentioning anyone by that name. Did this Mr. Tate give you his first name?"

"Yes. Yancy Tate from Texas."

Shiloh smiled. "Must be a very old friend. Did he have a drawl like Clay?"

"Didn't notice any. But he did have a kind of funny voice. Sort of like he had a cold or something."

"I'll tell Clay. He'll be up in a minute."

"I'm sorry if I kept two old friends from getting together."

"I'm sure it'll be all right," she assured Wilkins. He left, and Shiloh glanced around the depressing, nearly empty room and wondered about Jared. Was he up to something, now that he knew about the quicksilver? He had accepted her hospitality, lied about having a wife, twice sneaked into her room, and now knew about the cinnabar. Shiloh was concerned that he would try to think up some way to gain monetarily from the quicksilver mining possibilities.

Deciding not to borrow trouble, Shiloh sat down at her desk as the door opened again.

Victoria came in. "Am I too early?" she asked with a friendly smile.

"No, you're right on time. Clay will be back in a minute. Please hang up your coat and make yourself as comfortable as possible on what little furniture we've got left."

As Victoria moved to the coat pegs, Clay returned.

"Good!" he said, smiling at both women. "We're all here. Now we can discuss what to do next about this cinnabar situation."

The meeting went faster than expected. Shiloh mostly listened while Clay outlined the plans he had worked out. Victoria kept her eyes on him, nodding and smiling encouragement from time to time, but Clay didn't seem to notice.

Finally, he turned from the counter where he had spread out a few papers and faced the women. "Then it's agreed," he said, "I'll go to the Mount Saint Helena property and bring back as many rock samples to be assayed as I can carry. Shiloh, you keep the office open here until I get back. There won't be much activity until spring when the roads improve. Victoria, you will look into the legal and financial angles to developing the mine—if the ore samples I bring back prove to be worth anything."

"They'll be worth something," Shiloh declared firmly. "Aldar believed the quicksilver was the answer, and I believe Aldar."

"I'm sure you're right," Victoria agreed. "My late husband was a very practical man when it came to money. I wouldn't be surprised if he and your husband had that ore assayed before. It's just too bad that Clay has to make the trip in such uncertain weather."

"I don't mind, and it's worth it," he assured her. "Now, if there's nothing else, I've got to get ready."

⌒

A short time later, Duggan stopped to rest his ankle before struggling up another of San Francisco's steep hills. He had left Sacramento because military authorities were diligently searching there for deserters from Camp Far West who had gone into the foothills to hunt for gold. The cold autumn rains and high water in the streams had driven most of them out of their old tents, rag shanties, and brush huts to Sacramento, where it was warmer and buildings were more substantial.

Duggan was hungry and short of money when he saw a possible solution drive by in a horse and buggy.

"Clay! Clay Patton!" Duggan yelled, hobbling across the newly laid boardwalk toward the muddy street. "Hey, Clay! Stop!"

Several passersby stopped and looked at Duggan, but Clay, apparently deep in his own private thoughts, did not hear him. The mare carried Clay up the hill and out of sight.

Duggan stood awkwardly at the curb, shaking his head. *I bet he would have bought me a big steak if I could have told him that Alvin Brakken is after him with a rope.*

⌒

Clay came by to pick Shiloh up after a quiet day at the office. He had tied a saddled horse behind the buggy. "I'll ride the gelding back to the stables," Clay explained, "and leave the horse and buggy for you. That way, you'll be able to get around until I get back. I hired feed for the mare delivered to your place this afternoon. You'll be fine until I return."

He explained that he planned to take a boat across the bay and rent a horse for the final overland leg to Sonoma and the mine. He would return with the ore samples in a few days.

Shiloh nodded, her feelings mixed over the rapid changes taking place. Then she remembered what Wilkins had said about Yancy Tate looking for Clay.

"I don't know anybody by that name," Clay replied, careful to keep the sudden sense of concern from his voice. "What did this man look like?"

"I forgot to ask."

"Well, I guess it doesn't matter," Clay replied.

☙

Preparing for bed that night, Shiloh opened her New Testament and gently fingered the lock of red-gold hair she kept there. Did she dare hope that she had finally found a clue to her unknown mother? Or was she stirring up a hope that would wither and die when Clay returned?

Suddenly, she remembered something Wilkins had said about the stranger inquiring about Clay. It was something regarding his voice, "like he had a cold."

I should have remembered that when Clay asked if Wilkins had described Tate. Oh, well, it's probably not important.

⌒ CHAPTER XIX ⌒

T HE MORNING Clay left for Sonoma and Mount Saint
Helena, Victoria sat eating breakfast in the hotel dining
room when Jared walked in. Without invitation, he joined her.

She angrily glanced around to find Elijah, who was pouring
coffee for two men at a nearby table. Lowering her voice so
only Jared could hear, she snapped, "How dare you?"

"Now, now," he replied in a low voice as though admonish-
ing a child, "you shouldn't say such things before you know
what I have to tell you."

"I don't care what you have to say!" Victoria spoke vehemently under her breath, her eyes flashing. "I don't want to
sell, and neither does Shiloh."

The lawyer ignored her outburst. "Don't you want to know
where I've been?" he asked.

"Why should I?" Out of the corner of her eye, she saw
Elijah approaching. "Tell him you're not staying," she whispered to Jared.

"Oh, but I am staying until you hear me out. That is, unless you want to create a scene."

The waiter, holding a silver coffeepot, stopped beside Jared.
"May I get you something?" Elijah asked.

"Cup of coffee, please," Jared replied.

When Victoria remained silent, the waiter poured for Jared,
then left. Jared smiled at Victoria. "I believe you were about to
ask me where I've been."

"I am asking you to leave."

Jared ignored the venom in her quiet voice. "I've been back
down to the New Almaden Mine. I wanted some facts and figures. Of course, they're confidential, but there are ways to find
out things if you know how."

"And you know how?" she asked skeptically.

"Judge for yourself." He produced a paper from his inner coat pocket, carefully unfolded it, and placed it on the table.

Curiosity made Victoria peer at the inked writing on the page.

Getting up, Jared drew his chair around so it was close to hers. He lowered his voice as he quickly reseated himself and jabbed a forefinger at the top figures. "Just this last summer, New Almaden stockpiled enough cinnabar ore to produce more than two thousand flasks of quicksilver."

He shifted his eyes to gauge her interest, then continued, "A flask is what they call the cylinders in which mercury or quicksilver is transported. Each flask weighs about seventy-five pounds. Prices range from as little as eighty-five up to one hundred and fifteen dollars a flask."

He paused, sensing increased interest in her attention. "You with me so far?" he asked.

"Go on." She tried to sound noncommittal.

"Multiply the lower figure of eighty-five dollars per flask by the two thousand flasks, and that comes to a total of a hundred and seventy thousand dollars."

Jared watched Victoria's mouth open very slightly as she began to breathe a little fast. "Yes?"

"Now, at the higher price of a hundred and fifteen dollars per flask, those two thousand flasks are worth a total of two hundred and thirty thousand dollars. That's a little less than a quarter of a million dollars, and full production hasn't yet started. Next year, they expect to produce nearly eight thousand flasks. At one hundred and fifteen dollars a flask, that's a total of nine hundred and twenty thousand dollars, or just under a million."

He leaned back and replaced the paper in his pocket, adding, "And that's just the beginning! What do you say to that?"

"That's all the more reason why I won't sell," she replied, "so why are you wasting time telling me this?"

"I have a plan whereby we can both reap enormous benefits.

If you want to hear about it, let's get out of here and I'll tell you."

She thought quickly, confident that Jared's plan involved her selling at least half of her share of the property to him. He would undoubtedly also try to do the same with Shiloh. If he owned half, and the two women each only owned a quarter, he would essentially have gained control.

Victoria's mind raced on. If Clay returned with cinnabar samples that showed the property was very valuable, she would certainly not sell. However, if the assay report was disappointing, she would keep that secret from Jared. Then she would allow him to coax her into selling all her share to him, at a price she set.

Smiling at her prospects, she replied, "I need some time to think about it. Now, I'm sure you must have other pressing business elsewhere, so I won't keep you."

Brakken had located the offices of Laird and Patton Stage Lines, but Clay seemed to be out of town. On the second day, Brakken decided that, even though the roads were very muddy, Clay must be out on some extended stage run. Brakken was impatient, wanting to get on with his business of repaying Clay for hanging Alben. The delay pushed his impatience into anger, but there was nothing he could do until Clay returned.

Entertaining himself in San Francisco's countless gambling houses, Brakken rapidly lost the money he had blackmailed Victoria into giving him. In a black mood, he drifted toward the waterfront to search out the best place for his act of vengeance.

Five days after Clay had left, Shiloh and Mara silently sat in the parlor near the fire, sewing baby clothes.

Finally Shiloh spoke. "Clay should have been back by now."

"Don't fret, Shiloh. It's a long, hard trip. I'm sure he'll be back as soon as . . . listen!"

Shiloh heard footsteps on the wooden porch and got up quickly, dropping her sewing. "That's his step!"

She hurried to the door as Clay knocked and called, "Shiloh? Mara? You home?"

"Yes!" Shiloh exclaimed, swinging the door open.

She smiled in relief upon seeing his tall figure in the pale light from the room. "I'm so glad to see you!"

Instinctively, she took a half-step toward him. His arms instantly enfolded her, drawing her against his chest. He bent his head toward her, then abruptly stopped.

Awkwardly, he released her and stepped back to remove his hat. "I'm mighty happy to see you, too, Shiloh."

She lowered her eyes, feeling slightly embarrassed at her action, which had initiated their embrace. "Come in, please," she said.

"I hired a hack to bring me out. If it's all right, I'll take the horse and buggy back tonight, then come by to get you in the morning."

She nodded her assent and Clay said, "I'll pay the driver and be right back."

When he returned, he removed his hat and coat while saying, "I hoped you wouldn't mind if I came out tonight instead of waiting for tomorrow."

"Of course not!" She took his gear and hung it on pegs by the door. "I've been eagerly waiting to hear about the trip."

Mara excused herself, saying, "I'll fix some coffee."

When she had left the room, Shiloh and Clay looked at each other, each obviously glad to see the other but unable to freely express those emotions.

"Sit down," Shiloh said, impulsively taking his hand and leading him to the sofa.

He stood there, towering over her, keenly aware of the touch of their hands and reluctant to let go.

Shiloh realized for the first time how much she had missed him. She released his hand and sat in the straight-backed chair. "How was the trip?"

"Fast but rewarding." He sat on the sofa, facing her. "I brought back ore samples, which I promptly took to the assayer. You should have seen his eyes light up when I handed him those 'specimens,' as he calls them."

"That sounds promising."

"I hope they are. I ran into an old Indian on the property who had some especially bright red rocks. He said his people have been getting them from a cave for centuries, and he showed me the cave. Actually, it's a tunnel about twenty feet deep. The Indians use the color to decorate their bodies and small pieces of rock as ornaments on their clothes.

"I brought a sample from the cave as well as some black rocks I found lying out in the open. Those had more of a dull pink color among the black. Homer, the assayer told me that's because cinnabar turns dark when it's exposed to the elements for a year or so. He's positive all the samples I brought are cinnabar, but he won't have the report on their value until he completes some tests."

Shiloh observed, "I'm sure that Aldar knew the value before he bought that property."

"Well, we'll know tomorrow. Homer asked if I'd found them near the New Almaden. When I told him no, he said that a couple of quicksilver mines have been found in that area but none as rich as the Almaden. He also told me that cinnabar is found around fumaroles, which he explained are underground holes where hot gasses and vapors escape in volcanic regions."

"Is our property on a volcano?" Shiloh asked with some alarm.

"I wondered the same thing and asked the assayer if volcanoes in other places in California had formed cinnabar deposits. He said that he didn't know of any although he sometimes wondered about Mount Saint Helena. I think he was trying to see if I'd react.

"When I didn't, he said that there probably wasn't any cinnabar up there. He figured that because it's not really the remains of a single volcano even though it still resembles one. There haven't been any eruptions there for countless years."

Shiloh said, "I don't understand how quicksilver got in those pieces of rock."

"I asked the same question, and Homer explained that great heat, formed far underground, sends up vapors that follow cracks in the rocks as they are forced toward the surface. The quicksilver also becomes a vapor and seeps into the cracks. It's trapped there when it cools.

"Gold is formed somewhat the same way, except it's never a vapor. It melts under the earth's heat, and the gasses below force it toward the surface. The gold cools in the rocks, and some of these break off and end up in places like rivers. As the rocks get ground down or broken, the gold is released. That's what miners are getting with their picks and pans."

Shiloh asked, "So the gold and the quicksilver have been in these mountains for countless years?"

"Sure have. Oh, Homer also told me that before the war, the Mexican government had a standing reward of one hundred thousand dollars for discovery of a quicksilver source."

"Really?" Shiloh's excitement sounded in the word.

"Really, but let's wait until we get the assay report before we get our hopes up too much."

She nodded. "Of course. But I've thought about Aldar buying that property. I mean, he borrowed the money from Vallejo to make the purchase, and Aldar was too smart a man not to have first known the value was there."

"You're right. And remember, Victoria once said her husband was not only a farmer back in Missouri, but he also had mining interests."

"Yes, I do remember that!" Shiloh exclaimed. "That's why he invested in the property with Aldar."

"No doubt, but let's not get too excited until the assay report shows how high a grade your mine has."

"I'm trying, but it's hard," Shiloh admitted, then asked, "Do you think the assayer suspects something?"

"No doubt. He told me that a few years ago an older man had brought in some specimens that looked very much like what I gave him. Homer said he never saw the man again."

Shiloh guessed, "That must have been Henry Barclay."

"I think you're right. Maybe Aldar didn't want to be seen with the specimens because Homer probably would have recognized him. Or maybe Barclay wanted to make sure that he got the straight facts direct from the assayer.

"Recently," Clay continued, "Jared took the rock he borrowed from your room. After that, a young blond woman, who had to be Victoria, came in with questions. And now I show up."

"Do you suppose this Homer will tell anybody?"

"It won't matter even if he does because he doesn't know where the specimens came from. Neither does anybody else, except those of us who are directly involved."

Shiloh had heard about gold miners having their claims jumped, but that was different, she thought. The gold seekers were claiming open land. She and Victoria held the deed to their property. Even if somebody did find out where it was, and what it contained, the land couldn't be jumped.

Clay added, "Homer says that gold is found in a lot more places than cinnabar, which is rarer than gold. So if the assay report turns out to be good, then we should begin to see Aldar's dream come true. Incidentally, have you come across any more detailed plans on routes for the stage lines?"

"I've looked everywhere," Shiloh replied. "Nothing."

"Maybe he never wrote it down."

Mara returned with a small tray containing a coffeepot and three cups. While she poured, Shiloh briefly recounted Clay's news.

Mara replied, "If the cinnabar is rich enough, how are you going to deal with Victoria in all this?"

"Good question," Shiloh admitted, meeting Clay's eyes. "What are we going to do about her?"

"It's your choice since you own a half interest."

Shiloh pondered that. "Well, my only interest in the quicksilver is using it to see the stage line developed, as Aldar dreamed of doing. So I have no objection to her as half owner as long as we're both legally protected and I get my fair share of any profits from the cinnabar."

Mara suggested, "What happens if either you or Victoria dies? Oh, I know it's not a cheerful thought, but maybe you two should have a legal paper giving the survivor first right to buy the other person's half."

Clay nodded. "That makes sense, Mara."

Shiloh sipped her coffee before asking about the second part of Clay's trip, which interested her on a more personal basis. She suggested, "Tell us about the rest of your trip."

Mara sat down beside Clay. "She means, did you deliver her message to that man?"

"I did. His name is Merritt Keene."

Shiloh waited impatiently, hoping Clay would reach into his pocket and hand her a written reply to her note. Instead, Clay casually sipped his coffee.

"Well?" Shiloh demanded, embarrassed about having written to the stranger, and yet eager to know what his response had been.

"He came back with me," Clay replied quietly. "He wants you to have breakfast with him at eight-thirty tomorrow morning."

⚭

Brakken knew that Clay would eventually return and decided it wasn't necessary to watch the office this morning. Instead, having squandered all the money Victoria had given him, he stationed himself across the street shortly after eight o'clock in the morning. He stood where he could watch both the dining room window and the entrance to the hotel. He hoped she would come outside. He didn't want to anger her by approaching her at breakfast.

He was relieved when she finally left the hotel and started walking along Washington Street. He followed and caught up with her.

Casting a sideways glance at him, she hastily lowered her voice. "What are you doing?"

He smirked. "I just came to see my banker."

She increased her stride. "Get away from me!"

"Just as soon as I get a payment on your account."

She was trapped and knew it. "I can't keep giving you money! I don't have any coming in!"

"That's your problem. You can and will keep paying me." He held out his hand, palm up.

After quickly glancing around, she handed him two double eagles. "That's all I've got. Now get away from me and stay away."

"Is that nice?" he asked mockingly. "After all I've done to keep your secret? Anyway, I can't leave right now because you and I need to talk about when we can get together for . . ."

He broke off and stared down the street, swearing vehemently. "There he is!"

Victoria halted without thinking and turned to look behind her. A light hotel coach was approaching, followed by a horse and buggy.

"There who is?" she asked.

"Clay Patton! With his woman partner!" Brakken whirled around, turning his back to the street.

"Where?" She was startled that Brakken knew Clay.

"In the horse and buggy. I don't want him to see me."

Victoria didn't want Clay to see her with Brakken either, so she quickly turned away from the traffic. "How do you know Clay?" she asked.

He fixed her with suddenly suspicious eyes. "I could ask you the same question."

"I met him a while back when some drunken hack driver tried to get out of line with me. Clay was driving by and threw him into the street."

"What do you know about him?" Brakken could hear the sounds behind him, indicating that both vehicles were passing without slowing.

"Well, only that he and a woman named Shiloh Laird own a small stagecoach company." Victoria had no intention of mentioning the quicksilver property that she and Shiloh owned jointly. "How do you know Clay?"

Brakken stole a glance over his shoulder. Both vehicles were moving steadily down the street. "We go way back," Brakken replied evasively. "What's this woman like, besides being young and pretty?"

"She's going to have a baby."

Taking Victoria's arm, Brakken gently started walking, forcing her to fall into step with him. "Clay's kid?" he asked.

"No, no. Her husband was killed last spring. Clay was his best friend."

Brakken slowly turned enough to see Clay as he guided the horse to a hitching post in front of a small restaurant. Brakken turned back to look at Victoria, satisfied that Clay was unaware of being observed by the two people on the boardwalk.

Brakken asked, "They real close? Clay and her?"

"I don't know. Maybe. I've seen the way he looks at her sometimes. Why are you asking all these questions?"

"I've been looking for Clay for seven years."

Sensing something sinister, Victoria demanded sharply, "What did he ever do to you?"

"Not to me, to my twin brother." Brakken turned toward her, his face contorting in fury. "You remember that rope I had the first night I came to your room?"

When Victoria nodded, he explained, "Well, Clay used that same rope to hang my brother."

Victoria studied Brakken with new appreciation of just what kind of a man stood before her. "You've been following him all these years?"

"Sure have. Oh, I'd have to stop and work now and then, like when I couldn't steal the money I needed. But yes, I followed him across the country."

Brakken's voice dropped and he finished by speaking through clenched teeth. "Now it's my turn to do the hanging!"

∽ CHAPTER XX ∾

SHILOH'S NERVOUSNESS showed as Clay helped her from the buggy in front of the restaurant where Merritt Keene waited for her.

Clay escorted her across the boardwalk to the door. "Want me to come in with you?"

"I have mixed feelings. I'd like to have you with me, but I probably should go in alone. Do you mind?"

"I think you should. Besides, I've got to be at the assay office when it opens. So I'll leave the horse and buggy here for you. I'll see you at the office when your meeting is over." He hesitated, then said softly, "I hope this turns out well for you, Shiloh."

"Thanks." She turned and entered the restaurant, lightly touching the New Testament in her purse. It gave her hope that the enigma in the two locks of hair and the single word, *Shiloh,* would be answered today.

All the tables were filled with men. Shiloh felt a moment of panic, then relief as she saw Merritt Keene rise quickly from his small table and come to meet her.

She hadn't gotten a really good look at him during their brief encounter in Sonoma. Now she saw with approval that he stood about six feet tall with a fairly slender build. His bright blue eyes welcomed her from beneath dark, wavy hair with few gray hairs. She guessed he was in his middle forties.

"Thanks for coming!" he exclaimed with a broad smile of greeting. "I know that it was presumptuous of me to come back with Clay instead of replying to your note . . ."

She interrupted, "I've been embarrassed since I wrote it."

"Please don't be." He led her to his table and pulled out her chair. "But I must again apologize for splattering eggs on you in Sonoma."

She assured him it was all right as the waiter approached. She only ordered coffee, feeling too nervous to eat anything. Merritt ordered bacon, cornbread, and coffee. When the waiter left, Merritt told her that he had learned a little about her from Clay on their trip back from Sonoma. Shiloh guessed he meant about Aldar, the baby, and the stage line. She listened politely, but was eager to ask her burning questions.

Finally Merritt cleared his throat. "If you don't mind, I'll get right to the reason I wanted to see you."

"That will be fine," she assured him. She was inwardly tense with excitement, wondering if the questions she had asked for twenty years were about to be answered.

"Ever since I first saw you, I've been unable to think of anything except how much you reminded me of someone I used to know." Merritt's face tightened. "You have no idea how seeing you affected me."

Shiloh could see he was moved, but she had her own emotions. Whom did she resemble? Shiloh shivered with the possibility that this man might know her mother. Otherwise, why had he accompanied Clay back from Sonoma after receiving her note? But she warned herself not be too disappointed if this meeting failed to confirm what she hoped it would be. She sipped her coffee and waited in silence until Merritt raised his eyes to meet hers.

"After you left that day," he continued, "I deeply regretted that I had let you walk out of my life without even learning your name or where you were from. I prayed that someday I would see you again."

She looked quizzically at him as he continued, "Those prayers were answered when your friend Clay returned with your note."

"After I sent it, I was sorry . . ."

"Don't be!" he broke in. "I think it was the most wonderful thing you could have done. It gave me the opportunity to come see you and try to settle something that's troubled me for years." He hesitated before asking, "Would you mind if I asked you some questions?"

"No, of course not."

"First of all, where are you from?"

"Pennsylvania."

A shadow of disappointment showed in his eyes. "I see. Your parents still live there?"

"Yes, well, the couple who adopted me do."

"Adopted?" Keene's voice shot up sharply.

She looked closely at him. "Yes. I never knew my birth parents. I was a foundling."

Keene twisted in his seat and looked at her with great interest. "In Pennsylvania?"

"No, in Virginia. A small, slave-holding family there took me in. When I was about a year old, an older couple visiting from Pennsylvania saw me. They adopted me, along with a two-year-old girl named Mara. Her mother was a slave who wet-nursed me. Mara and I were so close that the people who adopted me bought Mara and freed her from slavery. She and I are still close as sisters."

"Do you know how old you are?"

"Edgar and Martha Edgeworth, the couple who adopted me, figured out that I must have been born about 1829. So I will celebrate my twentieth birthday this Christmas."

"Christmas?"

"Yes. When I was little, I chose it because I thought it would be wonderful to have such a special birthday. Right now, Christmas is coming up fast, but I've had so many other things on my mind that I've barely thought about it."

"What was the couple like who adopted you?"

"They took good care of both Mara and me, giving us food, clothing, and shelter. But they weren't much for hugging or showing affection. That's why Mara and I are so close. We had each other, even though we sometimes disagreed, and still do."

Shiloh opened the testament to show the two locks of hair. "These were found . . ."

"Let me see those!" He gently touched the strands of long red-gold hair that matched Shiloh's.

Excited by Merritt's interest, she explained, "I think that belongs to my mother. The dark ones must be my father's."

He slowly returned the long, red-gold strands and reached into his watch pocket. "I want to show you something," he said. Producing a large gold watch, he opened the back and handed it across the table to Shiloh.

She gingerly took it and leaned forward, taking in a black-and-white pen bust sketch of a pretty young woman with shoulder-length hair and facial features that closely resembled Shiloh's.

Shiloh exclaimed, "She looks like me!"

"She certainly does. Now you see why I reacted as I did at Sonoma and why I had to see you again?"

She stared at the drawing for several seconds. "It's uncanny," she said softly, handing the timepiece back.

After all these years, she wondered, was it possible?

He looked tenderly at the girl in the sketch before closing the back with a soft click. He replaced the watch in his pocket and took a long, slow breath.

Watching the obvious emotions play across his face, Shiloh asked, "What was her name?"

"Rebekah." He said it softly, almost reverently.

Shiloh asked quickly, "Your wife?" Then she held her breath, anxiously watching the man across from her.

He nodded, his jaw muscles twitching before he softly explained, "I was told she died a long time ago."

Shiloh's hopes were instantly shattered. She could barely whisper. "Died? She's dead?"

Sighing, Merritt replied, "It's a long story, but the gist of it is that her family didn't approve of me. However, Rebekah and I fell in love and secretly eloped. She had a friend who made that sketch. Rebekah gave it to me as a wedding present.

"When we got back from our honeymoon, she insisted on going alone to tell her parents. I shouldn't have let her, but she convinced me that it was better to do it her way. I later learned from neighbors that Rebekah's parents and two brothers were furious."

"What did they do?"

"They said she was seventeen and couldn't legally marry me. They wouldn't let her leave the house, so one night I tried slipping in to take her away. The brothers were waiting for me. They started firing, but it was dark and I got away.

"Then I persuaded some mutual friends to try reasoning with Rebekah's family. That didn't work either. Neighbors brought word that Rebekah had been taken out of state to live with relatives, but on the way, she had jumped out of the wagon and run away."

Merritt fell silent.

Shiloh asked, "Did she come to you?"

"I was hoping for that, but when she didn't, I went looking for her. When I got back, neighbors said that her family had reported she was dead."

Still dazed, she asked, "How did it happen?"

"They never gave me any details. At first, I wouldn't believe it. I thought they were just trying to make me give up. But I never have, so when I saw you . . ."

Shiloh looked intently at him, feeling her hopes rise as she anticipated his next words.

But Merritt abruptly asked, "Where did you get your name, Shiloh?"

"From here." With hands that suddenly trembled, she gently touched the white leatherbound testament. "This the only thing they found with me."

She pushed her cup and saucer aside and carefully opened the front cover, resting her forefinger on the word as she read it aloud, "Shiloh."

Merritt took a long, shuddering breath and swallowed hard. "Shiloh," he repeated in a whisper.

"The Edgeworths christened me Rachel Ann, but Mara always called me Shiloh. I liked it because it seemed to connect me with my past although I don't know how."

She looked at Merritt and thought he looked pale. Slightly unnerved, he touched the testament. "You're right, Shiloh. That *is* a lock of her hair, and mine, from twenty-one years ago, and . . ."

Shiloh wanted him to complete his sentence, but she was suddenly so emotional she couldn't even prompt him to finish.

"There's something else," he continued in a barely audible voice. He picked up the testament. "I gave her this as a wedding present."

Shiloh thought her heart had stopped.

He opened the front cover and gingerly touched the single word written there. "We were married in Shiloh, Kentucky, so Rebekah started to write that down, along with the date, but I guess she got distracted."

Merritt's face contorted as he fought back tears. He said in a husky whisper, "I didn't know there had been a child, but—here you are."

Shiloh could not speak. She was overwhelmed by the realization that she had found her father, but after waiting all these years, she would never meet her mother.

Merritt abruptly stood and took Shiloh's hands. "Come, my precious daughter," he whispered huskily, "Let's get out of here before we make a scene."

⁐

Mara had finished dressing and was combing her hair when there was a knock at the front door. She frowned and went to cautiously open it.

"Jared, what are you doing here?"

He smiled, "I came to see you, of course." He stepped past her without invitation. "I saw Shiloh drive off a while ago, so I assumed you were alone."

"You've been watching the house?" Mara's tone held a hint of disapproval.

"Why not?" Jared turned to face her. "I had reason to believe that you were expecting me."

She was irritated at his arrogant attitude. She also remembered with distaste his last visit. She asked, "Why would I be expecting you?"

His eyelids drooped so that he seemed to be looking dreamily at her; a faint smile played on his lips. "I remember when you stood in front of the light in your bedroom with almost nothing on. You did that deliberately, knowing I would be watching. But when I came to you, you put me off. Well, don't try that again."

There was frost in her tone when she replied, "You didn't answer my question."

"Yes, I did. When you got what you wanted, you played coy. You still owe me." His tone softened as he added, "You are without doubt the most strikingly beautiful woman in this town."

"I didn't promise you anything for helping me get that lot. Your imagination is acting up if you think different."

"Look, I'm getting tired of this foolishness! When you needed help buying that lot downtown after Locke told you

Negroes couldn't own land in California, I got it for you. You owe me."

"I have some gold . . ."

"Stop it!" Jared reached out quickly and roughly placed his hands on her shoulders. "I let you get away with it once, but not this time."

She did not resist his grip but asked quietly, "Even though you took advantage of me?"

"What's that mean?"

"Since then, I got a copy of the Monterey constitution and read it carefully."

"Where I come from, it's against the law for coloreds to read or write."

"Well, we're here now, but I could read a long time before I moved here. So when I reviewed that constitution, I saw that there were delegates present who tried to keep free Negroes from living in California, but that idea lost. In the end, the only prohibition was that you had to be a white man to vote. Nothing was said about Negroes not owning real estate. You knew that, didn't you?"

"How could I? I was new to California."

"Well, anyway, I now own a lot that you bought for me with my money," Mara said thoughtfully, "for which I thank you."

"Your thanks isn't enough," he said huskily, his hands sliding down her shoulders and around her waist.

She did not resist, nor did she respond.

"Not nearly enough." His hands began to move again. "Which room is yours?"

She reached behind her back and caught his hands. "Wait," she said softly.

He looked expectantly into her flawless face.

"You're not very romantic," she complained. "Aren't you going to kiss me?"

"Kiss you?" There was genuine surprise in his words.

"It's customary, you know, at times like these."

He hesitated, confusion dancing across his face. "I didn't come for that, and you know it. Now, come on."

"No!" Her tone hardened and her dark eyes flashed with sudden anger. "What you're saying is that I'm good enough to go to bed with you, but you can't bring yourself to kiss me because of my color!"

"What's gotten into you?" he demanded. "This is no romantic rendezvous. You know your place!" He reached down to pick her up and forcibly carry her down the hallway, but she spun away.

"Get out!" She screamed so violently that her throat hurt. She ran to the door and jerked it open. "Out! Out!"

"Not this time, you ungrateful black . . ."

"Get out while you still can!" She took a few quick steps to the sofa and reached under a cushion. She turned around, a revolver in her hand.

"You wouldn't dare!"

She cocked the weapon. "How sure are you?"

He delayed, then swore under his breath but stepped onto the porch. Mara slammed the door hard, then leaned against it, the pistol dangling at her side.

Hot, angry, painful tears seeped out of her eyes and burned bright glistening trails down her cheeks.

◌

After leaving Shiloh to meet Merritt, Clay walked to the assay office, but it was still locked. Restlessly, he walked down the street to kill some time, and he saw Denby Gladwin approaching, also on foot.

Clay would have preferred to avoid their meeting, but Gladwin greeted him, "Glad I ran into you."

"You're out early, Gladwin."

"I had a quick errand to run," he replied, chewing on a dead cigar stub. He was a man who always knew what he wanted, and his quick temper made many people afraid to cross him. "You got a minute?"

"I've got an appointment," Clay replied, "but I can always listen for a minute. What do you have in mind?"

"I've been thinking about the bullheaded way you and Shiloh won't cooperate with Jefferson Locke and me on our business proposition."

"We've already been over that," Clay said mildly. He didn't want to get into another discussion, especially now, when the assay office was about to open with news about the cinnabar Clay had brought in.

"I think you and Shiloh got the wrong idea, Clay." Gladwin removed the cigar from his mouth and used it to emphasize his words. "You think the idea of California as a separate nation is ridiculous, don't you?"

"I just favor it being a state, that's all."

"One separated from the other thirty states by a couple thousand miles of wilderness? That's not nearly as logical as California being a separate nation. Locke and I aren't the first ones to think that. Back in 1836, the Mexican governor, Juan B. Alvarado, planned the Free and Sovereign State of Alta California. Mariano Vallejo toyed with the idea of setting up his own state. Sutter tried to get John Marsh to help establish the Republic of California. Lansford Hastings also wanted a separate nation. Three years ago, a few Americans started the Bear Flag Republic in Sonoma. Of course, that didn't last long, as you know.

"Those were all efforts from within, but don't forget that Russia, France, and England all had their eyes on California during the Mexican period. In fact, the Russians had a toehold on California with their base at Fort Ross on the coast. England was ready to grab not only Oregon but also California. You can bet that if the United States hadn't gone to war with Mexico, France and England would both have tried to seize California. Did you ever hear how England was within days of trying to claim California just before Commodore Sloat did it for the United States at Monterey?"

"I've heard about all that." Clay kept his answers short, trying to discourage Gladwin and noticing out of the corner of his eye that the assay door was open.

"California could easily have been a separate nation, and it still can be. So why don't you and Shiloh come to your senses and reconsider our business proposition?"

"Thanks, but we've already made that decision."

Gladwin's temper showed in his next words. "The deadline for applying for that mail contract is coming up fast. You two can't swing it, but if you'll work with us, you can meet all the conditions to qualify for the franchise. Then you'll have everything you want without any of the problems."

"Thanks for the offer, but again, no thanks." Clay started to turn away, then stopped. "Why do you keep trying to buy our little struggling company? There are other small outfits around who would surely be glad to jump at your offer. So why us?"

"That's none of your business!"

"No, I suppose not. I was just curious. Now if you'll excuse me . . ."

"Locke is right!" Gladwin exploded. "The only way you and Shiloh are going to learn is to lose everything! Well, in just a few weeks, you're going to learn plenty!"

Clay watched Gladwin waddle down the street, trailing vile language. After waiting for Gladwin to turn the corner, Clay headed for the assayer's door. His heart thudded against his ribs, but he wasn't sure if it was because of his controlled anger over Gladwin's threat or his anticipation of the assay report.

He ignored the clutter of specimens on the shelves and tried to sound casual as he entered and greeted the thin, gray-haired assayer behind the counter.

Before Clay could speak, Homer chuckled. His grin made his age-mottled skin stretch tight across his prominent cheekbones. He greeted Clay by saying, "I figured you'd be chomping at the bit to find out about your specimens. Follow me."

Puzzled, Clay rounded the counter and entered the back room. A single candle burned in a reflector wall bracket, casting shadows on a shallow trough placed on a long plank bench.

The assayer stopped there. "You're mighty lucky you came to me because I'm the only one who ever worked around the New Almaden mine. I'm probably the only one in town who knows about cinnabar."

"Then I'm very grateful that I came to you, Homer," Clay replied. He tried to suppress his anxiety.

"Hmm," Homer mused. "It's certainly unusual, but you're the third person recently to ask about cinnabar. Four if you count the older gentleman who came in a few years back. But I'd swear the specimens all came from the same location."

It was a leading statement, but Clay ignored it except to say, "Yes, you mentioned that when I first brought these in."

"Strange." Homer shook his gray head. "Something's going on, but I don't suppose you're going to tell me what it is?"

Clay forced a smile. "'Fraid not. What did your tests show?"

Homer crooked a finger, inviting Clay to come closer.

He joined the assayer in leaning over the trough. What looked like two common gold miner's pans rested under water. In one a dark sediment showed at the bottom. In the other pan, bright red sandlike material had settled, showing clearly through the water.

"Here are two of the specimens you brought me. In the first pan is what's left of that black rock. I pulverized it and washed it the same as I would a shovel full of gold-bearing river rocks." Homer lifted the first pan out and poured off the water.

"Cinnabar is found around fumaroles," he continued, "or where there has been thermal activity. The dark specimens were mudstone. It was formed under an ancient seabed ages ago."

"That so?" Clay asked without enthusiasm. He didn't care. He wanted to know about the cinnabar's value, but he didn't want to rush Homer.

"If you'll remember, there was a white streak in that mud-stone. That was quartz. Based on my findings in that and the other similar specimens you brought, I'd say the cinnabar ore is probably going to run around one percent."

"Only 1 percent?" Clay was so disappointed he let the words slip out before he thought.

Homer snorted. "Don't go looking down your nose at 1 per-cent! That's only from the first specimens." He set the first pan down and lifted the second, saying, "But you're in luck, be-cause in this one, the red sandlike material you see will run about 65 percent mineral."

The number sent Clay's hopes up, but he hesitated, want-ing to make sure of the meaning. "What do you mean by mineral?"

"I mean cinnabar."

"It's very pretty," Clay observed, trying to control his eagerness.

"It's more than pretty!" Homer reached out and grabbed Clay's right hand and pumped it heartily. "It's going to be pro-cessed into quicksilver—enough to make you rich! Real rich!"

Clay grinned happily and clapped Homer on the back. "That's the best news I've heard in years. Thanks! Now there's someone special I have to tell."

He dashed out the front door, hoping he could find Shiloh still at breakfast with Merritt Keene.

⁕

On the short drive from the restaurant toward the office, Shiloh sat stunned. She kept looking at the man whom she had just discovered was her father. His face was radiant as he reined in the mare before the offices of Laird and Patton.

After leaving the restaurant, they had briefly embraced, their first as parent and child. They were both beaming with joy, yet there was a strangeness in their new relationship. It had come about so abruptly that the countless questions and comments each had harbored for years suddenly burst out in spontaneous laughter.

When Merritt hitched the mare to the rail outside of the office, Shiloh didn't even notice an untidy young man with a wild beard and uncut hair leaning against the side of the building.

As Merritt came around the back of the buggy to help Shiloh down, the bearded man hurriedly approached her. "Mrs. Laird?" he inquired, removing his hat.

In a quick glance at Shiloh, Merritt gathered that she did not recognize the man, so he stepped in front of her. He asked brusquely, "Who are you?"

"No offense, Mister, but if this is Mrs. Laird, I have something terribly important to tell her."

Something in the stranger's sincere and sober manner caused Shiloh to touch her father's arm and stand beside him. "It's all right," she assured him in a quiet voice. She faced the stranger. "I'm Mrs. Laird."

"Excuse me for bothering you, but my name's Arthur Duggan, and I knew Clay Patton back in Texas."

Relieved, Shiloh smiled. "You knew Clay?"

"Yes ma'am. I was just a shirt-tail kid of fifteen or so, but I remember him. I hope he remembers me."

"I'm sure he will," Shiloh replied, "and he will be glad to see somebody from his hometown again."

"I ain't so sure." Duggan lowered his head and rocked uneasily on his feet. "I come to warn him."

Shiloh stiffened in alarm. "Warn him?"

"Yes, ma'am. A spell back, when I was coming from the east, on the other side of Johnson's ranch, I ran across another man from back home. He's aiming to hang Clay."

"What?" she exclaimed in disbelief.

Merritt said grimly, "Young man, if you're lying . . ."

"I swear on my mother's grave!" Duggan raised his right hand, then looked squarely at Shiloh. "I'm plumb sorry to tell you like this, but he could be watching me this very minute, and if he knew what I was doing, I'd be as good as dead too . . ."

Merritt interrupted, "Get to the point, Duggan!"

Shiloh nodded, asking breathlessly, "Why is somebody after Clay?"

"Well, ma'am, several years ago, back in Texas, this man's twin killed Clay's wife and little boy, so Clay hung him."

Memories of something Clay had told Shiloh about that tragedy gushed up, constricting her throat but confirming the truth of what Duggan said. She managed to ask weakly, "What is this man's name?"

"He calls himself Yancy Tate, but . . ."

"Oh!" Shiloh's startled exclamation interrupted Duggan. She remembered when the bookkeeper down the hall from her office told her that a man calling himself Tate had been looking for Clay. Tate had claimed he was a friend of Clay's.

"His real name's Brakken," Duggan continued. "Alvin Brakken. Clay hung his twin brother. Now Alvin's brought the same rope that Clay used so he can . . ."

"Enough, Duggan!" Merritt interrupted brusquely as Shiloh suddenly grabbed his arm.

"I'm right sorry," Duggan exclaimed in alarm. "You going to faint, Mrs. Laird?"

"No," she said without conviction, fear squeezing her heart so she could hardly breathe. She turned to Merritt. "We've got to tell Clay, fast!"

She started back to the buggy. "He was going to be at the assay office when it opened. Maybe we can catch him there."

☙

It had been a long time since Clay whistled, but he felt like doing so as he walked briskly away from the assay office. Suddenly, a man stepped in front of him and blocked his way.

It had been seven years, but Clay stopped dead still upon recognizing Alvin Brakken.

He stood with his feet spread and braced, a grim smile on his face. "I been waiting for you, Clay," he said.

Noticing the bulge a revolver made under Brakken's coat, Clay asked evenly, "What do you want?"

"I come to pay you back for killing my brother."

Over the first few years after he had buried Elizabeth and Mark, Clay had thought Brakken would follow him. Lately, Clay had assumed that Brakken had given up. Clay now realized how wrong he had been.

He replied calmly, "I'm unarmed, and I don't think you'll kill me with witnesses around."

"I don't plan to; not here and not today. That would be too easy. I had years to work out the best way to make you pay for what you done."

"What are you going to do?"

"Just what you did to Alben. I'm going to use the same rope you used on him. But not just yet. When I'm ready, you'll come to me!"

Brakken abruptly turned and crossed the street, dodging horses and vehicles. He entered a building and Clay lost sight of him.

Staring after him, Clay felt perplexed by the strange warning yet like a man unexpectedly coming upon a keg of black powder with a short, fast-burning fuse—and no way to escape.

⌒ CHAPTER XXI ⌒

ALMOST IN a daze, Clay wandered down the street. He repeatedly told himself, *I can't believe it! It's been seven years!*

A few minutes before, Clay had felt like whistling. He had wondered how Shiloh's meeting went with Merritt. He had also happily anticipated Shiloh's joyful reaction when he told her that Aldar had been right, that the assay report showed that the property could pay for the stage line.

Moments ago, it had seemed to Clay that it was just a matter of getting the proper papers drawn and delivered to the courthouse on time. With proof of financial responsibility, plus careful plans for developing extensive stage service, government agents could see that it was safe to award a mail franchise to Laird and Patton Stage Lines. Then Brakken had showed up.

Clay somberly warned himself that there were only two possibilities: *Either he kills me, or I kill him.*

His grim musings were interrupted by the sound of hoof-beats behind him. He looked up to see Shiloh and Merritt in the buggy. Glancing at her face, he wondered if it would indicate whether she had found out about her mother. Instead, he was startled to see that she looked badly frightened.

She leaned out of the buggy and blurted, "Clay, a man named Duggan came to our office a while ago looking for you."

"Duggan? Arthur Duggan?"

"Yes. He said he knew you back in Texas."

"That was a long time ago. He was just a boy . . ."

Shiloh interrupted, "He said somebody named Alvin Brakken is in town. Brakken wants to kill you."

Clay stared at Shiloh, sorry that she knew. He had not planned to tell her about his encounter.

Merritt explained, "We came looking for you right away."

Clay sighed and lifted Shiloh from the buggy. He set her feet on the boardwalk, but did not release her. He looked down into her face and lightly brushed a wisp of hair from her forehead. "I know. I met Brakken on the street a few minutes ago."

"Oh, Clay!" She clung to him. "What happened?"

He hesitated, unwilling to say, but realized he must. "He threatened me."

"Oh, no! Duggan said Brakken has a rope he claims you used to hang his twin . . ." Her voice broke.

Clay saw the anguish in her eyes. "It'll be all right," he assured her.

"How can it be?" Shiloh cried. "I remember what you said about a twin brother killing your wife and son. But you said that was years ago!"

Clay bowed his head until his cheek rested against hers. "It was. I thought that Alvin had given up."

Shiloh realized that his danger was also hers. His future was intertwined with hers on a deep basis that had nothing to do with their business association, but she had not acknowledged it, not even in her private thoughts. "How can we stop him?"

Clay slowly released her. "I don't know." He looked at Merritt, who had stepped down from the buggy and stood a few feet away, holding the mare's reins. "Do you mind if Shiloh and I go someplace and talk?"

"Of course not." Merritt met Clay's eyes, knowing that Clay must choose between two terrible alternatives.

Merritt added, "Clay, if I can help you . . ."

"Thanks," Clay interrupted, "but this is my problem."

"I understand, but my offer stands. You take the horse and buggy. I'll meet you later at your office."

"That will be fine," Clay replied.

Merritt nodded, then reached out a little awkwardly and took both of Shiloh's hands. He didn't say anything, and neither did Shiloh. Impulsively, she moved toward him. He dropped her hands and embraced her.

"God be with you both," he whispered, then released her, shook hands with Clay, and walked away.

Shiloh had been so anxious to tell Clay the joyful news that Merritt was her father, but that would have to wait. In sober silence, she let Clay help her into the buggy. He climbed in beside her and turned the mare west.

⌒

Mara still smarted from the way Jared had treated her. There wasn't anything she could do to Jared, but there was something she could do with confirmation of the information she had picked up. That included making Locke squirm because of the lies he had told her in their first encounter. But that would happen after she took care of some business near the plaza. She walked there carrying a small carpetbag. In it, carefully wrapped so that they would not clink together, she carried enough gold coins to accomplish her purpose.

Through Elijah, Mara had learned that a haberdasher named Malberg was hurting financially. Mara entered his small establishment on Kearney Street. The short, balding man pushed his wire-rimmed spectacles up onto his forehead, laid down a pair of trousers he had been sewing, and rose to greet her.

After exchanging greetings, Mara asked, "Are you Mr. Malberg?"

"I am. What can I do for you?"

"I understand that you own a lot on Sacramento Street off of Dupont near the Plaza."

He looked carefully at her as though wondering why a Negress was interested in land. "I do. Are you representing someone interested in buying this property?"

She smiled. "Yes, I am."

He considered that before venturing, "For a quick sale, I could maybe let it go for only ten thousand."

Her smile disappeared. "I have friends who told me you were asking seven thousand dollars yesterday."

"Prices rise very rapidly in this place."

"Perhaps it will go down for gold?"

She caught the flicker of interest in his gray eyes. He said, "I have heard it said that money talks."

Mara looked around to make sure they were still alone. "Listen to this." She opened the carpetbag and turned back one corner of a towel, revealing some twenty-dollar gold pieces. She picked up four coins and gently shook them. "Isn't that a pretty sound?"

"It is musical," he agreed.

"A thousand today," she said, her voice taking on a brisk quality. "The balance tomorrow, all in gold."

"Nine thousand more first thing in the morning."

"Six." She clinked the coins again.

"The lot is worth . . ."

"Seven thousand," she said sharply and began putting the coins back into the towel.

"In a few days, I can get twelve or thirteen . . ."

"Maybe, and maybe not. But today you can get seven for sure. Who knows what tomorrow will bring? Seven. Last chance." She started closing the carpetbag.

"Wait! You drive a hard bargain. Come in the back and I will write it up."

Mara opened the bag again. "I knew you were a good businessman. Make the receipt out to Mara Edgeworth."

In the cramped office, Malberg swept clear a tabletop and lowered the glasses from his forehead. He watched carefully as she began counting the coins out in stacks of five. When the last double eagle was neatly in place, he went to a small desk, dipped a pen in the ink bottle, and wrote out the receipt.

"Thank you," Mara said, blowing on the ink to dry it before putting it in her now empty carpetbag. "I'll see you when you open up in the morning."

"I would like to meet your Mrs. Edgeworth," he said, his fingers lightly touching the golden stacks. "Perhaps she would be interested in some other property . . ."

"It's Miss Edgeworth," Mara interrupted, heading back through the store, "and she wouldn't be interested right away. But maybe someday."

The merchant beamed with anticipation. "When can I meet her?"

"You already have." Mara started for the door.

For a moment, Malberg stood in silence as her meaning became clear to him. Then he called, "Hey, wait! Are you saying that you're buying this lot for yourself?"

She kept walking but said over her shoulder, "Yes, I'm the buyer."

"I can't sell it to you!"

"Why not?" She whirled on him so suddenly that he stopped in surprise and took a short step back. "There is no law that prohibits me, or anyone of my color, from owning property. A lawyer assured me that the Monterey constitution says that's my right."

"But you don't understand! If the rest of the men around here find out I sold to you, especially those who own property in that neighborhood . . ."

She snapped, "Then don't tell them!"

His voice rose in desperation. "It'll get out, sooner or later. I could be ruined! Let me give the money back to you."

"I'll see you in the morning," she said, "and believe me, there's no way you can back out of this deal, Mr. Malberg, so don't lose any sleep trying."

Feeling both angry and exhilarated, Mara walked purposefully south of Market Street to Jefferson Locke's land office shack.

He turned from a map on the wall, smiling automatically, then the smile quickly vanished. "It's you again," he said curtly. "I told you before, no nigras allowed in here."

"And I told you then that I wanted to buy some property, which you refused to sell me. You said it was against the law in California, but that's a lie."

"So?" he challenged belligerently.

"So I want you to know that somebody else sold me two lots. I paid in gold. You not only didn't make that sale, but you also missed out on selling my new lot which is next to the three lots you own on Sacramento Street."

She could see him squirm as he realized she was his new neighbor, but he quickly recovered and demanded, "How do you know I own property there?"

"I know many things. If you want to sell those lots, let me know. I'll buy them, but only at my price."

"You can't threaten me!"

"As your new neighbor, I suggest you remember what I said."

"Get out!"

"In a minute," Mara replied coolly, ignoring the dark rage spreading over Locke's face. "The last time we spoke, I told you to remember that day because the time was coming when I would be able to buy and sell you."

"You're a vindictive nigra! Now, get out!"

"I'm going because I have finished what I came here to do." She paused, then added with a pleased smile, "I have taken the first step in making that promise come true."

He glared, livid with rage as she walked out, pulled the door shut, and swept triumphantly down the street.

❧

In her hotel room, Victoria mulled over the ongoing leeching of her resources by the blackmailing Brakken. He was becoming more bold and had even accosted her on the street. Her plans to attract a wealthy and respected San Francisco escort would be seriously hurt if word got around that she had been in the company of a disreputable man.

She had first vainly hoped that Jared would be able to stop Brakken, like get him jailed on some charge. But she hadn't even suggested it because she realized Jared wasn't the type to get such a job done. She had known from the beginning that Clay would, but she could not manipulate him.

Now that she knew Brakken's plans to kill Clay, Victoria could use that knowledge to make sure that Brakken died by Clay's hand. The question was: How?

She knew Brakken would never dare face Clay in a duel.

Ambush was more in Brakken's character. But his obsession with hanging Clay meant he must have some kind of special encounter planned. Unless she discovered what, Brakken had such an enormous advantage that Clay might not get a chance to get rid of Brakken for her.

If Brakken lived, he could continue to blackmail her and make her life miserable. She could never marry wealth without fear of his greed. She also knew that it was only a matter of time until Brakken again made crude advances to her.

She shook off a feeling of revulsion, recalling how he had first showed up, soaking wet, dirty, and unshaven. He had made it clear that he wanted more than money from her. He wasn't the type to give up, she told herself, remembering the rope he had carried into her hotel room. He had plainly said he planned to hang somebody, but she hadn't suspected he meant Clay.

How, she wondered, staring out the window, could she work it so that when those two met, Brakken died? What if both men died? That would leave Shiloh with the stagecoach line and half-interest in the quicksilver mine.

Victoria pondered that and decided she needed two things for her own security and peace of mind. First, she had to find some way to get hold of Shiloh's half. Next Victoria had to be sure Brakken was killed when he and Clay met.

The question in both cases was still, How?

She took a couple of agitated turns around the room. Then she stopped and looked at herself in the armoire mirror. "Of course!" she said aloud. "That might work! It will, if I handle it right!"

⌒

Brakken sat on the waterfront, ignoring the rough-looking men who worked there. They paid no attention to him, either, because he looked like one of them. He stared thoughtfully at about five hundred dead ships. They had been anchored as close to shore as their crews could get them before abandoning them to go search for gold.

Over the years since he had found Alben dead with Clay's rope around his neck, Brakken had thought of many ways to make Clay suffer before he died. At first, Brakken had thought of physical tortures, then he had broadened that to an emotional level. That meant Clay had to be alone where nobody could help him, no matter how long it took to die.

Brakken had worked out all of the details, but he wanted to again review them to make sure he hadn't overlooked anything. His gaze skimmed the assortment of closely packed, seagoing vessels that rocked gently in the bay. There were brigs, schooners, barges, and whalers, among others.

Their black masts, stripped of sails, clawed at the gray, threatening sky. Who would think to look for Clay on a dead ship? And even if someone did, how would he pick out the right one from all those hundreds?

It had taken Brakken a while to select the one that best suited his purpose. His cold eyes skimmed the clustered mass of ghostly ships to rest on one that was square-rigged.

Anchored in the middle of the other ships, she was identifiable because the crew had abandoned her so quickly. Her sails had not been removed, but the winds had torn away all but a few tattered pieces of canvas. These flapped from the yardarms where they had been fastened horizontally at the center to the three masts.

Brakken congratulated himself. *The perfect place!*

He lowered his gaze to the water. The bay was miles wide, and its water could be rough. Normally it was no place for an inexperienced person like him to row a boat at night without lights.

However, the ships were so close to shore that some were tilted in the mud flats. Those in deeper water were sheltered enough from the wind that Brakken felt sure he could row that far.

He had proved that by finding an unguarded twelve-foot rowboat and practicing in daylight. At first the boat was difficult to control, but he gradually gained enough skill to maneuver among the ships.

He had grunted with satisfaction upon seeing that the Jacob's ladder still dangled over the blackened side of the chosen square-rigged sailing vessel, the *Narnak*. He had climbed aboard, sending rats squeaking for cover. His brief inspection of the yardarms on the forward mast satisfied him that he had everything he needed.

Rowing back to shore, Brakken had hidden the rowboat under a larger four-oared pinnace that had been dragged up on the sand when its bottom rotted out. With a final look around, Brakken started walking inland.

"Now," he said aloud, "it's time."

꩜

Clay and Shiloh rode up and down the less steep San Francisco hills while they talked through Clay's alternatives in dealing with Brakken's threat.

Clay's fingers played with the reins while he frowned, deep in thought. "There was a time when I would have gone looking for him and killed him."

"But now?"

Grimly, he told her, "I don't know. It would be self-defense, but I wish it didn't have to be that way. Yet I know it will never be over until one of us is dead."

"Oh, Clay!" Shiloh impulsively reached out and clutched his hand. "Isn't there any other way?"

"After he spent seven years trying to find me?"

"You were in the war. Aldar told me that you know how to handle a gun, but what if he ambushes you?"

"He might try that. He's like his brother was in that respect. They'd face a lone woman and a little boy alone, but not a man in a fair fight."

The implications were frightening to Shiloh. She desperately tried to think of alternatives. "We could go to the constable. What was the name of the one who helped when Aldar got killed?"

"Logan. Constable Logan. But it would be my word against Brakken's. He can't be arrested for threatening me, and a warning won't stop him."

Anguished, Shiloh exclaimed, "You can't live like this forever! This has got to be resolved!"

"I know. I have nothing against Alvin, as I did against his brother." Clay sadly shook his head. "But Alvin's not going to leave me alone. I hope there's some way other than one of us getting killed."

"If anything happens to you . . . !" she blurted, then stopped, not knowing what to say.

He didn't answer but was aware of her hand on his and of the fervency of her remark. He was also aware that if anything happened to him, Shiloh would be alone again. He not only didn't want to die, but he also did not want to leave Shiloh with another death to grieve.

"Nothing's going to happen to me," he assured her, moving his hand to cover hers. "There should be another way to end this, but I can't think what it is. I just have to think this through."

She needed the protective feeling of his strong hand over hers. She wanted to believe his words, so full of confidence. Yet common sense told her that Clay was right: Brakken's menace existed as long as he lived. She knew Clay well enough to know that he would end up doing what he felt had to be done. That terrified Shiloh, but not as much as if he did nothing. Would he even get the chance, or would he be gunned down in an ambush?

She looked up at him and saw his eyes were closed. She was sure he was silently asking for guidance. She closed her eyes and did the same.

When she looked up again, Clay abruptly changed the subject. "We got so worked up about Brakken that I forgot to ask how your breakfast went with Merritt Keene."

"Oh, it was wonderful!" Shiloh exclaimed, and breathlessly reported that she had found her father and learned something about her mother.

When Shiloh had finished her account, she remembered to ask, "What did you find out about the assay report?"

"It's everything we could ask for."

Her eyes brightened with hope. "You mean . . . ?"

"Yes, Aldar was right! That property will make enough to fund the development of the stage line!"

He added silently and solemnly to himself, *If I can stay alive until then.*

∽ CHAPTER XXII ∾

SEATED BESIDE Clay as he guided the mare west, Shiloh ruefully reflected on their situation. This should have been a joyful day. She had at last learned the identity of her birth father. The assayer's quicksilver report proved they could make the stage line flourish. Everything should have been wonderful, but Brakken's threat forced everything else into the background.

At Shiloh's urging, Clay told her again why Alvin Brakken had come to kill him. He found it painful, even after seven years, to recall finding his wife and son murdered. Speaking in a low tone and fighting the emotions that tore at him, Clay explained how he had learned that Alvin's twin, Alben, had killed his family.

"I knew the Brakkens were vindictive," Clay concluded, "so even before I hung Alben and left his body on his brother's doorstep, I figured that he would come after me. That's why I left Texas and never went back.

"Now, all these years later, he has found me. I can't believe he even warned me. He must get some sort of sadistic pleasure out of trying to make me sweat."

Shiloh reached out and grasped Clay's hand.

After a thoughtful moment, Clay continued, "I've changed since then, Shiloh. I never asked anyone to fight my battles for me. Now I would hate to take any man's life, but I don't want anyone to take mine, either. Especially not now." He turned soft eyes to hers. "You make my life worth living."

Shiloh desperately cast about for some way to guarantee Clay's safety. "Maybe you can buy him off," she suggested. "We don't have the money now, but Mara would loan it to us. We could repay her from the quicksilver mine or the stagecoach line process."

"That wouldn't work with Brakken. He wants blood."

"We could leave." Shiloh began to sound desperate. "Go somewhere else."

"We really can't; not after knowing about the quicksilver. We both shared Aldar's dream. It's about to come true, but it won't if we fail to keep faith with him. Besides, Brakken would follow, just as he did here."

Clay reined in the mare on a bluff overlooking the Golden Gate and the Marin headlands. He recalled fleetingly that it was near here where they had watched the stricken clipper ship limp into the bay with the Concord stagecoach tied to the deck.

Shiloh and he had grappled with the problems facing them, but those were minor compared to their present predicament. Clay briefly reflected on the comparison between their troubles and the ship. It had struggled on for a while before sinking, taking the coach down with it.

But Clay was determined that the comparison would stop there. They were close to triumphing in the struggle to win the mail contract and develop the stage line. Yet that could still be lost, along with his life.

Shaking his head, Clay silently vowed that he would not let Brakken kill him. Self-defense would keep Clay from being convicted by other men, but that would not ease his conscience.

He stepped out of the buggy and gently lifted Shiloh down. Holding her close, he wrapped his arms around her and looked into her upturned face before releasing her.

"I don't want you hurt by this, Shiloh. It's my problem, not yours."

"It's ours," she corrected him gently. She reached out to him, but he turned away from her, facing the bay.

She stepped over beside him. "Look at me, Clay," she said quietly but firmly. As he did, she continued, "Until Duggan told me that you were in danger, I hadn't allowed myself to admit how very much you mean to me. All the excuses I've made suddenly became too flimsy to hold any truth. Whatever happens to you, happens to me. I know that now. You must know it too."

He didn't answer her directly because he did not agree. He could be killed but she would be alive, alone again. He gazed across the bay while his thoughts tumbled over each other.

"There are some things that must be done quickly," he mused. "We must finish the proposal and submit it in person to be eligible for the mail contract."

"That can wait . . ."

"No, not really. The deadline's just days away, and there's no way of knowing when or where Brakken will make his move. I'm going to do my best to live, but if I don't make it, then you must be at the courthouse on time with all the papers."

"We'll be there together!" she cried, but she knew that she might be wrong. She suppressed a shudder at the thought of losing Clay. It had been terrible when Aldar was murdered. If it happened again so soon . . . She drove the dreaded possibility from her mind.

He reached out to encircle her shoulders and gently pull her tightly to him. "I'm trying to be practical and realistic, Shiloh. Please help me by letting me say what's got to be done."

She forced herself to nod.

He released her shoulders to take her hand and lead her to the buggy. "Merritt's been waiting a long time. We can talk on the way back to the office."

∽

Jared squirmed in his chair while Denby Gladwin leaned across the desk in his new brick hotel. Gladwin removed the usual stub of dead cigar from his mouth and jabbed it across at the lawyer.

"You're telling me that when you talked to the assay man this morning, he said that somebody had just brought in cinnabar specimens that were going to make them rich?"

Nodding, Jared explained, "Homer's description fits Clay perfectly. Of course, the assayer doesn't have any idea that I know exactly whom he meant. But I thought you should know . . ."

"You thought?" Gladwin exploded, standing suddenly so that his bulging middle hung above the desk. "You were paid to get Aldar's plans, not to think! That quicksilver will bring them all the money they need to go ahead with the stage line."

"I know, but . . ."

Gladwin waved him to silence. "When you first came here, wanting to represent my interests, I gave you the simple task of finding those papers. Aldar had personally told me that he had worked out details for developing a complete stage system to serve not only California, but overland to the Missouri River as well!"

Stalking around the desk, Gladwin jabbed his right forefinger into the lawyer's chest. "Nobody but Aldar had that kind of vision," Gladwin continued hotly. "Nobody! But we've got our own vision for the Empire of Pacifica, and we need that stage system to help reach enough people in California to make it happen."

"I looked all over the office while they were gone up north, and I even searched Shiloh's house . . ."

"You couldn't find your nose with both hands at high noon!" Gladwin interrupted. He chomped down on the cigar stub and returned to his chair.

"Locke and I have repeatedly tried to buy out that line, but neither Shiloh nor Clay would sell. But I still want those plans! I know they exist, and if we get them in the next few days, we can still submit our bid for the mail contract. With Aldar's plans, we'll beat out everyone. Without them, we lose not only a stage line, but also everything that such a system represents to our cause."

"I'm not the only one who tried to . . ."

Gladwin broke in angrily. "I don't want excuses! You're a southerner! You want to be rich and powerful like a lot of us in this new place. The best way to get what you want is to help us establish the Empire of Pacifica. For that we need a stage line to cover the West where we can send our people, our message, and our newspaper, which we'll have. We need Aldar's plans—now!"

Jared protested, "But Shiloh herself said they'd never found a will or any of her husband's papers, except for the agreement that gave her and Patton the rights to the express business."

"Which they promptly sold to start up a stage line!" Gladwin stuck the cigar stub back in his mouth and strode back to his chair. "That line couldn't really get started without money, which Shiloh and Clay couldn't even borrow. Now they don't need it; or won't when that quicksilver gets into production."

Gladwin added hotly, "Oh, one more thing you forgot. Besides the will, they found a copy of the deed to that property. That had been overlooked until this blond woman showed up with her copy. Aldar's plans for that stage system must be around somewhere."

"Maybe not. Maybe they got lost. Anyway, I did my best."

Gladwin yelled, "Doing your best isn't enough. You wanted to do some work for us, and we gave you that opportunity. It would have made Locke and me rich, and moved us a long way toward our ultimate goal."

"I'm sure Shiloh hasn't found those plans. Maybe I can still . . ."

"No, you can't!" Gladwin thundered, waving his hairy arms. "When they told you that you couldn't manage the office because they had caught you in a lie, you were through being of any value to them, or us!"

Jared rose reluctantly. "Trying to purloin documents isn't what I had in mind when I came to you. I can still represent you in legal matters."

"You've got more nerve than a stagecoach driver on a cliff-side road! Thanks to your blundering, there will be many people eager to invest in that quicksilver venture. When the roads are dry this spring, Shiloh and Clay will be well financed, and they'll have the mail franchise. I'll have nothing. Now, get out of my sight!"

Jared hurriedly left, but he hadn't given up.

∽

Brakken followed Victoria to the new post office at the corner of Clay and Pike streets. Postal service ended at San Francisco, so when the mail arrived by steamer once a month, men lined up for blocks, day or night, enduring rain or cold fog. Each hoped there would be a letter from home. But the steamer was not due until next week, so the little postal facility was nearly empty when Brakken entered.

He saw Victoria pay a dollar to a man who had just received a six-month-old newspaper. She took it to a small side counter where she skimmed news from the East.

Her back was to the half-dozen patrons waiting for the two clerks, so she attracted little attention as Brakken eased up beside her.

"I got some real news for you," he said quietly without looking at her.

From behind the newspaper, she recognized his hoarse voice and stiffened, fearful of having anyone noticing him talking to her. She whispered, "I can't talk here."

"I didn't come for any money," he assured her in a low tone. "I just thought you might like to know that I'm about ready to hang Clay."

She became fully alert. This was what she had wanted to know. Now she had to act her part well to make sure her plan worked, and Clay killed Brakken. "Why are you telling me?" she asked from behind the paper.

"Well, you knew when I was going to kill your husband, so I thought you might like to also know that your friend is about to die."

She thought of protesting that Clay wasn't really her friend but realized that would not accomplish her purpose. She went into her act by lowering her voice and saying, "That somehow excites me."

Waiting until a postal patron walked by, Brakken asked. "How do you mean?"

She made sure nobody was watching, then slid her foot over to touch his. Hearing his sharp intake of breath, she lowered the paper slightly and peered over the top. "Does it matter how, as long as it does?" She raised the paper again and added provocatively, "It's exciting enough to make up for all the time you've waited."

His voice was more husky than usual when he said, "I'll meet you at your hotel in fifteen minutes."

"No, not now. Somebody might see. Tonight, about nine o'clock."

"You'd better be there," he said with a hint of suspicion in his tone.

She assured him in her most seductive voice, "I'll be there." She turned without looking at him, folded the paper, and walked out.

So far, so good, she thought. *His blackmailing days are about over.*

☙

On the drive back to the office, Shiloh's eyes were drawn to San Francisco's massive mountain called Fern Hill. She remembered Aldar's promise that someday he would build her a fine house up there among the chaparral where now only wild goats frolicked.

He was buried in a cemetery at the foot of Signal Hill, but his dream lived on. The stagecoach system he envisioned now seemed certain to soon become a reality. Or would there soon be another fresh grave near Aldar's final resting place?

Clay's voice broke into her melancholy reflections.

"Are you listening?" he asked.

Suppressing a shudder, she realized he had been saying something. "I'm sorry. My mind wandered."

"I said that when I was in the war, I learned that the best defense is a good offense. It's hard to win a war when you're just defending yourself. Winning usually means going on the attack."

She cried out in alarm, "You're going after Brakken?"

"I can't wait for him to choose the time and place. He could strike while I'm asleep or driving passengers. He could even shoot when you're riding with me. I can't take the risk of you getting hurt like that."

"But you said that he threatened to hang you."

"He did, but I don't intend to give him that opportunity."

"Where will you look for him?"

"I've got a couple of places in mind."

"Please be careful."

"I will. Now, I had better take you to the office and then return to my place and get ready."

Upon reaching the stagecoach office, Shiloh suffered mentally while Clay filled Merritt in on all that had happened that morning.

"While I go after Brakken," Clay concluded, "there are a number of things that must be done. Merritt, I hope you'll help Shiloh with everything."

"She's my daughter," he replied softly. "I'll be here for her; for both of you."

"Thanks. Now, let's go over what's left. The most important thing is to get the papers ready to present at the courthouse before noon on December 10.

"Fortunately, we've already worked out the proposed routes, the towns to be served, the number of horses, stages, and drivers needed to serve California.

"It's too bad we don't know Aldar's plans for the overland routes. But even without those, the government can't very well keep us from getting a contract to carry the mail if the cinnabar papers are all in order."

Shiloh forced aside the fears that gripped her to remind Clay, "Victoria was going to look into that."

"Fine," Clay replied, "but I'd also like you or Merritt to talk to Sledger. Ask if he can recommend someone he trusts to draw up the legal papers for both the mine and the stage line."

"I'll take care of it," she replied.

"I know you will. The government will want proof that we have the financial backing to carry the stage line until it becomes self-supporting, so you'll need a detailed assayer's report on the mine's value."

"I'll see to that," Merritt volunteered.

"Thanks." Clay continued, "We'll also need a plan for developing the mine. Once we have that, the government would have no reason to deny us the mail franchise. Just be sure you take everything to the courthouse by noon of the deadline. After that, there's every reason to believe that we'll meet Aldar's goals."

Shiloh protested, "We can't do all that without you."

"Sure you can. The preacher and your father will help. Oh, there's one more thing: Shiloh, I think you should follow up on Mara's suggestion to get some written agreement with Victoria. Make sure that it gives each of you the right to the first option to buy the other's share of the cinnabar property if either of you decides to sell."

"I'd rather give you the first right," Shiloh said, "or maybe split it between you and my father."

Merritt shook his head. "I've done well enough in life that I don't need anything else."

"I don't want that right either," Clay declared. "If anything happens to me, my share of the stage line goes to Shiloh. Merritt, you're a witness to this."

He nodded and shook Clay's hand but did not reply.

"Well," Clay said, turning back to Shiloh, "I think everything's settled. I'll leave the horse and buggy for you. I've got the gelding if I need him."

She nodded, trying to swallow the lump of fear that caught in her throat. She asked in a barely audible voice, "When will you be back?"

"When this is over, I'll come straight back to you."

"Promise?" she whispered, her eyes misting.

"I promise, with all my heart."

∞

Walking down the street that afternoon, Jared still silently smarted from Gladwin's blistering remarks when he heard someone call his name. He turned around to see Victoria trying to catch up with him.

"I've been looking for you," she greeted him as he walked back to meet her.

Having this pretty woman indicate an interest in him made Jared smile in anticipation. "I'm glad I ran into you too," he replied. "I suppose you've heard about the assay report?"

She hadn't but wasn't going to admit that. "What about it?" she asked.

"It's going to make you and Shiloh wealthy."

That was delightful news, and all the more reason to talk with Jared. Still, Victoria was careful. "How do you know that?" she asked.

"That assayer can't keep his mouth shut. Oh, he didn't give me any names, but he was so excited that he told me about some cinnabar specimens that he had assayed for somebody. I knew he had to mean Clay."

Jared was surprised when she linked her arm through his as they walked on together. He felt her gently brush against his upper arm. When she didn't move away, he smiled to himself. She was finally thawing toward him.

She enjoyed teasing him. "You think Shiloh knows about the quicksilver?"

"She must. Homer, the assayer, said that the man who brought in the specimens was waiting when the doors opened this morning. I guess he and Shiloh planned to tell you the next time they saw you."

"I'm sure they will." Victoria wondered how rich she was going to be, then thrust that thought aside to focus on her reason for seeing Jared.

Since she had last talked to Brakken, Victoria had carefully rehearsed what she would say tonight when he came to her room. She had to convince him to let her be present when he attempted to hang Clay. Before that, Victoria had to be sure her interest in the quicksilver mine was protected.

She lightly brushed against Jared's arm before asking, "If anything happened to Clay, do you think Shiloh will stay in the stagecoach business?"

"Hmm? Well, she certainly has been determined to see her husband's dream come to fruition. Now, with what the quicksilver can provide, the stage line seems certain to get a mail franchise. That is, if the papers are filed on time. So I'd guess that she will stay in the business. Why do you ask?"

"If she gets the mail subsidy, do you think she will want to remain as a partner in the quicksilver mine?"

Jared started to get an inkling of what Victoria was thinking. He said, "I doubt it. That would be too heavy a load for her, especially since she's expecting a child."

"Do you think she would sell her share?"

"Why should she—especially now?"

"I see what you mean. But if anything happened to her, then who would inherit her share?"

"Probably Clay, or maybe Mara. Then you might have a partner who's not as easy to get along with as Shiloh is. But look at this from her viewpoint. If anything happened to you, who would get your half?"

Victoria flashed a knowing smile. "It wouldn't be you. On the other hand, I have no husband, children, or family. So I thought that if I offered Shiloh an option on my share, she might do the same for me with hers."

"The right of first refusal," Jared nodded. "She might. After all, she's got more to gain than you do."

Victoria wasn't sure about that, but didn't say so. Instead, she said, "That's why I was looking for you. I want a legal document saying that if either Shiloh or I die, the survivor has a first option to buy the other party's share."

"You expecting her to die?"

"No, of course not. I'm sure she doesn't expect me to either. There's no danger to either of us, so I think I can convince her that this is just a good business precaution."

Jared looked suspiciously at her. "What do you know that I don't?"

She ignored the question. "How soon can you have that paper prepared?"

"Tomorrow."

"Good." She disengaged her arm from his.

Jared said softly, "When I found your note, I hoped that it meant you and I could get together later."

She made her tone sound promising. "Let's see about that after those papers are signed."

⟲ CHAPTER XXIII ⟳

T HAT FRIDAY afternoon at his Spartan Cow Hollow
quarters, Clay prepared to defend his life. He reached into
the tiny closet and removed his 1848 pocket Colt from the
shelf. A fairly new invention capable of firing several times
without reloading, the Colt would be his principal armament.

Knowing how dangerous Brakken was, Clay also considered
carrying Aldar's Remington derringer as a backup weapon. From
the corner of his closet, he removed a square tin box. It had once
contained a saltless, hard bread called hardtack. Clay opened the
lid and carefully lifted out the papers that protected the gun.

Clay's thoughts were elsewhere as he methodically cleaned
and oiled his guns. He wondered why a peaceful, God-fearing
man like himself had no choice but to face such an adversary
as Alvin Brakken.

I don't want to kill him, Clay assured himself. *There was a
time when I wouldn't have hesitated a moment. But not now. A
lot of things have changed since I last saw Alvin. One of the most
recent was falling in love with Shiloh. I certainly didn't plan on
that. I never expected to love anyone after Elizabeth.*

Sighing heavily, Clay strapped the holstered pistol around
his waist and picked up the derringer. He slid it into his boot
but didn't like the feel. He tried putting the little pistol inside
the waistband at his back, but wasn't comfortable with that
either. After a moment's reflection, he decided to leave the
derringer behind.

Clay stepped to the window and carefully peered out before
going to the stables to saddle the gelding.

Clay had considered where he was most likely to find his
adversary and what he might expect from him.

He's got to try to surprise me and take me prisoner, Clay
thought. *Judging from what Duggan told Shiloh about the rope
Brakken's carrying, Alvin wants me alive. When I asked him what*

he was going to do, he said something like "just what you did to Alvin."

Clay finished saddling the gelding and swung into the saddle, still trying to recall Brakken's exact warning. *What did he say just before he turned and walked off?. . . . "But not yet." Yes, that's it! Then he said, "When I'm ready, you're going to come to me!"*

Shaking his head, Clay muttered, "He's right; I'm going after him. But how could he have been so sure of that? And how would I know when he's ready? I'm overlooking something, but what?"

Clay felt the short hairs on the back of his neck tingle as he warily began his search.

∽

The candles had been lit and Merritt put fresh logs in the fireplace while Mara carried a steaming dish in from the kitchen. Shiloh fretted about Clay and absently began to set the table for dinner.

In trying to keep the conversation away from the dreary direction it had taken most of the day, Merritt told Shiloh, "In all those years of living alone after I lost your mother, my loneliest times were always at Christmas. It would have been great to have a child to watch open Christmas presents. Just think, Shiloh; it's just a little over two weeks until we have our first holiday together as father and daughter, plus your twentieth birthday."

"It's hard to think about that right now," she responded quietly as she walked to the window to peer into the darkness.

Mara placed the dish on the sideboard and approached Shiloh. Lowering her voice, Mara said, "You can't fall apart over this Brakken situation. My friends are already starting to look for a man of his description, especially the voice. They'll find him, if Clay doesn't, and then it can be settled. Clay will be safe and everything will turn out all right."

"I know, but I can't help being very concerned."

"You've done all you can," Mara added, "except finish getting things in order at the office against the December tenth deadline. Don't get discouraged, and don't drag your father's spirits down."

"You're right." Shiloh turned to face Merritt across the room. "I'm sorry. I'm just so upset about Clay." She paused and then added shyly, "Father."

He walked over and kissed her on the forehead. "I like the sound of that. Could you say it again?"

"Father," she said softly, kissing him on the cheek. "My very own father."

He put his arms around her. "My dearest daughter."

Mara said, "I could use a hand in setting the rest of the table, Shiloh."

"I'll help," Merritt said.

"Thank you," Mara replied. "You can set the plates around." Then she asked, "Shiloh, what else do you need to do before Clay returns?"

Walking around the table, Shiloh replied, "I just have to complete the financial accountability statements based on what the quicksilver mine is expected to produce."

Her father declared, "I can help with that."

"Thank you." Shiloh continued, "Victoria is having a lawyer check into the best ways to set up a company to operate the quicksilver mine."

She turned to Mara and added, "Remember when you suggested that Victoria and I draw up some legal papers giving each other an option to buy out the property?"

"I remember," Mara assured her.

"Well, Victoria had the same idea because she came by today with papers already legally drawn. I read them, and they looked fine to me. Then I gave them to Father."

"I checked them over," he said, "and they looked all right to me."

"So I signed them," Shiloh concluded.

"Good," Mara said approvingly, placing the potatoes in the center of the table.

Shiloh nodded. "Yes, everything looks good. But I really wish we'd found Aldar's plan for developing the stage line. I remember him saying that he had worked out everything for California as well as the overland route to the Missouri River."

"You've looked everywhere?" Merritt inquired.

"Yes. My pastor found a small box at the office with a note from Aldar regarding the Mount Saint Helena property. That's why we first went north where you and I met."

"Did you go through everything in that box?" Merritt asked.

"Yes. Well, not at the time," Shiloh explained. "It was about then that Victoria came in and introduced herself. Later we looked for clues as to what Aldar meant about the property but never found anything."

"Mind if I take a look tomorrow?" Merritt asked.

"No, of course not, but tomorrow's Saturday. I hadn't planned on going into the office, but we may as well take one more look."

Mara warned, "Remember, even if you don't find Aldar's plans, you've got to have everything else ready to submit Tuesday noon or you can forget about that mail franchise."

Merritt volunteered, "I'll see that everything else is ready, and I'll even take them to the courthouse myself."

"Thanks, but the rules say that one of the owners has to be present in case the government representatives want to ask questions. Now, please sit down at the table. Father, would you return thanks?" He nodded and she added, "And please remember Clay, wherever he is."

⌒

A few minutes before nine o'clock, Brakken made sure no one else was in the hotel hallway before knocking on Victoria's door.

She opened it slightly and asked softly, "Did anybody see you come here?"

"No," he replied, sliding through the door, which she quickly closed after him. He grinned appreciatively at her, taking in the inviting curves barely concealed by her silk dressing gown. "I wasn't quite sure you'd be here," he admitted.

She saw in the light of two candles that he had shaved and changed clothes. She gave him an encouraging smile. "I told you at the post office I would be."

He reached for her but she resisted, placing both hands on his chest. "There's no rush," she said seductively. "I thought you might like a drink first."

He forced himself to release her. After all, he needed her cooperation to make his plan work. "Just one."

"Make yourself comfortable," she suggested, going to the marble-topped stand that held a flowered ceramic pitcher and a matching wash bowl.

When she turned back to him holding two glasses, each containing a couple of ounces of amber liquid, he had removed his hat, coat, and boots. He sat in the large uncomfortable chair upholstered with coarse horse hair. He half-closed his eyes as he regarded her approach.

Handing him a glass, she clinked hers to his. "To us," she toasted, and sat on the side of the high bed, her bare feet well off the floor.

He echoed her words and drank quickly, anxious to get on with his planned activities. He set his empty glass on the floor and stood, his eyes bright with desire.

"Don't be in such a hurry," she said with a smile. "Help yourself to another drink."

"I'd rather . . ." he began, but she laughed softly and shook her head, making the blond curls jiggle.

"First, we need to talk. Then we'll have the whole evening if we want." She encouraged him with another smile, safe in her knowledge that she had arranged for the manager to knock on her door in twenty minutes.

"What about?" Brakken asked a little curtly, settling back into his chair.

"This afternoon you said you were ready to hang Clay."

"Yes, and you said that you found that exciting. I never thought about it that way before. Then I remembered how you were when we planned to kill your husband."

He paused, frowning in disapproval. "You got me all worked up then slipped away without meeting me as you promised."

"I'll make it up to you." She wet her lips and gave him a little tantalizing smile. "But first, I want to know more about your plans for Clay."

Picking up his glass, Brakken walked to the stand to splash a few ounces into it before explaining, "I need your help."

Victoria raised her eyebrows in surprise. She had planned on persuading him to let her be present when he and Clay met, but she had not expected Brakken would want her help. Instantly wary, she put her plans aside to hear what he had in mind, asking, "What can I do?"

"Bring him to me."

Victoria laughed. "You know I can't do that."

"Yes, you can. When I send you word, you find him and bring him where I tell you to."

Victoria regarded him with obvious doubt. "He won't come to his own hanging."

"He'll come; I guarantee it."

There was such a look of confidence in his face that she believed him, but she saw an opportunity to push for her own objectives.

"Why should I do that?"

"Because," he said bluntly, "if you don't, I'll tell the whole town about how you killed your husband."

She flared, "I didn't do that! You did!"

"You paid me," he reminded her coldly.

"Who would believe your word over mine?"

Shrugging, he explained, "They don't have to believe me. Rumors alone could ruin your life around here. No eligible rich man is going to risk marrying a woman accused of killing her husband."

Her anger rose, but she forced herself to keep her voice under control. "If I help you, you go away and never cross my path again. Agreed?"

He chuckled. "You're in no position to bargain, and you know it. So, are you going to help bring Clay to me?"

Trapped and furious, but recognizing the truth of Brakken's remarks, she sighed. "Tell me the details."

"You don't need to know them. Just be ready when I tell you. Clay will come. Afterward, we can celebrate." Brakken drained his glass a second time and stood again. "We've talked enough."

She started to slide off the bed, but he was too fast. He seized her roughly, his breath smelling of liquor. She struggled, but he said huskily, "This time, you're not going to get away."

Although she struggled, he covered her mouth with his and forced her backward.

When the manager knocked on the door as Victoria had arranged, it was too late. Victoria was bruised and hurt while Brakken nonchalantly searched her purse. His smug, self-satisfied manner aggravated Victoria so much that she had to use all her willpower to keep him from seeing the fierce hatred she had for him.

She warned herself not to let Brakken sense her soaring emotions. She had gotten what she originally wanted: the assurance that she could be present when Brakken and Clay had their final encounter. Now she had a more personal reason to want Brakken dead.

∽

The Saturday search yielded nothing new. On Sunday, Shiloh and Merritt took the buggy to church where she introduced her father to Pastor Sledger and told him about Clay.

The huge bear of a man welcomed Merritt warmly then tried to comfort Shiloh by saying, "Your faith is made stronger only by opposition." He raised his arms and flexed his muscles which threatened to burst the seams in his coat. "These muscles," he explained, "are the result of countless rasslings with men, animals, stumps in the ground, and all kinds of other things. They all offered resistance, some of which I hated. But it was the struggle that built my body, just as the struggles you're going through now will develop your faith. We're told that the trial of faith, which is more precious than gold, brings honor to Him whom we serve."

Through the next day, Shiloh fervently wished that her faith wasn't being tried so fiercely. Late Monday afternoon, Shiloh and Mara sat in the parlor while Merritt split firewood outside. Shiloh tried to be hopeful as she got up and paced the floor, periodically peering out the window. The baby reflected Shiloh's restlessness, kicking and moving more than usual.

"Why doesn't Clay come by and let us know he's all right?" Shiloh asked, vainly searching the road.

Mara looked up from the finishing stitches on a baby blanket. "I don't know why, but I do know you're going to wear a hole in the floor if you don't sit down. Pacing won't bring him back any sooner."

"I realize that, and I know I'm not supposed to worry but leave everything in God's hands. Yet sometimes that's very hard to do."

"Well sit down and pick up your sewing before you drive me out of my mind."

Shiloh reluctantly took her chair again and reached for her thimble but didn't put it on. "Why hasn't Samuel or one of his friends brought you word about Clay or Brakken? Surely someone must have seen one of them."

"I didn't ask them to keep an eye out for Clay, only to find

Brakken. The fact that nobody has reported seeing him means they're not having any better luck than Clay is."

"How do you know Clay hasn't found Brakken?"

"Simple. That would be big news, and Samuel or Elijah or someone else would bring me word right away."

Merritt entered by the back door and removed his jacket. "It felt good to swing an ax again," he said cheerfully. "There should be enough wood to last for a few days. I also fed and watered the horse."

"Thank you," Shiloh replied absently over her sewing.

Her father came over and put his hand on her shoulder. "You still fretting about Clay?"

"I can't help it. Just not knowing is terribly difficult."

"If it would make you feel better, I could go look for him," Merritt replied.

Shiloh looked up hopefully. "Would you?"

"Of course. I'll go harness the mare."

Mara shook her head. "No disrespect, Merritt, but you don't know this city. If you got into the wrong place—like along the Barbary Coast—you could get badly hurt or even killed."

Shiloh sighed and agreed. "She's right. It's too dangerous."

Merritt walked toward the fireplace and said over his shoulder, "I've got an idea. Mara, if I drove into town, would I be likely to find your friend, Samuel? I could ask him if anybody has seen either Clay or Brakken."

Shiloh's eyes lit up with anticipation. "That's a good idea. What do you think, Mara?"

She replied, "Samuel moves around, working at various places. But Elijah will be at the hotel about now, waiting on tables."

"Then I'll go see him," Merritt decided. He put another log on the andirons and stood up. "I'll get my coat."

Mara laid down her needle and removed the thimble from her finger. "Elijah doesn't know you, so he might be reluctant about talking to you."

Shiloh's face fell, causing Mara to exclaim with a light tone, "I saw that look! Your lower lip dropped so far you could step on it."

"I didn't mean for my feelings to show," Shiloh admitted.

Mara stood up. "Well, I don't like to see you looking sad. Merritt, if it's all right with you, I'll ride in with you to see Elijah."

"I would be delighted to have your company."

"Good." Mara turned to Shiloh. "You don't mind being alone for an hour or so, do you Shiloh?"

"No, not at all. I'll be fine," she replied, feeling greatly relieved.

"We'll be back as soon as possible," Mara assured her.

"Thank you both," Shiloh said fervently.

After they left, she walked into her bedroom and picked up her New Testament to seek solace and reassurance. As she picked up the two locks of hair, she felt sudden tears start. After all these years, she had finally solved the mystery of their origin, and her own roots.

How many times had she prayed about that? She could not remember, but it didn't matter. Now she had the answer, or at least part of it. She had found her father. She turned the pages and almost reverently touched the word that had been her preferred name: Shiloh.

Grateful tears squeezed out of the corner of her eyes as she silently expressed her gratitude for knowing the origin of her life. Now if Clay could return safely . . .

Dabbing at her eyes, Shiloh turned to the Psalms. She began reading the poetic words of the twenty-third: "The Lord is my shepherd . . ."

She broke off reading, startled at the sound of the front door opening. There had not been time for Mara and Merritt to find Elijah and return.

"Clay!" Shiloh cried joyfully, leaping up and almost running down the hallway. "Oh, Clay! I'm so glad . . ."

She stopped abruptly at the sight of the stranger who stood just inside the door.

"Shiloh Laird," he said in a rasping voice, "you're coming with me."

She had never seen Alvin Brakken, but his voice helped her to recognize him. She started to back up until he reached under his coat and produced a long-barreled revolver.

"Move!" he commanded harshly. "I need you for bait!"

✆ CHAPTER XXIV ✆

CLAY WAS FRUSTRATED, lonely, and cold after searching again in all the places he thought Brakken might have hidden. No hotel had a Yancy Tate or Alvin Brakken registered. Riding through San Francisco's streets, still muddy after the recent rains, Clay had found no trace of Brakken. He had even tied his horse in front of a hotel and walked to Montgomery and Pacific streets on the Barbary Coast.

This area near the waterfront was the city's roughest and home of the British prisoners who had chosen here over Australian penal colonies. Every form of debauchery and crime existed. In the rats' warren of grog shops and prostitute cribs a man might be drugged and shanghaied or killed by the sudden flash of a knife or a quickly drawn gun.

Clay was clearly armed, and he walked with the confident stride of someone not to be bothered, so the rowdy drinkers drifted out of his way. As he passed, disappearing into the shadows between burning pine torches, they returned to their wild celebrations.

Clay decided that Brakken was deliberately hiding or waiting in an ambush. He struggled with an overpowering longing for a hot stove's warmth and Shiloh's company. He returned to his horse, thinking he would ride out to her home to reassure her.

As he neared the house, he was cheered by the faint glow of lights inside. However, as he reined in the gelding, he noticed the buggy was gone and the front door slightly open.

In sudden alarm, he dismounted and rushed inside, calling, "Shiloh?" He shoved the door open, tense and alert. "Where are you?"

Except for the crackle of the dying fireplace and the faint sputtering of the candles, the room was silent. Pulling out his Colt, he dashed through the house, searching each room and calling frantically, "Somebody answer me!"

His horse neighed and was answered by another. With pistol in hand, Clay rushed outside, hearing the familiar crunch of the buggy's wheels on the sand. "Shiloh?"

"No, it's Mara, with Merritt."

"Where's Shiloh?" Clay asked anxiously as the mare stopped at the end of the short gravel patch.

"Isn't she in the house?" Mara's voice carried immediate alarm.

"No!" Clay ran to the buggy as the two passengers disembarked. "The door was open. Her coat's gone, but the candles haven't been blown out."

Merritt whispered hoarsely, "Good Lord!"

Realization struck Clay like a blow. "Brakken! Oh, I should have known!"

Merritt cried in dismay, "You think he's got her?"

"I'm sure of it! That's what he meant about me coming to him! But where is he? I've looked everywhere for the past few days and nights without finding even a trace of him. It's my fault! I should have realized what he meant and protected her!" He turned toward his horse.

"I've got to find her!"

Merritt said firmly, "There's no use in castigating yourself. Let's go inside and figure out what to do."

After Brakken left the rented horse and carriage in the shelter of a sand bluff by the cove, he checked Shiloh's gag to make sure it was secured across her mouth. Then he forced her into the rowboat and carefully eased it through the clot of dark, dead ships. The night was made even darker by the schooner's looming black hull as the rowboat bumped against it. The dangling Jacob's ladder was faintly visible in the light of a moon crust.

"All right," Brakken said softly, the raspy voice made more ominous in the darkness. "Grab hold and climb up."

Shiloh tried to protest through the dirty gag that smelled sickeningly of fish as Brakken roughly yanked her to her feet. Afraid of trying to climb in her condition, she realized that she had no choice. She took a step toward the ladder, which caused the rowboat to tip sharply. Shiloh staggered and started to fall overboard.

Brakken roughly caught her, commanding, "Climb!" Her fingers clutched wildly at the swinging ladder as she lifted her skirts from around her ankles and began to awkwardly climb. Feeling her way in the darkness, her fear was made worse by her tortured thoughts.

This can't be happening, she told herself. *This man really intends to kill Clay and me. Aldar's child will never have a chance at life. Oh, Lord, please, no!*

With her fingers sore and bleeding from the climb, Shiloh reached the broad, steady deck and stood up. She sighed with relief.

"In there," Brakken directed, pushing her forward. He slid a wooden cover back from the companionway hatch. A faint light showed from below. Brakken commanded, "Now climb down."

Trying to suppress her frightened whimpering, Shiloh cautiously made her way down a narrow ladder, afraid of falling and injuring the baby. One deck down, she saw the faint glow was made by a smoky whale oil lamp suspended from a ceiling beam.

As her eyes adjusted in the thick gloom, she made out a small table with stationary benches on either side and a narrow bunk against one wall. She had horrifying thoughts of what her captor planned to do.

"I'm going to take off your gag," he said, "because you could scream your head off and nobody would hear you. I'll leave your hands free to fight off the rats while I'm gone."

He laughed at his own humor before adding, "I'll lock you in from the outside, so don't bother trying to escape."

She fought her panic down and momentarily felt relieved that nothing terrible would yet happen to her. Not wanting to antagonize him by speaking, she merely nodded.

He started up the ladder. "Make yourself comfortable. I've got to leave a message for someone, then return the rig to the livery stable. After that, I'll be back, and we can all prepare for the sunrise."

Shiloh frowned, trying to imagine why Brakken had mentioned the sunrise. He closed the companionway hatch and bolted it from the outside, leaving her alone in a dead ship that barely rocked in the calm waters of the cove. Then she understood what Brakken meant. Clay had hanged his brother at daybreak. Instinctively, Shiloh clutched her throat which suddenly constricted so she could barely breathe.

⌒

Riding double, Mara clung tightly to Clay as he rode the gelding hard through the night. After a hurried consultation, a devastated Merritt had reminded them, "Shiloh's my daughter, and she's carrying my grandchild. Now that we've found each other after all these years, I'm not going to lose them."

Merritt had volunteered to drive the buggy to the preacher's house to see if Shiloh might have gone there.

If not, Merritt would find Logan, the constable, and alert him to her disappearance.

Nearing the lights of the gambling houses and grog shops, Clay slowed the lathered horse in front of the building where Mara's friend Samuel held a janitor's job.

"If he doesn't know anything," Mara said, sliding to the ground, "I'll go to the restaurant and ask Elijah. They'll get everyone looking and listening."

"So far as I know, Brakken had no horse, so he might have rented one. I'll go check the livery stable." He dug booted heels into the gelding's flanks and rode off at a trot.

Clay's anger at himself turned to fury as he fumed silently at Brakken. *I didn't want to kill you, but if you've harmed Shiloh, I won't hesitate, so help me God!*

As he passed Victoria's hotel, he saw her getting into a carriage. He pulled up and called to her. "Wait a minute! Shiloh's disappeared!"

Victoria turned away from the carriage and hurried toward Clay. "I just heard."

"You did? How?"

"It's a long story; I'll tell you later. I was just going to find you to take you to her."

Clay shook his head in bewilderment. "You know where she is?"

"I know how to get where she is. Come with me."

"You bet your life I'm going with you! Where is she? If he's harmed her . . ."

"I don't know, but I think she's all right for now." She glanced dubiously at the horse. "I don't think this dress will let me ride double with you."

Clay dismounted and tied the gelding to a hitching post. Pointing toward the carriage Victoria had almost gotten into, Clay said, "I'll hire that carriage, then you'd better tell me what you know that I don't!"

At the foot of Market Street, Victoria called to the driver to stop. Clay hastily paid him, and they stood overlooking the cove while the carriage headed back up the street.

Clay pulled out his Colt and scanned the quiet water, straining to see in the dim light from the fragment of moon. He saw only the reflection of moonlight on small waves and the ghostly black hulks of abandoned vessels anchored as close as a hundred yards offshore.

"I don't understand," he said brusquely as the night silently settled around them. "Where is she? And why won't you tell me how you know?"

"I told you it's a long story," she said, keeping her voice low although there didn't seem to be another living person anywhere around. "Come on, we've got to get down to the water's edge."

Clay hesitated, feeling skittish about Victoria's unexpected role in the situation. Gun ready, he followed her down the slope of the bluff and across the flat sand, which crunched under his boots. Suddenly, he stopped, reaching out to grip Victoria's arm.

He could barely see two small shacks nestled in a sandy niche about ten feet from the water. The one on his left was perhaps ten feet wide by fifteen feet long. It had a pitched roof, in contrast to the flat roofed, ten-by-ten structure to the right. No hint of light shown from inside, and there was no smell of smoke from the chimney.

"I'm not going another step until you tell me what I want to know," Clay said flatly.

"You want to see Shiloh again?" Victoria parried. Without waiting for an answer, she added, "I think I see a rowboat. Come on."

"A rowboat?"

"Yes. Follow me."

With every muscle and nerve taut, Clay advanced slowly, sweeping his head from side to side and holding the Colt steady in his right hand. As Victoria started between the two buildings, Clay suddenly veered off to his right.

Victoria asked in an agitated whisper, "Where are you going?"

He didn't answer but slipped behind the small building that he hoped had no windows in back. He was right, he realized, as he pressed himself against the wall and eased forward, pistol ready. Coming to the far corner, he turned, again glad there was no window.

Holding his breath, he crept around the corner to the front, his eyes trying to make out where the door should be. As he neared it, he heard a slight sound from inside, right next to where he crouched.

He started to swing the pistol around just as something hard jammed into his spine.

"Don't move, Clay!" Brakken's hoarse voice warned. "I thought you might try something like this, so I loosened a board so I could stick this gun through."

Reluctantly heeding the round muzzle of Brakken's revolver against him, Clay stood still.

"Good boy," Brakken said. "Now, take your pistol by the barrel and hand it to me, butt first. Nice and easy. That's good. Now, raise your hands and move over to the door. It's open. Stand there where I can see you."

Obeying, Clay silently chided himself for falling victim to Brakken. "If you harm a single hair on Shiloh's head, you'll regret it," Clay warned.

"That's pretty brave talk from a helpless man," Brakken said mockingly, coming out of the door. "Now, let's all go down to the water. Victoria, get in the boat and sit down in back. Clay, you sit in the middle. I'll push us off."

When the sand quit grating on the boat's bottom and the craft floated free, Clay whirled to face Victoria. "I never expected you to do something like this!"

"I didn't have a choice," she replied.

"Both of you, shut up!" Brakken commanded. "Clay, grab those oars and get to work."

"I never rowed one of . . ."

"Learn fast!" Brakken commanded. "I'll tell you where to go."

It took Clay several minutes to get the small craft pointed into the cove and moving on a fairly straight course. He silently raged, feeling betrayed by Victoria and knowing that he had failed Shiloh. Now he regretted not bringing the little derringer.

All he could do was silently pray and hope he had another opportunity before it was too late.

Brakken directed Clay toward the ship and said, "There's a ladder hanging there. Feel for it, Victoria, then climb up. Clay, you follow."

She had a struggle climbing with her purse, which banged heavily against the ladder.

"I'll hold that for you," Clay volunteered.

"Thanks," Victoria replied, "but I can manage."

On deck, Clay glanced apprehensively at the three tall masts, naked except for the yardarms, which were faintly visible in the moon's cold light. One arm had broken off and swung gently, silhouetted against the sky.

Brakken held the gun on Clay and raised the latch that he had used to lock the companionway hatch. Then he pushed Clay forward. "You first. Slide the cover off and get below deck."

As he climbed down the companion way, Clay noticed a faint light and heard a muffled sound. Then he saw Shiloh. She leaped up from the bench.

Clay recklessly rushed to her and swept her into his arms. "Are you all right?"

"Just frightened," she whispered against his chest.

Brakken said mockingly, "A regular homecoming. Isn't that touching, Victoria?"

When she didn't answer, he warned, "Clay, if you get any brave ideas, remember I'll shoot her first. Victoria and I are going up on deck to wait for the sunrise."

Shiloh seemed to recognize Victoria for the first time. "What are you doing here?" she cried in disbelief.

Victoria started to reply, but Shiloh spoke first.

"Now I understand! The option clause! You got me to sign it, knowing this was going to happen! How could you?"

Clay said coldly, "I trusted her, and she led me into this trap."

Brakken warned them harshly, "That's enough! Now, I thought you might like to know what's going to happen."

Through clenched teeth Clay demanded, "Let her go. You can do what you want with me."

"Really? How very generous of you!" Brakken mocked. "You have no bargaining power and you know it. Don't tempt me to do anything before the time comes for both of you."

Victoria asked with a hint of concern in her voice, "What are you going to do with her?"

"I vowed when I found my brother dead that I would find Clay. Then I would learn who or what was important to him and take it away."

Shiloh sucked in her breath.

"Clay," Brakken continued, "I've watched you and her together." He waved the gun barrel at Shiloh. "I know how important she is to you, so you can suffer with every thought in your head for as long as you live."

He laughed. "Get it? As long as you live." His voice dropped to a growl. "Clay, when I've taken everything away that's important to you, then I'll take what little you have left: your miserable life."

Clay suddenly tensed and started to step toward Brakken, but Brakken pointed the gun at Shiloh. "One more move, Clay, and she's gone."

He stopped, teetering as he held himself in check in spite of his terrible fury.

Victoria protested, "She's going to have a baby. Surely you don't mean you'd hurt her?"

"I already told you what I'm going to do," Brakken snapped. "You're the one who wanted to be here."

"What?" Shiloh gasped, turning anguished eyes on the other woman.

"Why?" Clay asked.

Brakken chuckled. "It seems she gets some kind of strange pleasure out of watching men die."

Victoria made a strangled cry, raised both hands, and struck at him with clenched fists. "You filthy beast!"

He caught her hands and easily held her at arm's length. "If you don't like the way I do things . . ."

"I'm sorry!" Victoria interrupted, fighting to gain control of herself.

"I'll let it go this time," Brakken replied. He again turned to leave, then stopped to face Clay. "I brought the rope you used on my brother."

Clay silently fumed as his captor turned to Victoria. "You stay down here and keep an eye on them. Not that I'm worried. The only way out is past me and both these pistols." He shoved his into his belt beside the Colt he had taken from Clay.

When Brakken disappeared through the companionway, Clay and Shiloh turned bewildered eyes on Victoria.

"Look," she explained, "I didn't know it was going to be like this. I have nothing against either of you. He threatened to . . . to lie about Henry's death if I didn't bring Clay to him. Shiloh, I'm sorry."

They stared at her in silent disbelief.

"Believe me," Victoria exclaimed. "He's an evil man! Really evil! I'm sorry for what I did, and I'll try to help you both."

Clay replied in a flat, hard tone, "I don't know whether to believe you or not. But if you're sincere, get my gun back for me."

"I'll try."

"I hope you're telling the truth," Shiloh said. "If you don't mind, I'd like time alone with Clay and with our God."

Victoria nodded, gathered her long, heavy skirts about her, and moved away from them to give them privacy.

It seemed only moments before Brakken called down. "Sun's coming up. Everybody on deck."

Shiloh appreciated Clay's steady arm around her as they stepped into the cold morning air. Her legs were so weak she could barely walk, so she sought strength by silently reciting the comforting words, *"though I walk through the valley of the shadow of death, I will fear no evil, for thou art with me."*

Clay had anguished over the moment now upon him. It did not seem possible that this was the last day he and Shiloh would be together. There was a nightmarish quality to the scene.

In the hours after their anguished prayers, the words had run out and a silence settled over them. In that stillness, broken only by the occasional squeal of a rat in the bulkheads or the slight creak of the wooden hull, Clay faced the reality of their situation.

As he saw it, either he passively let Brakken kill them, or he would have to force an opportunity to do something, anything, that might give Shiloh and the baby a chance to live. Clay desperately wanted to survive but understood that he might not make it. He refused to surrender his hope for Shiloh and frantically sought some action to save her.

"Hold me," she whispered.

He complied, saying softly, "I want to hold you forever."

Slowly walking beside her across the deck, Clay saw the hints of a new day. The sun had not yet started to appear, but its first rays struck the eastern horizon across the bay.

Red sky; it's going to rain. He shook his head at the irrelevant thought, then remembered that noon today was the deadline to file for the government mail franchise. What had seemed so vital yesterday had become insignificant in their urgent situation. Clay dropped his gaze from the distant horizon to the hundreds of silent ships surrounding their vessel.

He had no faith that Victoria, who had betrayed them, would help them now. He furtively looked for something he could use as a weapon but didn't see a thing except the various supports that had once held the sails.

The loose spar he had noticed last night tapered toward the ends to support and help spread the head of a square sail. It creaked slightly as it swayed, held captive by a length of line beside the mast.

He heard Shiloh gasp and followed her eyes. A noose dangled from one of the mast arms.

"Recognize it, Clay?" Brakken asked cheerfully. "It used to be yours. I brought it all the way from Texas." He paused, then added mockingly, "Let's try it on you to see how it fits."

Brakken almost playfully slipped the noose around Clay's neck. It felt rough against his skin. He heard Shiloh sob as he automatically reached for the rope.

"Uh-uh!" Brakken exclaimed, knocking Clay's hand down. "Your hands will have to be tied behind you."

Brakken stepped back and cocked his head to look at the noose. "I've been waiting seven years to do this," he said with satisfaction. "I must say it looks pretty good on you, Clay."

Brakken slid the noose back over Clay's head. "Let's see how it works on your lady friend, then it will be your turn."

Desperately, Clay tried to reason with his captor. "Let Shiloh go. She's done nothing to you, and she's going to have a baby."

"Can't do that, Clay. You need to suffer the agonies of the damned by what's going to happen to her. Now, turn around."

Shiloh tried to keep from breaking down, but she felt the tears of terror start.

Clay whispered to her, "Hang on." He raised his voice to Brakken. "Can I ask one question?"

"Make it quick. The sun's coming up fast."

"My question is for her." Clay turned to Victoria. "Why did you do this?"

"He gave me no choice."

Brakken exclaimed, "That's right! She hired me to kill her husband back east, and she has to do what I say or I'll tell the whole world what she did."

Victoria's face darkened with sudden rage. "You liar!" She whirled to face Shiloh and Clay. "He's lying!"

"No, I'm not, but it doesn't make any difference to these two. They're not going to tell anyone."

"You lied to me!" she shrieked and rushed at him.

He shoved her so roughly that she fell to the deck. Clay started toward Brakken, but he whipped out his pistol and leveled it at Shiloh.

"One more step," Brakken warned, "and she's gone."

Slowly, Clay relaxed, reaching out to take Shiloh's hand.

Brakken picked up two short pieces of rope from the base of the mast and ordered, "Turn around; both of you."

Clay knew that he'd lose his last chance if his hands were bound. But Brakken might shoot him if he resisted and that wouldn't help Shiloh. He closed his eyes and silently prayed, *I've got to do something, and fast!*

CHAPTER XXV

CLAY'S HEART pounded violently as he prepared himself. Brakken had shoved Clay's pistol into his waistband but advanced with his own revolver drawn and the two short lengths of rope in one hand.

"I said, turn around," he commanded.

Clay slowly started to obey while taking a step toward the mast with the dangling spar. "Let Shiloh go," he again urged.

"Don't be telling me what to do!" Brakken roughly shoved Clay. "Now, for the last time, turn around!"

Clay played off the shove and staggered as though slightly off balance. It took him a couple of steps before he seemed to regain his footing. Brakken again moved toward him.

Victoria volunteered, "You can't tie those ropes and hold the gun. Here, let me help you."

Brakken regarded her with a grim smile and handed over the rope pieces. "You really do get some kind of strange pleasure out of this, don't you?"

Victoria didn't reply but hung her purse over her left arm and took the pieces of rope from Brakken with her right hand. Stepping behind Clay, she whispered, "Open your hands. I'm going to slip my derringer into . . ."

Brakken interrupted. "Wait a minute, Victoria."

Clay felt her stiffen as he anticipated feeling the small weapon in his open hands.

Brakken continued, "You had better tie the woman first, then him."

Hidden behind Clay's back, Victoria tried to retrieve the small two-shot weapon from her purse. "I'll have him tied in just a second."

"Don't argue with me!"

Clay still kept his hand open to receive the derringer while Victoria hesitated. Then she slowly moved out from behind him, leaving his hands empty. Feeling his last chance slipping away, Clay tensed while fighting back a disappointed groan.

Brakken noticed Clay's movement and quickly shifted the barrel of his gun toward him. "You want to be a hero? Now's your last chance."

Clay forced himself to pause and wait for Brakken's eyes to shift away from him to the women.

Shiloh began to shiver violently and crossed her hands across her swollen abdomen.

Victoria hesitated beside her, the ropes in one hand and the purse in the other. She turned to Brakken. "The baby. You can't . . ."

"Shut up!" Brakken yelled, angrily pivoting toward both women. "Get on with it!"

In that moment of distraction, Clay reached out and grabbed the dangling spar. He didn't dare take time to pull it toward him but shoved it forward with all his strength.

Brakken whirled, swinging his pistol toward Clay with his right hand and throwing up his left to deflect the heavy spar. It struck his upraised hand and the force of the blow spun him off balance. The gun clattered to the deck as he tried to regain his footing.

Clay leaped for the pistol, scooped it up, and aimed toward Brakken in one quick motion.

Brakken started to reach for the gun in his waistband.

"Hold it!" Clay commanded.

Brakken's hand froze on the grip.

"That's better," Clay said. "Now, very carefully, lift your hands."

As Brakken obeyed, Clay reached down and swiftly snatched the second pistol from Brakken. Shifting guns, Clay held his familiar weapon on Brakken while sliding the other into his belt with his left hand.

Victoria cried, "Kill him, Clay! Kill him!"

"No need for that," Clay replied quietly without taking his eyes off Brakken. "He's under control. We'll save him for the constable."

Clay motioned to Shiloh, who rushed into the comfort of his free left arm.

Victoria's voice rose. "He's evil! Shoot him!"

Brakken swore at her. "I'll ruin your life for this, Victoria! No matter how long it takes, I'll . . ."

He broke off as Victoria plunged her hand into her purse and withdrew the derringer. Before Clay could stop her, she fired.

The ball struck Brakken in the chest. He staggered against the base of the mast, then slowly slipped down to sit on the deck. He stared in shocked disbelief at Victoria.

Standing with the gun in her hand, she shrieked hysterically to Shiloh and Clay, "He lied about my husband! Don't believe what he said! He lied about me!"

Clay replied softly, "I think what you did just now proves the truth."

Brakken stirred as though trying to get up, and Victoria rushed toward him, pointing the pistol at his head.

Too late, Clay realized the derringer had two barrels. He dropped his arm from around Shiloh and leaped to stop Victoria.

Desperately, Brakken reached out and grabbed her hand. As he struggled to point the gun barrel away from him, it fired, striking Victoria who crumpled on top of him.

Clay kicked the now useless derringer across the deck and bent to examine the victims. As he slowly straightened, Shiloh rushed into his arms.

"Oh, dear Lord!" she sobbed, turning away from the horror and burying her face against Clay's chest.

He held her close, whispering comforting words against her hair. Suddenly he stiffened and lifted his head. "Listen!" he exclaimed. "Someone's coming!"

Shiloh lifted her tearful face. She sagged with relief when she recognized Merritt and Mara as Samuel deftly rowed them toward the ship.

CHAPTER XXVI

EXHAUSTED AS she sat before the fireplace that evening, Shiloh silently stared into the flames. Mara entered the room with a tray containing two steaming cups of tea.

"Here," she said, offering a cup to Shiloh. "This will make you feel better."

"I feel fine," Shiloh replied, taking the cup. "It's just been a terribly long day." She cocked her head to listen. "I wish Clay and Father would get here, so I can find out if we got the mail franchise."

Mara set the tray down and sat beside Shiloh on the sofa. "The important thing is that Clay realized the scribbled notes he found in the hardtack can with Aldar's derringer were his overland stage plans. I'm so glad he found them and got to the courthouse before the deadline."

"Yes, I'm grateful for that. And I understand why he and Father wanted to wait to hear the results, but I do wish they'd get back. I'm dying to know if we received the mail contract."

"Relax. They'll be along soon."

Nodding, Shiloh took a sip and commented, "Tastes just right. You always make things just right."

"It didn't look that way last night and early this morning," Mara replied with a sad shake of her head. "We were rowing fairly blindly among those abandoned ships at dawn when we heard two shots."

"Tell me again how you and Father found us. I was too excited to really listen before."

"Well, after we returned home and realized you were missing, Merritt decided he would go ask John Sledger if he had seen you. If not, Merritt would go find the constable. Clay figured that Brakken had rented a rig to kidnap you, so Clay went to check livery stables."

Shiloh suppressed a shudder, remembering how frightened she had been when Brakken forced her to accompany him to the ship graveyard in the bay.

Mara continued, "I went to find Elijah and Samuel and asked them to spread the word to their friends to be on the lookout for you or Brakken. Elijah started asking around, and Samuel insisted on going with me because he said it wasn't safe for a woman alone."

"That man surely loves you, but you don't give him any encouragement."

Mara's voice hardened. "He's a runaway slave who could be caught and sent back east. He's a good friend, and right now, that's all I'm looking for."

Shiloh regretted having said anything. "Go on with your story," she suggested.

Mara sipped her tea before continuing. "After about two hours, we talked to one of Samuel's friends who works at a waterfront saloon. He claimed that he had seen a white man and pregnant woman get out of a runabout at the foot of Market Street. They rowed out toward all those ships rotting in the bay. Then the man came back alone and drove off in the rig. I knew that had to be you and Brakken."

"But how did you know which ship we were on?"

"I'm coming to that. Merritt arrived at the waterfront just as Samuel used a flaming pine torch to point out some footprints in the muddy sand. That puzzled us because there were four sets of prints. We were only expecting three. Two were obviously men's, and the other two were women's."

"Clay's and Brakken's; Victoria's and mine."

"Yes, we eventually figured that out. But we didn't know how she was involved. Only one thing was certain: All of you were somewhere on one of those ships, and at least you and Clay were in mortal danger."

"Listen!" Shiloh interrupted, suddenly sitting up. "It's Clay and Father!" She set the cup down and moved as fast as possible toward the door. She quickly opened it and the men walked into the light from the open door.

"I'm so glad to see you both!" she cried, searching their faces for any sign of what she waited to know.

Merritt gave her a quick kiss on the cheek as Clay put his arms about her.

He closed the door and asked teasingly, "Are you glad to see us, or do you just want to hear whether we have good news?"

"You got it?" She guessed, her voice rising.

Clay nodded, took her hand, and led her to the sofa. Mara

got up and took one of the side chairs while Merritt seated himself in the other.

Clay announced, "Our stage company now has an official contract to carry the United States mail."

"Thank the Lord!" Shiloh exclaimed, impulsively standing on tiptoes to kiss him on the lips. "Oh, Clay! How wonderful!"

He raised an eyebrow in amused surprise. "I thought you weren't the kind of a woman who kissed until she was engaged?"

"Didn't you ask me to marry you?"

"Yes, but . . ."

"I just accepted!"

Mara and Merritt joyfully extended their congratulations. After everyone had settled down somewhat, Mara said, "Merritt, before you came in, I was telling Shiloh how you and I met at the mud flats last night."

"Actually," he replied, "it was this morning. After midnight, anyway."

"I guess that's right," Mara agreed. "It took us a few hours to figure things out." She summarized what she had just told Shiloh, then added, "Merritt, why don't you tell them what happened before we met?"

"Well, my darling daughter," he replied, smiling tenderly at Shiloh, "I went to ask Brother Sledger if he had seen you. He hadn't. We agreed that Brakken must have kidnapped you. The preacher volunteered to find the constable, and I went to the livery stables because that's where Clay had gone."

Clay looked at Shiloh and added. "I knew Brakken didn't have a rig, so he would have had to rent one. In your condition, he wouldn't risk having you ride double on his horse. I headed out to check the livery stables but ran into Victoria, who knew where you were."

Shiloh said softly, "But she betrayed you, and me."

"Yes," Clay agreed. "She led me into a trap, and Brakken forced me at gunpoint to get into a rowboat with them."

Merritt continued, "But I found the right stable. I described Brakken, and the liveryman started cussing. He said, 'That's the man! He left smelly boot prints on the floorboard after he returned the rig.' He told me the only place around here that has mud like that is the flats at the foot of Market Street."

Merritt explained, "Those muddy footprints confirmed what Samuel's friend told us. We knew we had to find you fast. But with some five hundred ships in the cove, we didn't even know where to begin looking. Time was obviously running out, and very fast at that.

"Samuel found a rowboat and we spent hours rowing among all those big black ships. We looked for lights, but didn't see any. We were feeling pretty hopeless.

"Then," he finished softly, "just as dawn was breaking, we heard a shot. We started rowing furiously toward the sound, but we still weren't sure which ship it came from. Then there was a second shot."

"We thought we were too late," Mara added quietly.

Clay slid his arm around Shiloh to pull her close.

She sighed heavily. "I have such mixed feelings about Victoria. She did a terrible thing, yet she saved our lives."

Clay agreed. "When she stepped behind me to tie my hands as Brakken wanted, she whispered to me that she was going to slip me her gun. But Brakken didn't give her a chance."

Shiloh said with a catch in her voice, "When he started to hang me, Victoria protested to him about the baby." Shaking her head, Shiloh admitted. "I don't understand her. Did she ever really change?"

Clay replied, "I don't know. But I'm sure Brakken was black-mailing her, so she planned for me to kill him. When she couldn't slip her derringer to me, she lost her head, and shot him. Most derringers fire only one ball. I didn't realize until too late that Victoria had a second shot. So they both lost their lives."

Shiloh looked up at Clay to ask softly, "Would you have killed Brakken?"

Clay hesitated before replying. "I guess we'll never know, will we?"

There was a thoughtful pause when no one spoke, then Mara said, "Shiloh, I guess you're now sole owner of the quicksilver property. Right?"

"Yes, according to the contract that Victoria insisted I sign."

"You're going to need money to develop the mine. I'd like to lend you enough to get it started. This time, I won't let you tell me no."

"She won't have to," Merritt assured Mara. "I have made more money selling property than I'll ever need. You're a good friend, Mara, but as Shiloh's father, I claim the right to . . ."

"Wait! Wait, both of you!" Shiloh interrupted. "You really are wonderful to me, but I've got another idea."

All eyes turned to her as she explained, "Brother Sledger knows lots of good men who have money to invest. We could form a company with several investors. The only problem is that I need someone trustworthy to manage it. I don't know how, and I'm going to have my hands full raising my child and helping Clay with our stage line."

Merritt cleared his throat. "I have a suggestion. I know a man near Sonoma who used to successfully operate a coal mine back east. He's honest and competent, and I'm sure he could profitably operate a quicksilver mine. Would you like to meet him, Shiloh?"

"Of course, but . . ."

"But what?" Merritt prompted as she hesitated.

"Well, I'm afraid I would be a little anxious about having someone take charge of a property that's so far away. I wouldn't often get to see firsthand how things were going."

"I have a solution for that as well," Merritt replied. "I want to move from Sonoma to where I can be near my daughter and soon-to-be grandchild, but I'll have to make periodic trips back up there to check on my real estate investments. I could check on the mine at the same time."

Shiloh glanced at Clay. When he nodded, Shiloh turned to Mara, who also bobbed her head in approval.

Looking back at her father, Shiloh said, "That sounds wonderful. Thank you."

"Not so fast," Merritt answered with a hint of smile. "There are two conditions."

"Which are?"

"I get to be here to see you married and to help my prospective son-in-law pace the floor while the baby is born."

Shiloh laughed with delight. "All right, but in this case, the marriage comes after the baby. I don't want to walk down the aisle looking like this. Some people might not know it's Aldar's child."

Grinning, Clay asked, "When will these two events take place? I'd like to make plans to be there."

"The baby should be born in March." Shiloh's voice became somber. "Aldar will have been dead a year in June. How about sometime in July for our marriage?"

Clay nodded. "That's fine with me. I want to give you something special for a wedding present, and it may take six months or so to get it ready."

"Goodness!" Shiloh exclaimed. "What kind of a present could that be?"

"You'll see after the wedding," he replied mysteriously.

⌀

In early March, Clay disembarked from a steamer after a business trip to Sacramento. He hired a carriage to take him to Shiloh's home, knowing the baby was due any day. He couldn't wait to tell her that arrangements had been completed for the first mail-carrying stagecoaches to roll as soon as the ground was dry.

Nearing Shiloh's home, Clay suddenly tensed at the sight of an unfamiliar horse and buggy hitched outside. After quickly paying the driver, Clay hurried down the path toward the porch.

Merritt stepped outside. "Hurry up, Clay."

He broke into a run across the wooden porch. "Shiloh? The baby?" he cried anxiously.

"Relax," Merritt replied, slapping the tall man on his shoulder. "I need you to teach me how to pace."

Clay stopped abruptly. "What?"

"Well, we've both been fathers," Merritt explained mildly, "but I never got to wait while my daughter was born because I didn't even know I had one."

"Tell me about Shiloh!" he demanded, anxiety making his voice rise sharply. "Is she . . . ?"

"She's been in labor a couple of hours. Mara and the doctor are with her. I was afraid you weren't going to get here in time."

Clay started walking again. His long legs carried him across the parlor toward the bedroom. "Are you sure she's all right?"

"As much as a woman can be at a time like this." Merritt followed Clay and laid a restraining hand on his arm. "Now, you'd better stop where you are before Mara throws us both out in the cold."

Slowly, Clay turned and faced the older man. "You said you wanted some lessons in waiting for the birth of a child," he reminded Merritt with a grin. "Well, let's see if I can remember. Oh, yes. You start like this . . ."

An hour later, Clay's lighthearted humor had given way to anxiety. "I wish someone would let us know what's happening," he said from in front of the fireplace where he had momentarily stopped pacing.

Merritt looked up from the sofa. "They're too busy right now. Anyway, I'm sure everything's going along just fine, Clay."

"Just the same, I wish . . ."

He broke off abruptly as a high, thin cry came from down the hallway.

"Listen!" Clay cried.

The sound came again, uncertainly at first, then rapidly

settled into a steady, strong, lusty series of cries that announced a new life.

Merritt leaped to his feet and Clay started to let out a joyful yell, then checked himself. He grabbed the other man's hand and vigorously pumped it.

"Congratulations, Merritt! You're a grandpa!"

Mara hurried into the room. "It's a boy," she announced with a wide smile. "He and his mother are both doing fine!"

∞

Four months and a week later, Shiloh started down the aisle on her father's arm. The guests rose as one, turning to watch as Shiloh entered at the back of the church.

Her red-gold hair, swept up to her crown, fell gracefully down her neck in a cluster of long curls.

Her gown, made by Mara, was a creamy ivory silk with a fitted bodice and a deep collar of lace. The layers of graduated flounces in the skirt were alternately edged with ruffles and lace, and the sleeves were fitted to just below the elbow. From there, they were finished with a deep ruffle of lace that met her matching off-white gloves. The tips of her dainty little button-up boots showed beneath the skirt.

Nervous but happy, and glad for her father's supporting arm, Shiloh matched her pace to the organ's measured tempo. They moved slowly down the center aisle between the packed pews toward the flower-decked altar.

There Brother Sledger waited with Clay. Mara stood up as Shiloh's bridesmaid, and the best man was a stagecoach driver named Frank Simmons with whom Clay had worked in the past.

As she passed the last row of pews in front, Shiloh glanced down at her son as he slept peacefully in the arms of a matron from the church. Sudden tears erupted at the sight of her infant with his light head of pale blond hair who so resembled his late father. They both shared the same name of Aldar, but

Shiloh didn't want to call the baby Junior, so they called him A. J.

Shiloh blinked back her tears, unsure whether they were of joy over the baby and Clay, or of sadness for her first husband. Although he had died young, his son and his dreams were alive and well.

Shiloh gave her attention to Brother Sledger as he began the wedding ceremony. "Dearly beloved, we are gathered here in the sight of God and these witnesses . . ."

It seemed to take forever, but Shiloh had no hesitancy when she looked up at Clay and said quietly but firmly, "I do."

Then Clay took her hand and rapidly led her up the aisle and through the joyous exclamations of approval from the congregation. When they reached the outside door at the top of the stairs, Shiloh suddenly stopped and stared toward the street.

"What's that?" she cried, momentarily forgetting the well-wishers who crowded around.

Clay squeezed her hand. "Remember that Concord stage that sank when the clipper ship went down last year?" Without waiting for a reply, he continued, "I had it raised and cleaned."

"You didn't!"

"Oh, yes, I did. That coach is as beautiful and solid as the day she was made. All those months in salt water didn't hurt her a bit. Oh, I had the red paint touched up, and the gold trim redone, but she's an original. Our line is going to be the very first in California to have a genuine Concord stage. That's the special wedding present I told you about last December."

"It's perfect! I couldn't ask for anything better!"

⌒

After kissing her still-sleeping son now safely in Mara's arms, and hugging her father, Shiloh let Clay assist her into the coach. When he was seated beside her, their guests threw a final hail of rice and shouted good wishes before the driver on the high outside box loosened the reins.

The six mustangs leaned into their harnesses, and the magnificent coach with its comfortable seats rocked gently on leather thoroughbraces, starting their short honeymoon with a rattling of cans and old shoes tied behind the high rear wheels.

Inside, Clay and Shiloh embraced in their first moments alone since being married.

"Happy?" he asked after kissing her.

"Oh, yes." She gently touched the upholstered seat beside them. "This coach is such a symbolic way to start our lives together. When that clipper ship sank with this stage on it," Shiloh confessed, "I had a feeling our future had gone down too."

"It didn't look as if we had any future at all when we stood on the deck of that abandoned ship as the sun came up and Brakken . . ."

Shiloh gently laid her fingers across Clay's lips. "I know. Everything looked so hopeless, but here we are." She moved her fingers and rested them on Clay's before adding, "Love and faith are mighty powerful forces. And Brother Sledger was right. Faith, like muscle, grows stronger through resistance."

Clay gently bent to lay his cheek against hers. "Thank God for all that." We've still got a long way to go, but we've won three battles so far. Our financial and business problems have been met. The quicksilver mine will make a profit from the cinnabar, and with the mail franchise, the stage line should be lucrative.

"Now there's every opportunity for us to fulfill Aldar's vision. One day, Laird and Patton Stage Lines will extend not only all over California, but also from here to the Missouri River.

"We also survived Gladwin and Locke's best efforts to stop us, although I don't think they're through trying to establish California as a separate nation."

"I agree. I doubt we've heard the last of them. Especially," Shiloh added, "since Locke threatened Mara, which I take personally."

"If the threat of Civil War keeps growing, those two men could become a real problem," Clay said.

"Clay, if war comes, what's going to happen to all of us? If California becomes a state, will it secede from the Union as some southern states are already talking about? Or will California become a separate nation, as Gladwin and Locke and their people want?"

"Let's not think about that today," Clay urged.

"You're right." She snuggled close to him. "Now that these other troubles are behind us, I'm grateful that I have learned to trust and love again."

"Yes," Clay agreed, holding her tight. "There have been some hard times, and there may be some ahead. But let's remember this Concord coach, and how it was raised to roll again. On our fiftieth wedding anniversary, I'll remarry you and take you for a ride in this very same coach. And A. J. can drive."

"It's a date," she said, offering her lips.